TH
BLACKSMITH
PRINCE

BERYLL & OSIRIS
BRACKHAUS

So happy we got to know you!

Beryll + Osiris

Editing and proof: Chantal Perez-Fournier
Layout & Book Design: Julia Schwenk
Cover: Anna Tiferet Sikorska | tiferetdesign.com
Map: Kosmic | kosmicdungeon.com

ISBN-13: 978-1542456104
www.brackhaus.com

Acknowledgements

Once again thank you so much to our wonderful beta readers
Aljoscha, Tiferet, Aleks, Uhu, Talomor, Alana and Eija.

Special thanks go to our lovely editor Chantal
for a mackerel at the perfect time.

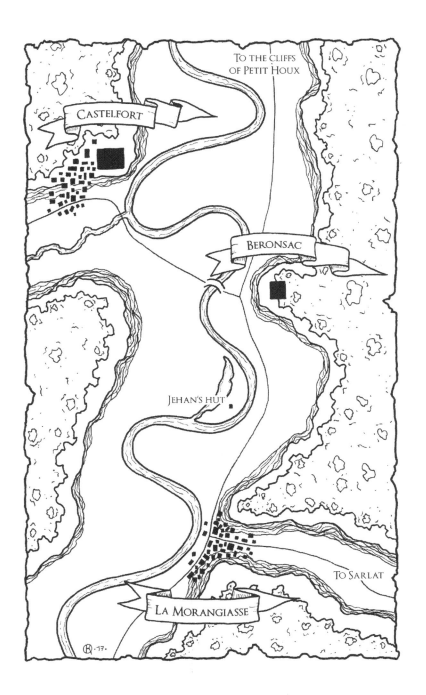

TO THE CLIFFS
OF PETIT HOUX

CASTELFORT

BERONSAC

JEHAN'S HUT

TO SARLAT

LA MORANGIASSE

Chapter One – The Scent of White Oleander

Afternoon sunlight flooded the market square of La Morangiasse, gilding the stone houses that clung to the cliffside like swallows' nests. It struck sparks on the languid waves of the river, where mosquitoes played over the embankment, and the lengthening shadows brought the first relief after a scorchingly hot, late summer day.

It was the time of day when the cats came out of their hiding places, still drowsy after having spent the entire day sleeping through the worst of the heat, looking around the market stalls for the occasional bite of food to steal or beg from the sellers. Of course, the fishmonger's stall was the first place they turned to, and as always, Jehan had kept enough scraps for each of them to get a bite or two.

All around the marketplace, the merchants were packing up their stalls, filling the square with amicable chatter over the last few bartered deals and bits of gossip. Someone in the entourage of Comte Rainaud had ordered an entire bolt of orange silk, the smith's wife had broken a toe, and brigands had been sighted on the road to Bergerac. So nothing out of the ordinary had happened since market day last week.

A gaggle of young men passed Jehan's stall, laughing and chatting. Apprentices and journeymen from the various shops, mostly, happy that the day's work was finally over.

"Are you coming with us, Jehan?" one of them asked. "We're going down to the river, for a swim."

Some had already taken off their shirts, their skin glistening with a sheen of sweat where it wasn't covered in dust.

Jehan took off his frazzled straw hat, fanned himself and ruffled his close-cropped brown hair. It had been a long day, and he wasn't much looking forward to spending time with healthy young men, bathing and laughing and jumping off the rocks into the river, as naked as they could possibly be. Or rather, he was looking forward to something like that way too much.

"You just go ahead, I still have to pack up. You know Marianne, my niece? It's her birthday today, and I wanted to pass by their house for dinner and say hello."

The group accepted his answer with a nod and walked on, still chatting, drifting across the market square towards the river. Jehan already had his eyes back on his crates of smoked trout when a shadow fell onto his wares.

"Really? Not even for a little while? You're the best swimmer of all of us, and you've been sweating all day, just like the rest."

Jehan looked up with a bittersweet smile. Giraud, the smith's son, stood right in front of him, the lower third of his long trousers covered in soot and speckled with burns up to where his leather apron usually started protecting them. Only now, he was wearing nothing but those trousers – his belly and chest clean, tanned skin over sinuous muscle. His arms, neck and shoulders were covered with soot and striped with sweat. Around his neck, his simple cast-iron necklace had left lighter areas where it touched his skin. Giraud's face was black with soot, almost as dark as his hair, but his green eyes sparkled like the back of a dragonfly over the water.

Boys like Giraud were the reason Jehan preferred not to join the crowd, even after a day like this.

"Really not."

Giraud cocked his head and put on a tiny frown.

"Nothing I can do to convince you?" he asked, his smile revealing teeth as white as salt. Not quite as tall as Jehan, yet, but Giraud seemed to grow more and more handsome with every year.

Jehan looked down to hide the colour rising to his cheeks, but the only thing he could look at was the trail of fine black hair rising from Giraud's trousers towards his belly button. He closed his eyes firmly.

Don't stare, he reminded himself. Don't stare, don't stammer, don't blush.

"No," he replied. "I have work to do."

"Is it anything I can help with?"

"No. Thank you."

"Jehan, we all have work to do," Giraud countered amiably. "Yet we all find time to have a little fun now and then. So why don't you?"

"Maybe I am just different."

"'Course you are. But did you ever wonder if maybe that's a good thing...?"

Jehan looked up in surprise, just catching Giraud giving him a lopsided smile, all good cheer and friendship. Little wonder the other boys in town looked up to Giraud the way they did. He was just the smith's son, but for all the townsfolk cared, he was a young hero in the making. He even looked the part these days, with his dark locks and the fashionable moustache and narrow goatee he was growing of late. He was lithe and agile where Jehan felt just tall and angular, running and laughing where Jehan just tried to stay out of trouble.

Besides, Giraud just wanted to be nice – a friend – as he was to almost all the young men in La Morangiasse. How could he be expected to understand that Jehan had good reasons to keep a certain distance from everyone?

The silence between them grew awkward until Giraud gave a little sound, that half-chuckle, half-scoff he did so well.

"Whatever it is that you are, I'll be down at the river." He turned to leave, but not without a friendly nod of his head. "If you change your mind, you know where to find us."

"Thank you," Jehan forced out, even managing to add a credible smile. "Maybe another time."

But Giraud was already on his way towards the river where the other boys were shouting and laughing by the shore. For a heartbeat, Jehan thought he smelled white oleander flowers in the air, even though there were no shrubs nearby, but the impression was gone in an instant. Lost in thought, he allowed himself to watch Giraud cross the square with lithe steps and pass the road along the riverside. He skipped down the few steps to the water where he was greeted with more shouts and some handfuls of mud thrown from several directions. When Giraud undid his belt to slip out of his trousers, Jehan turned his eyes back to his trouts as if he had been stung.

Don't stare, don't blush.

Being different could get a man killed, and there were more than enough ways he wasn't like the other men in town.

Inside their crate, the trouts looked up at him with dead eyes, one next to the other, indifferent to his worries.

"You know, he has a point there," a mumbling voice almost made him jump out of his skin. "Hiding yourself like that isn't healthy."

"Grandma!" Jehan turned around, staring at the old woman on her stool, half hidden by the shadow of the house behind them. She hadn't said a word all afternoon, and he had all but forgotten about her. "You can't seriously suggest that I – "

"What?" She laughed, showing her last tooth, her wrinkled face lighting up with mirth. "Of course I can. I am old, no one gives a wet rat about my thoughts."

"I care what you think."

"Yeah, you do, don't you? And yet you don't hear what I am saying." With a sigh that was half insult and half resignation, she leaned against the wall behind her and turned her attention back to the cat she had been nursing in her lap, gently muttering to the small creature.

Only, it wasn't a cat.

"Grandma. There's a *lutin* in your lap."

"It's been here all afternoon, just like I have been." The old woman continued scratching the head of the little humanoid creature that held its red woollen cap in both hands and stared at Jehan balefully. "And no one has noticed either of us."

"You can't just – "

"Don't tell me what I can or cannot do, Jehan *le Pêcheur*," she snarled at him, and for a heartbeat, her grey eyes didn't seem as blind as usual. "Others have tried and failed miserably. And besides, it is not as if anyone but us will ever notice."

Jehan gave a defeated sigh. There was little sense in arguing with his grandmother when she was in this kind of a mood. And in a way, she was right. They were the only villagers with the second sight, the ability to see and talk to all the creatures that weren't quite human, to the spirits and fae and ghosts they shared this world with. And it had served them well – while not exactly among the rich or powerful in town, his family was happy and healthy and well respected all around. So he gave a polite nod to the little fae in his grandmother's lap, and continued stacking what remained of his wares without a second thought.

From the narrow street that led up towards the houses built higher into the cliffside, *Père* Ancel appeared and began to make his customary round. The priest inquired about the families that lived farther away from the village and reminding everyone that the weekly market was over now. His church was situated up on the last street before the cliff got too steep, and his face was slick with sweat from the exertion of hauling his belly all the way down here. But he carried himself with good humour, as always. He was a kind man, if mostly clueless to what happened around him.

At the far end of the market, in the direction of the castle, Jehan saw the captain of Comte Rainaud's guard approaching for pretty much the same reason as the priest, trailed by two of his men in the Guard's black and green colours.

The little creature in his grandmother's lap made a satisfied little grunt, straightened his strawlike hair and gave a deep, almost courteous bow before putting his cap back on and hopped down. He threw a last baleful glance at Jehan, put up his chin and walked off around the corner of the nearest house. Jehan followed him with his eyes, lost in thought.

"How do you know we are the only ones able to see them?" he asked.

"Huh?" His grandmother made a few mumbling sounds. "Everyone can see them. They just prefer to believe they don't."

"You know what I mean." He turned over the wide straw basket that had held the perches and slapped it onto the cobblestone ground to clean out the last scales. "I am just worried that – you know what happens when people notice we talk to ... them."

"What wouldn't I give to have another one who could do my job. I won't live forever, you know?" She fiddled with something in her lap and reached out to Jehan. "Here, for you."

Jehan put down the boards that had served as a makeshift table for the day. The thing in her bony hands turned out to be a small, grass-woven satchel, tied with a length of vine. Inside, he found over a dozen small berries, their wrinkled black skins waxy and dull, but their scent unmistakeable.

"Juniper berries?" he asked, incredulous. Those were a precious spice down here, especially after the droughts of the last years, and priceless for smoking fish. "How did you...?"

"A generous payment for an afternoon of head-scratching." She shrugged. "Need to earn my gruel, after all."

"You have earned your keep for many years to come, Grandma."

She merely scoffed. "Still need someone to replace me when I am gone."

Jehan rolled his eyes. It wasn't as if they were having this talk for the first time, today. "But I thought Alienee was doing such a good job. You even said so yourself."

"As a midwife, yes."

He just gritted his teeth and took down the last racks and boards that made up the bulk of his family's stall. Last was the faded awning, and he folded it up with a few practised motions.

"You know I wasn't talking about replacing me as a midwife, do you, Jehan?"

"Yes, Grandmother."

"And?"

Now it was Jehan who gave a sigh. He surveyed his pile of crates and boards and declared his work finished, stretched and sat down on the cobblestones next to his grandmother.

"I am not a ... 'midwife'."

"Are not or do not want to be?"

"Both, I guess?"

She put her hand on his shoulder, like she had always done when Jehan had still been a little child, and he leaned his head against her leg.

"You don't have to be a woman to be 'not a midwife'."

"And how is that supposed to work? As soon as anyone gets even a little suspicious, I'll end up hanged. They might even burn me at the stake, just for good measure."

"And how's that different? Do you think that is even a cat's whisker more of a risk for you than for a woman?" Her cool hand patted his shoulder. "You wouldn't even need a husband to justify your every movement. I'd say it would be a lot easier for a man to do my job."

Whatever reply he might have had, Jehan swallowed it. There was just no point in arguing.

"Though, on the other hand," she continued as if talking to herself, chuckling under her breath, "a strapping husband might do you a world of good in other ways."

"Grandma! No."

She took a deep breath, patted his shoulder again and leaned back against the wall. Silent, they waited for one of Jehan's nephews to come downtown with the donkey and pick up the stall and what little wares hadn't been sold today.

Of course she knew he wasn't looking at girls the same way as other boys. She might be blind, but her senses were sharper than those of most seeing people. And Jehan didn't mind – neither her knowing, nor him being different in yet another way. He would have vastly preferred living someplace where being different wasn't a bad thing, yes, but that was something he took like the weather, something to prepare for, but nothing to fret about.

Most of the other merchants had left the marketplace by now, only a small group remaining to argue with the captain of the Guard and *Père* Ancel about yet another brigand attack somewhere in another town on the far side of Castelfort.

There hadn't been any brigands near La Morangiasse in the last two years, but there were still plenty around in the region, at least enough to make for decent gossip.

Gently, Jehan's grandmother placed her hand onto his head and began stroking his hair. A loud splash from the river reached them, followed by a burst of renewed laughter. He didn't look. Moments later, a stray cat joined Jehan, a beautiful gold-and-red striped creature that dropped to the ground next to his knee, demanding his attention with loud purrs. Jehan started scratching between her ears, closed his eyes and lost himself entirely in the moment. Like so often, he wondered why life couldn't just always be as peaceful as this.

"*Grand-mère Matrone*, Jehan, a good day to you," a man's deep voice yanked him out of his reverie. It was *Capitaine* LaForge standing in front of them, politely reaching for the tip of his wide-brimmed hat. His expression was mostly obscured by a formidable dark beard that also hid his deeply scarred jaw, but his eyes were bright with genuine kindness. "As always – the one family in La Morangiasse that I don't need to worry about."

"Is that you, Bertrand? My eyes aren't so good any more..."

"Yes, it's me, *Grand-mère Matrone*, little Bertrand," LaForge replied, giving Jehan an amused eye roll. They both knew that her hearing was still so acute that she could identify anyone she wanted. If she wanted. "How are you feeling today?"

"Oh, I am fine. A bit tired, from the heat, but no pain in my bones, so there won't be a thunderstorm tonight." She muttered something unintelligible, then added: "And your wife, Bertrand, how is she? Is she better?"

"Yes, very much. The tea you gave her seems to have cleared up whatever she suffered from. Once again, we are in your debt."

There it was – that tiny note of unease in a man's voice when speaking to Jehan's grandmother about another woman's ailments. Jehan had grown up with those moments, and those hushed talks about things 'men should never know'. And just like he had done as a child, he now pretended not to have noticed anything, and just smiled politely, scratching the cat at his feet.

Jehan understood the ways of fish rather well, and the changing of the weather. Spirits of the wild were easy to understand, and the High Fae were predictably unpredictable. He could look at most of the plants around and have a rough idea whether they were helpful or harmful. Humans, on the other hand, were a complete mystery to him more often than not.

"I am happy I could be of help," his grandmother replied, maybe mumbling a little more than she had to. "Just tell her that she should come over and talk to me if anything else is amiss."

"I will, *Grand-mère Matrone*, I will. And how is Ugs? Is his leg still acting up?"

Ugs was Jehan's elder brother, and the nominal head of their family since their parents had died in a sudden flood six winters ago. Despite having a stiff leg since his childhood, he had managed to win the hand of the most beautiful woman in town – Alienee, a stunning beauty from far away Sarlat, the apprentice to their grandmother and new midwife of La Morangiasse. The two of them had a small army of children, and together with Jehan they covered the entire fishing business here in town.

"He is fine, he is always fine." Grandmother gestured wildly in the general direction of their mutual home. "That little brat has been complaining all his life, and I think he'd feel bored out of his mind if he wasn't yapping about this or that for a day. I can still remember when he was about this tall, and he came hobbling home, crying about this frog, you know?"

Jehan was just about to remind his grandmother that poor *Capitaine* LaForge really didn't have to hear the story about that frog yet again when he heard the familiar snort of their faithful donkey.

"Sorry, Grandma, but I'm afraid it's time to go home," he said and jumped to his feet. "You'll have to tell the story another time."

She muttered a few choice words, but Jehan chose to ignore it. Instead, he gave a friendly wave to Lucartz, his little nephew, who led the donkey onto the market place with an expression of deep, adult gravity. Little Luc waved back and quickened his steps, which was harder than expected with a donkey in tow that absolutely wouldn't hurry anything.

Jehan and LaForge shared a silent smile.

"*Grand-mère Matrone*," LaForge offered with another tip to his hat, "I'll bid you a good evening. Please send my regards to Ugs and Alienee, yes?"

"Thank you, captain," she replied, nodding in his vague direction. "Have a good day as well, Bertrand, and my greetings to your wife."

He gave a silent nod to Jehan and scanned the square. It didn't take him long to spot his two guardsmen in front of the '*Plume d'Or*', where they were busy chatting up a barmaid on the steps of the inn, so he jutted out his chin and strode off.

"So, Luc, how's it going at home?" Jehan asked when his nephew came up to them. "Everyone gathered for dinner already?"

The boy nodded eagerly. "As if anyone's ever going to miss dinner." He grinned widely, and when Jehan gave him a friendly nudge to the shoulder, he took that as the opener to an impromptu wrestling match with his uncle. Jehan didn't have children of his own, but he loved his brother's milling brood without reservations.

Packing their stuff onto the donkey was a well-trained task for both of them, and done in a matter of moments. Jehan checked the straps one last time before he handed the leading rope back to Luc and nodded him towards their family's home. Jehan himself helped Grandmother back onto her feet, took her stool and offered her his arm to steady her on the way back.

Together, they slowly marched down the street that led out of town. Luc told them of the many special treats his mother was preparing for tonight, of the bread and the snails and the roasted goose, about the cabbage and the rabbit and the walnut cake. Step by step, they followed the curve of the river until they reached the sturdy little house where Jehan had been born and where his brother now lived. It stood right on the riverfront in a large bend, and like every late afternoon in summer, the sun reflected off the river and painted glittering golden lines across its yellow stones. Right next to it, under the old walnut tree, a large table had been set up, white linens fluttering in the breeze. Ugs was already sitting there on a bench, his leg stretched out, smoking his long clay pipe, while his children chased geese around the table.

It would be a beautiful evening.

***

The sun had already set behind the cliffs when Jehan finally reached the old bridge of Beronsac.

A riot of red and purple clouds dotted the lavender sky, starkly offset by the black silhouettes of slender oaks that lined the horizon. Some last swallows zipped low across the river to his left, crickets were deafeningly loud all around and, overhead, the first bats came out of their holes in the castle ruins and started hunting for an early supper.

Normally, Jehan enjoyed his evening walks home. He liked being on his own, he liked the rugged, unbridled beauty of nature and the silence that never was actually quiet. Only tonight, he was tired. The rack on his back grew heavier with each step even though it weighed only half of what he had carried into town this morning, and most of it was from things he was really looking forward to – fresh bread, some figs, carrots and beets and a full dozen eggs. The evening among the whirling throng of his family had left him happily exhausted, and longing for the solitude of his hut.

But that solitude was a lengthy walk from town – almost a mile downriver to the old bridge of Beronsac, then across the bridge and back upriver again for half a mile more. Normally nothing worth mentioning, but tonight Jehan felt like taking a break and a little nap on the side of the road, just for a moment. Dinner had been good, and plentiful, as had been the wine. It looked to be a good year, with enough food to get everyone through the winter and then some. He had already seen more than enough famines in his lifetime.

Jehan was so focussed on setting one foot in front of the other that he didn't notice the man standing on the crossing that led to the bridge. Only when he caught the soft whinny of a horse did he look up and froze.

Was it some creature of the night? He was used to various kinds walking up to him every now and then – but not here. For whatever reason, they avoided the area around the old castle ruins of Beronsac, and this crossing that led to the bridge was right at the foot of the cliffs crowned by those crumbling walls.

Maybe it was a brigand ambush? There shouldn't be any brigands this side of town, there hadn't been any since... The man on the road moved, his shape separating from that of his horse, and Jehan breathed with relief. That sinuous form could only belong to one person.

"Giraud?" Jehan asked. "Is that you?"

"You really took your time tonight," the smith's son answered jovially. "I was already afraid I missed you."

He walked over to Jehan and tipped his forehead in greeting. Jehan noticed that he had changed into a clean white shirt with billowing sleeves, the lacing over his chest almost completely undone. It looked good on him, as did his tight suede pants. Without the soot, he looked all dashing and handsome, Jehan found, his tanned face with the high cheekbones just right between roguish and sweet.

But even Giraud's green eyes couldn't distract from the obvious questions.

"You were waiting here for me? Why?"

"My, you're slow tonight. Yes, I waited here for you." Giraud hesitated for a moment, wringing his hands as if not entirely sure how to proceed. A strand of dark hair had come loose from his short ponytail, and dangled over his eyes. "I need to ask you a favour."

"Couldn't you have done that in the market today?" Jehan's question came out a little grumpier than he would have wanted. Whatever Giraud wanted of him, it would be something weird, he could already feel it in the air. "My apologies. If you came here all the way, it must be important to you. So please, what is it?"

"It's ... difficult, and I didn't want anyone overhearing us." Again, Giraud hesitated. "Is it a bad time? Should I come by your hut tomorrow?"

"No! I mean, no, that really isn't necessary." With a huff, Jehan took off his rack and sat it down next to the road. "You're here, I am here, so let's talk. What is wrong?"

"I... I need your help."

"Yes...?"

"I ... think they have been cursed. My parents, I mean."

Suddenly, Jehan was wide awake, his entire body tingling with alarm right down to his toes. "If you think so, you should talk to *Père* Ancel. I am just a fisherman."

"Well, you know… I don't think the priest is the right person for the job." Giraud smiled winningly, his white teeth all but gleaming in the low light. "He isn't talking to the little folks, like your grandmother does. Or you."

"What in heaven or hell makes you think I talk to fairies?"

Giraud laughed again. "Because you do? All these little gestures, the nods and smiles, they look harmless enough if one doesn't see that there's actually someone on the other end, smiling back. When you stop to scratch your chin in the middle of the road, it looks just like that – unless someone sees the swamp cat you allow to pass the street in front of you, just to be polite."

"What the hell are you –"

"Please." Giraud sighed. For a heartbeat, the crickets in the shrubs on the cliffside were the loudest thing to be heard. When Giraud spoke up again, his voice was little more than a whisper. "I know you see them. I know because I see them as well."

Silence spread between them like ripples on a pond. That was something so unexpected Jehan had to let it sink in first.

"Oh." The little sound was not even coming close to what he was feeling right now, but Jehan just didn't have any words for it. Fear and worry and fascination mixed with the pure surprise of this revelation. "How come?"

"I have no idea at all." Giraud shrugged. "Must be something I have inherited from my father's side. My real father's side."

Jehan nodded. Giraud didn't like to speak of it, but everyone in town knew that he wasn't the smith's son, but his nephew. His mother had been the smith's sister, who had suddenly fallen pregnant and refused to name the father. Despite everything, she had carried the child to term, only to fling herself off the cliff a few days after giving birth – either in shame or from a broken heart, the town was still arguing about that even to this day. But her brother Segui and his wife had been hoping for a child for years already, so they had taken in Giraud as their own. And as far as Jehan could see, they were a happy family together, with Giraud bringing nothing but honour to their name.

"And you think someone cursed them? Why? Everyone I know likes them, or at least respects them."

"I don't know." Suddenly, Giraud looked rather sombre. "I am not good enough in those things, I can barely spot a spell when it bites me in the face. With all the things going wrong of late, with Mama falling ill, this isn't natural. I can only feel something evil is hanging onto them, and it's because of me."

Jehan gave him a sidelong glance. He was rather sure Giraud wasn't telling him the entire truth. "Why should it be about you? Did you anger someone important?"

"Well, apparently, I did." Giraud laughed again, but it didn't have his usual mirth. "I must have, I guess. Can you have a look at them for me, please?"

Again, a deep sense of warning tingled all over the back of Jehan's neck. He really should keep his fingers out of this one.

"I don't know. Maybe you really should talk to *Père* Ancel."

"Oh forget that chubby old fool, this is real magic." Giraud looked genuinely heartbroken, and it made Jehan's chest flutter as if he had a caged bird inside. "Please?"

"I am not trained for such things, I really – "

"You're much more trained than I am, or anyone else I know. And – I can even pay! I have a few *sous* I could give you."

"I really don't want money, Giraud, it's just that I – "

"If it's not money you want, I could pay with something else," the journeyman smith offered eagerly and utterly without guile. "Do you need a year's supply of fishing hooks? Or new door hinges, I am getting really good at those."

"No, no door hinges either, please – "

"What else? Just name it. My parents mean everything to me. If you help me, I'd do anything for you!"

"I..."

Jehan's rebuke died in a mumble when his mind flooded him with unsolicited images of what he actually would want of Giraud. Touching his hair, his face, the side of his neck. Maybe even a kiss... Those images drowned every other thought in his head.

"My goodness," Giraud remarked into the silence. "You're blushing like a girl."

Jehan was too embarrassed to do anything but turn away.

"So there *is* something you want." Giraud hesitated for a moment and then walked around Jehan until he faced him again. "When the girls in town blush like that, they usually want something from me. Something like the neckerchief I am wearing, or a kiss..."

Jehan opened his mouth to deny, but right then Giraud bit his lips – a tiny, thoughtful gesture that managed to blot out all the words in Jehan's mind.

"Is it a kiss you want, as payment for your help?"

"I ... don't..."

Inside Jehan's head, there were several voices screaming at him, to say yes, to say no, to run for his life. But he didn't do any of that. He was completely absorbed by feeling trapped, and being unable to decide which unwelcome solution to this would be less painful in the long run.

But apparently, Giraud didn't have any of those concerns.

"Alright then," he said lightly, "I am a good kisser, I am told. Never kissed a guy, though. But I shouldn't be surprised, you witchy folks got a reputation for being naughty." He gave a little laugh, somewhere between amused and daunted, and stepped forward to close the distance between himself and Jehan. "Kind of looking forward to this, you know?"

This close, Jehan noticed that Giraud was now almost as tall as himself, if still missing a few inches, and that despite his extensive bath this afternoon in the river, he still smelled of smoke and rust. But he also radiated warmth, and under all that smoke there was another scent hidden, exotic and yet familiar, like sweet flowers blooming in the night, like starlight and campfire tales of ancient heroes.

He should have stepped back, should have told Giraud that he was completely misreading him, that a kiss was the very last thing that he wanted. He really should have.

But instead, he just stood there when Giraud laid a hand on his neck and pulled him close. He just closed his eyes when Giraud rose to the tips of his toes and leaned in. Their lips touched, and Jehan allowed himself to drown in that moment, this singular heartbeat of a dream that would never come again.

It was the worst decision he had ever made, and the best one at the very same time.

Sensations chased through him like a flock of birds, chaotic, unsorted, uncontrollable. How strong and firm Giraud's body felt against his own, how Giraud's moustache tickled against his own stubble. Jehan's hands went up and pulled him closer into their embrace. He placed one of his hands behind Giraud's neck, entwining them further, pulling him tight, suddenly kissing him rather than allowing himself to be kissed.

Giraud gave a startled little breath and relaxed, his body melting against Jehan's, still kissing, searching. Feeling him suddenly lean against him, all supple and eager, fanned a hunger in Jehan he had never expected to be there. He kissed him with renewed fervour, with desire for things he couldn't even name, but was sure he needed to survive. Blood hammered through his veins, and he felt his heart beat in his chest. It felt good, it felt right and perfect and everything he had ever wanted.

Suddenly realising what he was actually doing there, he let go and plucked Giraud off him like a burdock.

The young smith gave a breathless, startled little laugh and staggered to the side.

"Are you alright?" Jehan asked, mildly worried.

"Huh?" Giraud blinked at him, twice, before his eyes focussed again. "All the Saints, that was..."

"I am sorry, I really shouldn't have – "

"Good Lord. Now I know why those girls always want 'just a kiss'." Giraud laughed, a bright, carefree sound that made Jehan's heart ring like a bell. "Oh my. I'll be fine, just a moment."

"Right..." Jehan took another, cautious step away from Giraud.

What the hell had he been thinking? How could he have let this happen? How could he have lost all control? And worst of all – Giraud seemed positively flushed, excited, happy.

"Yeah. It is getting late," Giraud finally said, giddy and insecure at the same time. He fiddled with the waistband of his pants and blushed, breathless. "So you'll help me with my parents, yes?"

Jehan wanted to say 'no'. But with a sinking heart, he realised he had already accepted payment for his help. And in a kind he would not be able to return. How could he have been this stupid?

"I will have a look at them," he replied instead. "Next time I am in town."

"Thank you." Giraud hesitated, then turned abruptly and climbed onto his horse, turning it back to La Morangiasse. When they passed Jehan, he stopped, adding: "You know, that kiss ... consider it a down payment, yes? Your help surely is worth more than that. And I don't think I would mind paying up to my promises."

He finished with a sparkly-eyed smile that was at the same time insecure and excited, gave Jehan a parting nod and rode off into the early night.

What in all the Saints' names had just happened?

Jehan sat down on the milestone that marked the border between La Morangiasse and the neighbouring town, Castelfort, on the other side of the river. Above him, bats zipped across the night sky, catching the moths that played in the warm air above the massive stone bridge. His mind felt as direly in need of repair as the old bridge – still functional, but only barely so.

He had given his word to help Giraud, and had even accepted payment, so he knew he would feel obligated to at least have a look at things. Yet he had the worst feeling about this. And what if Giraud told anyone about what had happened here? Or worse, what if he wanted more? And all that for what?

For that feeling of his body against yours, a voice in his head reminded him. For the feeling of his hair under your fingers, and for that tingling on your lips.

Unthinking, Jehan's fingers touched his mouth, retracing those sensations that still lingered inside him like embers among the ashes.

It had been a godawful idea back to front. It would probably lead to a wagonload of problems for both of them.

But that one kiss...

There had been magic in it.

Chapter Two - Wise Women's Counsel

"Cassanoë? Are you there?" Jehan smiled at his whispered question as he knocked against the tree's bark.

It was a silly question, of course. Dryads could leave their trees as much as pigs could fly. But, Jehan also knew it was never wrong to be polite.

"I have brought presents!" he whispered up into the thick canopy of the oak he was standing underneath, and sure enough, caught a swift movement among the branches.

"Presents?" Her voice was like the rustling of leaves, like the croaking of branches, and yet it was undeniably youthful and feminine. "Oh, I love presents..."

Another motion up in the crown and then she stepped around the trunk of her tree as if she had been waiting there all along. Dark brown skin like the bark of her tree, and her hair a muted green, piled on top of her head in playful, thick curls, she was too little human for her utter lack of clothes to register with Jehan as anything but entirely natural.

"Madame Cassanoë, always a pleasure meeting you," Jehan greeted her in a low voice, bowing politely. "You get more beautiful with every year."

She tried to give him a stern look for his flattery, but her black eyes sparkled.

"Presents?"

"Why don't we sit down for a while?" Jehan asked and gestured at the ground next to the trunk. "Please?"

She pouted most attractively, but sat down without another word, cross-legged with an elegance that few humans would be able to match. Jehan joined her on the shady ground, took off his straw hat and smiled at the dryad.

His compliment hadn't been insincere, not even remotely. She was still a young oak, merely a hundred years old, just reaching the age of full maturity among her kind, pretty in every sense of the word. For the first time since he had met her, he spotted small clusters of grey, tangled moss and brilliant green lichen growing on her earlobes, dangling as decoratively as the most precious jewels. A few leaves and acorns scattered among her hair were all the adornments she needed. Considering that she lived right on the fringes of the marketplace of La Morangiasse, it was a shame so few people came to visit her.

But every now and then, Jehan took his time and sat at the base of the tree, looking to all the world like a simple fisherman resting in the shade of a large oak. That he and Cassanoë had been friends since his childhood, well, nobody needed to know.

"Presents?" she asked again, this time with a purring hunger in her voice that clearly reminded Jehan he wasn't dealing with a human.

So he reached into his satchel and produced a small pouch of folded fig leaves, their warm scent hardly able to mask the pungent smell of their content.

Cassanoë's eyes grew wide, black shiny orbs full of excitement. "You brought me goat's horn?"

"Ground goat's horn, of course. I may be just a human, but I do remember your favourite."

She smiled at him, widely, and took the small packet with deep appreciation. She smelled at it, closed her eyes in bliss for a heartbeat, then tucked it away into a dark nook between her tree's roots.

"Thank you, Jehan *le Pêcheur*, that is very kind of you."

"And you are welcome. Also, I have brought you a second present." Jehan took a small waterskin out of his satchel, opened it and poured its contents over the tree's roots. "Water. From my own well."

"Oh." Cassanoë's eyes turned narrow, her expression concerned. Bringing water to a tree was a ritual older than both of them, and a clear sign he wasn't here today merely to chat. "Are you in trouble, dear?"

"Not me," Jehan replied even though he wasn't too sure about it. "A friend of mine is, and I am searching for answers."

She took a deep breath, and the whole tree above her rustled softly in response.

"Then ask, my friend. I will listen, and see if I can be of any help to you."

"You know Segui, the smith, and his wife Marette?" Jehan pointed in the direction of their house, a little uphill from the market place. "They have had a nasty string of bad luck, recently, with a shipment of coal getting lost, an anvil breaking, and now Marette has broken a toe and can hardly walk. They get by, but it's just piling on, and so I took a look at them earlier today. And indeed, there is a curse hanging over them, but it's like nothing I have ever seen. It is so very elegant, it took me time to even understand how powerful this curse is. I am afraid we have only seen the beginning, yet, and it's going to get much, much worse. Have you heard their entire larder was infested with maggots? If anything similar happens again, they will have trouble getting through the winter, in a good year like this, can you believe it? It's as if someone has enchanted the entire town to conspire against them, and I have no clue who would even – "

Jehan's babbling explanation died off when he noticed Cassanoë's expression. She stared at him, eyes wide with horror, her mouth working soundlessly.

"Cassanoë, what is wrong?"

She grabbed Jehan's hand with painful strength and shook her pretty head. "No, no, no, no," she whispered softly. Her hair moved on it's own whim, youthful curls rearranging themselves into straighter, sterner lines, losing much of their green and gaining strands of yellow and orange instead. "Please don't tell me that this bastard is dragging you into his troubles."

"His name is Giraud."

"Oh no." Deeply upset, she took Jehan's hand and pressed it against her chest. She felt warm and a little coarse, like tree bark in the sun. "But I was so very fond of you."

"Please, not you as well!" Jehan let his head drop back against the tree and groaned softly. "When I first noticed that the curse is way above my skills, I went down to the river and ambushed three of the little *lutins* that pester the area. I thought, they're a nuisance, but they hear and see so much, maybe they will help in exchange for a fig or a cuddle. They got so scared they just shrieked and ran all over the place before they literally fell apart in a pile of river pebbles."

Cassanoë just nodded sagely, still pressing Jehan's hand against her chest.

"So I walked out of town and up to the beehives of the old Loussignac. There is a spirit hanging out with them, and she usually gathers knowledge pretty much like her bees gather honey, Abelia, do you know her? She just yelled at me to get lost and sent her bees after me."

Jehan looked at his companion, but her dark eyes were still filled with deep sorrow.

"Please, let it go, little Jehan," she pleaded. "You were always so smart, you should know when you're in over your head."

"I can't."

"But you really should." She pointed up at the tree above them. "Do you know why there are no hornets here? Because I do not let them nest. And so should you."

"I can't let it rest. I gave my word."

She cocked her head, suddenly looking rather inside of him than at him. "You accepted payment already, didn't you? I can feel him pull at your heart."

"If it only were just the matter of payment..." Jehan sighed. "I really need to know who did this, Cassanoë. Please. Just a hint, then."

"Oh, my poor darling. I am going to miss you."

"Stop talking to me as if I am already dead!"

"Well, not to be rude, but it won't be long now either way, you know? You are just a human, after all, and your kind is rather short-lived. You've seen more than twenty summers, now, haven't you? You'll be lucky if you see as many more." She patted his hand as if telling some harsh truth to a little child. "I am young, but I have already seen more than four of your generations come and go. Your own grandmother played around my trunk when she could barely walk, and even though just a few years have passed, you have to admit she looks quite wilted of late."

There was no ill will in her alien eyes, just genuine concern for a friendly creature that was as strange to her as she was to Jehan.

"So nothing from you? Not even a clue?"

She sighed again and shook her head. "Not a word. I like you, Jehan, really. You are my favourite human. But I don't like you that much."

"You are scared," Jehan suddenly realised. "Even you are scared of whoever did this."

"That boy is entangled in the worst kind of trouble, hear me. Untangle yourself as fast as you can." She bit her lower lip in concentration, thinking hard. "You won't let this go, will you?"

"I am afraid not."

"Then know that you won't find answers among the spirits of nature. And neither among the Fae." Her face was dead serious now, and Jehan knew she was giving him as much help as she thought she could risk. "Of all creatures that might know the answer to your question, only humans might be stupid enough to give it to you."

"Humans?" It took Jehan a long moment to figure out what she could possibly mean. "So I do have to talk to grandma after all, don't I?"

He had tried not to involve her from the very beginning. Her lecture on his idiocy was something he could have lived well without. But looking at Cassanoë's unreadable expression, he knew he had little other choice.

"At least I know where to go now." He leaned over and put his forehead against hers, a gesture of friendship and comfort that had developed between the two of them over the years. "Thank you, my dear."

"I would deserve your gratitude if I had managed to talk you out of this madness," she commented dryly. "But as things are, all I can do is wish you luck."

"I'll take your luck over someone else's good advice any day."

This brought a tiny smile back to her face at least, and a few newly green strands of hair curled up on her head.

"There's little advice you need and would listen to," she said with a knowing smile. "As long as you remember that the people small and overlooked sometimes are your strongest allies against the mighty, you'll do just fine."

Not that Jehan could make much of that advice as it was, but Cassanoë's words had always proven helpful so far. So he nodded and smiled, trying to put her words into a special corner of his mind where he would be likely to remember them when needed.

"Thank you, dear."

"Those thanks I can readily accept." She cocked her head and added: "I think you should go now. The children on the other side of the square are already wondering if you are drunk, talking to a tree like that in broad daylight."

Jehan followed her look and found a gaggle of kids on the other side of the market square who tried very hard not to appear too curious.

"Then I bid you farewell, fair lady of the green house," he said with a sketched bow of his head. "And I look forward to our next meeting."

That brought a renewed shadow to her face, but she gave him a smile nonetheless. "I would very much like to meet you again, Jehan *le Pêcheur*."

Jehan rose, put his straw hat back on and swiped the dust off the back of his breeches. When he turned around, Cassanoë was already gone.

Now that hadn't turned out as expected. Or rather, this had been even worse than he had feared. He had suspected this would be bad from the very beginning, but that a fae as strong and independent as Cassanoë would let him down, that was hinting at the involvement of powers he'd really rather leave alone.

Had that kiss been worth all this?

Maybe. Maybe not.

But looking back, he wouldn't have missed it for the world.

At least, no one seemed to have heard about that kiss, Jehan decided when he picked up his satchel and strode off towards his family's house on the other side of town.

The kids that had been staring at him dispersed just like every other gaggle of kids when grown-ups approached. There were no unusual stares from townsfolk, no wagging tongues that stopped wagging as soon as he walked around the corner. Then again, why on earth should Giraud tell anyone about their kiss? He was one of the town's most popular men, and he had even more to lose than Jehan. But that was the nature of fear – it didn't care for rational arguments.

Early that morning, Jehan had rushed to bring out the crayfish traps and check his weirs before he made his way into town. He had wanted to have a look at Giraud's parents as soon as possible – if he was going to get involved in this, he at least wanted to be swift about it. Only, he hadn't expected the reluctance of his usual sources.

The curse was too subtle for any spirit of nature, and too powerful for anything small. Considering that even Cassanoë had been cautious to tell him anything, that left unpleasantly few suspects. Either some high-ranking noble fae, or a witch or sorcerer proper. But how on earth had Giraud managed to anger one of those? How'd he even crossed paths with them?

Ah well, Jehan thought with a soundless sigh, he'd get to the bottom of this and inform Giraud. At least, he hadn't promised to undo the curse, only to look into it.

He made his way to his brother's house undisturbed, greeting the people he passed by and leaving a few breadcrumbs at the little bridge for the *lutins* that frequently loitered underneath. As soon as he had passed, he heard their excited chatter, but took great care not to look over his shoulder. They were a wild bunch, and didn't particularly like being watched.

He reached the house when the church bell rang the eleventh hour, and could see that Alienee and her daughters were having laundry day. Next to the scaffolding where the fishing nets dried overnight, two girls knelt on flat stones on the riverbank, pounding lumps of wet linens with their paddles. Further up the bank, on the other side of the house, Alienee and her eldest daughter Marianne were laying out other pieces to bleach on the dry meadow. Their geese had sought refuge from the heat of the day in the shade of the walnut tree, from afar looking nothing so much as more bundles of wet linen on the ground.

Alienee put down her basket when she noticed Jehan, and exchanged a few words with her daughter. She bundled up her skirts and walked up to him, her brisk steps looking rather ominous. Had he done something wrong? Except kissing the smith's son, that was? He couldn't think of anything, so he just walked on and smiled despite the slight heat on his face.

"Of course you'd show up today," Alienee said instead of a greeting, stern and yet beautiful as ever. Her hair had come loose underneath her bonnet, and a few dark strands were framing her face. "You and Iolande have always had a connection, haven't you?"

She was about the only person who addressed his grandmother by her first name, Iolande. To all others, she was '*Grand-mère Matrone*', or simply grandma. Jehan tried to think of something to say that would make him look calm and in control, but this really wasn't how he was feeling today.

"Did I do something wrong?"

"I bet you did," Alienee replied, her expression softening somewhat as she turned to walk alongside him. "Iolande isn't well, you know? She's been trying to hide it, but her age is showing, after all. I think she finally accepts that there will come a day she won't be around any longer. And it makes her angry, all the work she didn't finish."

"Grandma's been talking about dying since I can remember. Is this different?"

"She's stopped talking about dying." Alienee tucked a strand of hair back underneath her bonnet, a weary shadow over her face. "I have never seen her this upset, this restless. Almost as if she is counting her hours."

Completely at a loss at what to say, Jehan only nodded. He had always known that Grandma wouldn't be around forever. But she always had that armour of self-deprecating humour and sharp wit around her that made it hard to believe. Yes, she was old and frail, but there would always be a lot of other people around that Death would come for rather than his grandmother. He had always thought she'd die one day far from now, older than anyone else in town, happy and mumbling and content with her life.

Of course, Jehan hadn't forgotten that night six years ago, when the flood had come. Their house had been over-run by the river, and they had barely made it out alive. Desperate to save their two youngest children, his parents had gone back and never returned when a wall of their house collapsed onto them. A part of his grandmother had died that day, together with her son and her grandchildren. She had worked tirelessly to get her surviving family back on their feet, but Jehan had noticed the minute cracks in her armour whenever she thought she was unobserved.

The thought she might be preparing to leave her life with a heart full of regrets rattled his soul.

"I know you're a good man, Jehan," Alienee offered after a few moments walking silently by his side. "I don't know why she's so mad at you. But if you can make it right, you should do it soon. There might not be much time."

"She's mad at *me*?" Jehan's steps faltered. "Why?!"

Alienee shrugged apologetically. "I have no idea. As I said, you two... I swear, there were days I thought she'd prefer you as her successor, not me."

He stared at her, wide-eyed, helplessly feeling another blush creep up his cheeks.

"Oh my god, of course not!" Alienee genuinely seemed embarrassed, even though a little smile played around the corners of her mouth. "It is called midwife, not midman, there's a good reason for that. Men just can't stomach those things..." She sighed and put a gentle hand on Jehan's shoulder. "Just talk to her. Maybe she'll tell you."

Jehan nodded. "I will try. I ... I am sorry if I have caused you any trouble."

"I know you are, and I know you never wanted to." She gave him a wry smile. "Don't worry about me. Just try and make your peace with Iolande."

He nodded again and returned Alienee's half-smile in like. They had reached the house by now, and with a last, encouraging look, his sister-in-law left him at the foot of the stairs leading to the entrance. After the flood had passed, there had been nothing left of their house but a stretch of tumbled yellow stones. They had rebuilt it on the same spot, only half a storey higher, on a massive fieldstone foundation. If another such flood came, their house would become an island, but nothing worse than that. And even in the unheard of case that there would be more water one day – their house would stand long enough for everyone inside to get to safety.

Seven steps led up to the door, hewn from the same yellow stone as everything else. Unlike most other stones they had used to rebuild the house, though, these still had sharp corners, the lines of the stonemason's chisel clearly visible. Grandmother had insisted that they would get new ones for the stairs, as well as the door's lintel stone and the hearthstone of the fireplace. At that time, it had seemed like an unnecessary expense to Jehan, a needless fancy of a grief-stricken, stubborn old woman. But now, he saw it under a different light. It had been a new start, a new household to be created. Not the remnants of a broken one, but a new one, with new hopes and possibilities.

Not using old stones for the relevant pieces might have been mere superstition, but if he had to make that decision himself, now, Jehan would chose new ones as well. There was little to lose but money, and much to gain.

As some part of him still considered this his home, he entered without knocking. The windows were open, with the shutters on the south wall closed, keeping the inside cool and well-aired. Dustmotes danced in the slabs of light that slanted the air. The main room that made up the entire ground floor seemed empty, and it took his eyes a few heartbeats to adjust after the gleam of the midday sun outside.

"What do you want?"

So that dark bundle in the alcove at the far end of the room near the fireplace was his grandmother. She seemed tiny, but her voice had lost nothing of her acerbic bite.

"I just came to see you, grandmother."

She made a sound that could just as well have been a swearword. "No, you didn't. At least have the decency not to lie to my face."

With a soundless sigh, Jehan took off his hat, pulled one of the chairs from the family table over to her alcove and sat down. Her face was ashen against her simple brown bonnet, with fine nets of bright red veins covering her cheeks, and her milky eyes watery and half-closed. She was very old, yes, but how could her health have failed like this from one day to another? Her all but toothless mouth worked soundlessly, mumbling to herself while she waited for him to speak up.

But for a moment, he was at a loss for what to say. What was there to say? Jehan took her hand into his, holding it in silence until he had gathered enough courage.

"I need your help, grandmother."

She coughed out a brittle laughter. "Of course you do, you sweet oaf of a man. Why else would you abandon your work and your nice little hut in the woods at this time of the day? In the middle of the week, huh? So, what do you need?"

"I ... It's about Giraud, the smith."

"So it is him, huh? Finally." She perked up, her expression changing to something like mild anticipation. That was a lot better than expected.

"So you know?"

"I had my suspicions." Indeed, she looked rather pleased.

"And, what do you say?"

"Spit works in a pinch, but oil is better. Olive oil in particular."

"Pardon me?" Jehan took a few heartbeats to roll that sentence back and forth in his mind, hoping to find any connection to the curse he was looking into, but to no avail. "Grandmother, I am sorry, but I really have no idea what you are trying to tell me."

"Oh you sweet innocent child... Of course you don't." She patted his hand and sighed with an expression that was equally indulgent as it was exhausted. "It'll make sense eventually."

So he had done something stupid, again, and they hadn't even been talking about the kiss. But there was no point in trying to avoid the truth if he wanted her to help him.

"Giraud asked me to look into the curse that's on his parents. And I did, and it's grave."

His grandmother only nodded.

"So you know about the curse? Why didn't you do anything?"

"Why should I? It's nothing that concerns my family, and I would only burn my fingers meddling with this."

"But this... It's really bad, Grandma. They're struggling to keep their shop open, they have barely enough food for the winter... It's only going to get worse."

"Yes."

Her reaction felt so unexpectedly callous that Jehan for a while couldn't find any words. Why wouldn't she help, even though she probably could have? That was so unlike the woman he had known all his life. Unless...

"You saved your strength for us, didn't you?" he finally guessed.

That brought a weak smile to her face. "So there *is* some smarts in you after all."

Oddly embarrassed by the unexpected praise, he looked down at his bare feet.

"That spell you mentioned, it is nasty business, yes," she agreed into the silence. "How much do you know?"

"Nothing, really. Everyone's afraid to tell me anything about it, though apparently everyone knows something. Even Cassanoë's scared. Seems Giraud has angered a sorcerer, or a noble fae, I guess. Nothing else would work that subtly."

"Good, good reasoning." A fit of dry coughs rattled her. Jehan reached for the pitcher of water on the small table next to the alcove, filled her cup and gave her a few sips to drink. It took a while before she could continue, her voice hoarse. "I don't know much more than you do. Only thing I know is that working against that spell would require more than the little tricks we usually do."

"What do you mean?"

"Oh, come on. We talked about the ancient crafts often enough. You still have that dagger and your wolf pelt, don't you?"

That sent a shiver down Jehan's spine. Of course, grandmother had talked to him about the ancient crafts, about the ways of the gifted people in times when the world was still wild, when humans were much closer to their animal nature. When magic wasn't a polite parlour game of exchanging gifts and observing customs, when magic had been blood and sweat and sex and death. He remembered those stories vividly. Only, he had never thought them anything else but stories.

"I still have that wolf pelt," he replied, his tongue so dry he took a sip of water himself. "Not sure about the dagger. So what do I have to do?"

"Hm." She cocked her head, thinking. "That depends. Why do you care?"

"I... " He wanted to tell her what had happened the other night on the crossing of Beronsac, but he just couldn't find the words.

"Eh. You did something stupid, didn't you?"

"I... I kissed him."

She didn't even flinch, as if that was the most normal thing in the world to her. What a strange, strange woman.

"And? Did he kiss you back? Or is he blackmailing you into helping him?"

Jehan was silently relieved she couldn't see the violent blush on his face. "He kissed me first."

"Ha. Good, very good." His grandmother seemed inordinately pleased. "So this might even work."

"You think so? It feels like a disaster to me, right from the very beginning."

"Don't be such a wuss. Some things in life are worth taking some risks for. How else will you ever learn what you are actually capable of?"

"I am not sure I want to learn that."

"Oh goddammit, *Jehan le Pêcheur*, grow some balls."

The force of her outburst made him flinch back. Did she really think him a coward?

"You have to decide what you want, Jehan, and you'll eventually have to fight for it, one way or another."

At least, his heart had a clear opinion for once. "I want to keep my word to Giraud."

"So there." She nodded, her breath going swift and shallow, like the one of a bird. She dropped her head against the wall behind her. "Cursed be this body. I knew this day would come, when the price to keep up my health would become too steep. But there are some things even I am unwilling to pay..."

"Get some rest, then grandmother," Jehan suggested, even though he didn't exactly understand what his grandmother had hinted at. "I can come back another day."

"And what did I say about growing a pair?" She moved her hand, feebly, but it wasn't enough to become a readable gesture. "Go, seek out the ancient Raëlle. Tell her I send you, and she'll help. She'll put you on the right path."

"The witch?!" The words burst out of him before he could think about it, and it didn't even need his grandmother's headshake to make him blush. Stupid, again. And a coward.

"Yes, that one. Who's a witch just like me. And you, for that matter." She took another laboured breath. "And take that smith's son with you. The path to her tower is dangerous, and you'll need someone who knows his way around a fight."

Being around Giraud for any prolonged time wasn't exactly what Jehan had planned. For a moment, he was tempted to tell her that he had crayfish traps out that needed emptying, but she would know that it was just an excuse. But if his grandmother said so, that's what he would do. Those traps and the little crustaceans inside could just as well wait another day.

"I will."

He wasn't sure how he'd explain to Giraud where they'd be going, or why, but he'd try.

"Good." She pulled his hand away from his. "Now leave. You have a long way ahead of you today. I am tired."

Jehan nodded silently and rose, picking up his straw hat again on the way out. His heart was pumping in his chest, and he didn't really know why. At the door, he hesitated, a knot of words in his throat that just didn't want to come out. But he had to say it, however hard it might be.

"Grandmother?"

"What?" Her voice feeble, but still gnarly like the roots of a mountain fir.

"I love you, grandmother. You know that, yes?"

"I never doubted that for a moment, my dear." In the dim recesses of the alcove, he thought there was a contented smile spreading on her weathered face. "Go with my blessing, Jehan, and with my love."

Chapter Three – Brigands in the Forest

"Good day, *Maître* Forgeron, is Giraud in?"

Jehan politely tipped the rim of his hat when he entered the open shed that made up most of the workshop. Giraud's father stood at the anvil, hammering a square rod of glowing red iron into shape. Short and stocky, *Maître* Segui was all rounded muscles and strong hands, his blackened face dominated by jolly eyes like polished marbles. He wore his thinning hair cropped close to the skull, but he had ample hair on his cheeks and shoulders to more than make up for that.

"The boy's in the back yard," he replied after a cursory glance at Jehan before eyeing his work critically. "Do you need new hooks?"

Not waiting for Jehan's answer, the smith turned around and stuck his iron back into the coals of the forge, gesturing a small boy in the corner to start working the bellows.

"No new hooks, this time." Jehan smiled politely in lack of any other words. He couldn't possibly tell the truth, of course, but then what else? He should really have thought of a fitting excuse to show up here in the middle of the day before actually doing so. "He ... offered to help me, and I came to ask if he had time this afternoon."

"That boy's supposed to be working here in in the smithy, not for the rest of the village." Segui gave a deep, rumbling laugh and shook his head. "Tell him as long as he's got those swords for the Guard repaired and packed, he's free to go wherever he likes."

"Thank you, *Maître*, I will." Jehan nodded and gestured at the narrow archway that led past the house into the yard behind. An irregular noise came from there, like chopping wood, only faster. "Can I just go through?"

The smith merely harrumphed something vaguely affirmative and turned his attention back to his forge. For any other observer, there would have been nothing wrong about the smith. But Jehan could not overlook the dark lines that hung off his form like a cape of gossamer shadows, lines that weighed him down and drained his every movement, every breath, little by little. The curse on him was a work of beauty, in a way, Jehan had to admit that. Dreadful beauty, though, and the thought that he was about to face a creature able to spin such clear malevolence into a work of art chilled Jehan despite the heat of the day. For a heartbeat, Jehan wondered if he could maybe exclude the fae from his list of suspects. Their magic didn't last well around cast iron, and forged iron wasn't much better.

But there was nothing to be done about it by standing there and staring, so he just nodded politely and picked his way through the workshop. He had to take great care not to step into some sharp shards of metal with his bare feet, or bang his head on one of the low beams that carried the roof. He could walk through the river shallows or the forest as easily as on any road, but this was genuinely unfamiliar terrain. Why hadn't he thought of bringing his sandals? Those would really have been useful now.

The house was one of the last in the back of the town, halfway up along the road that led up onto the cliffs and deeper into the forest. Two storeys of solid yellow stone, as nicely built as could be expected from a well-to-do smith in a town as small as La Morangiasse. The workshop was a large lean-to to one side of the house, and the cliff loomed over both of them, leaving a little walled backyard between the buildings and the rocky face. Jehan had never been inside, so when he passed the archway, he stopped in surprise.

The cliff didn't come straight down here, but had a little recess, almost like half a cave, so the yard was a lot bigger than it looked from the outside. A tiny stream of water trickled out in the back and gathered in a small, roughly hewn basin. Maidenhair ferns and moss grew wild in the shade, interspersed with low carpets of wild strawberries where the sun eventually reached the ground.

It was an unexpected, beautiful refuge from the heat of the day, but that wasn't what made Jehan forget to shut his mouth.

The table and benches that normally would take up most of the space in the backyard had been pushed aside. In the clearing, Giraud had wedged a large piece of timber upright between two rocks on the ground, and was currently busy attacking it viciously with a sword. Though viciously seemed the entirely wrong word here. Elegantly, Jehan corrected himself, skilfully, focussed. He had occasionally see the Comte Rainaud's guards sparring with their swords, but this was something else. Almost like dancing, he thought, if dancing had been about killing people.

For a long moment, he just stood there and watched, until Giraud unleashed a particularly flamboyant flurry of attacks onto his wooden target and caught sight of his unexpected audience. Startled, he paused, then burst into laughter.

"How long have you been standing there? Have you been watching me?" His face was flushed, and his simple linen tunic was drenched with sweat. "I'm making a fool of myself here, I know."

"Not at all." Oddly, Jehan's mouth was dry all of a sudden. "It looked rather ... competent."

Again, Giraud laughed. "Maybe from your point of view, it does. I'm just fooling around, really." With a sigh, he took a last glance at the sword in his hands, checked its edge and carefully put it down into a straw-padded crate together with the other repaired guard swords. "I wish I could work with proper rapiers. Much more elegant than these lumps of iron." He looked up again, a beaming smile on his flushed face. "Can you imagine, in Paris, the King's guards have the finest rapiers of all, Spanish steel, and muskets, one for each man! We'd have no problems with brigands here if we had that sort of equipment."

"Have you ever talked to LaForge about joining the Guard? I've never heard you sound this excited about smithing, have I?"

Giraud cast him a glance that was half amused, half insulted. "The captain has asked me a few times to join his ranks, yes. But I know my place, and it's here with my family." He pointed at the swords. "This is just me dreaming of some adventure." He chuckled again, waving as if the gesture could shoo away his dreams. For a moment, he wrestled with his tunic, then grabbed the garment by the hem and pulled it off over his head. "So what brings you here? Surely not just wanting to watch me make a fool out of myself?"

Speechless, Jehan watched Giraud bunch up his tunic and wipe himself down. He threw the tunic over the makeshift dummy, fetched a bucket from the corner of the yard and walked to the small spring in the back. With a long, well-trained motion, he scooped water from the shallow basin and poured it right over his head. Gasping with the sudden cold, he laughed under his breath, shook himself like a dog and sent droplets of water flying everywhere in high arcs.

"Much better," he stated. He squeezed the water out of his hair and wiped it off his arms and chest. "So, what brings you here?"

Jehan blinked, his mind reluctant to focus on anything other than fine rivulets of water on tanned skin, of sinewy muscles moving underneath with strength and grace in equal measure. The water running off Giraud's belly seeped into the waistband of his maroon breeches, making the fabric cling to his curves even more. He was doing this on purpose, Jehan thought, he had to be. No one in their right mind could show themselves off this advantageously and not be aware of it in the slightest.

But one look at Giraud's face confirmed once again that there was utterly no guile in him.

"I ... have looked into the matter you asked me to," Jehan started. Immediately, Giraud's expression changed from eager curiosity to hopeful excitement. "As you expected, it is serious, and unfortunately well beyond my skills. I have to consult other ... sources."

Giraud's expression turned progressively more thoughtful while Jehan spoke, and when he had finished, Giraud nodded and gestured for Jehan to come closer.

"So, what do you need my help with?" Giraud asked when they were both standing under the overhanging cliff, next to the spring. "You wouldn't be here if it weren't so."

This close, Jehan saw individual drops of water falling out of Giraud's hair, running down his throat and disappearing underneath his iron necklace. It made focussing on his words unexpectedly difficult. At least, the tinkling spring behind them would mask their words a little.

"I need to go to the tower of Raëlle. I would prefer not going alone, and if we leave soon, we could be back before tomorrow."

"The ancient Raëlle?" Unlike Jehan, Giraud reacted with eager anticipation to the name. "She really exists?"

"Yes." Jehan barely managed not to roll his eyes just like his grandmother would have done. "Yes, she does. But it's a long way to the cliffs of Petit Houx, and not without peril. Can you join me?"

"What? Of course! You're not going on this adventure without me." He looked around, all but humming like a bowstring. "Do you expect brigands? Or ... less mundane trouble?"

How could a man look so excited at the prospect of trouble? "Both."

"So ... I could bring one of the swords, you know? They don't expect them back before tomorrow." Giraud looked at Jehan pleadingly, as if it were his decision to take up forbidden arms and carry them through half of the Perigord. But he didn't have to reply. Apparently, Giraud could read the thoughts right off his face. "You think it's a bad idea, don't you? More trouble than it's probably worth? Yeah, you are probably right. I'll think about it."

A wide grin spread on Giraud's face, his delight so apparent that Jehan wondered if he had ever met a man whose emotions he could read so easily, or who could sway his own mood with nothing but a look or smile.

"I knew it was a good idea asking you for help," Giraud said and pulled Jehan into a tight and slightly wet hug. "I'll just go get dressed into something decent and then we'll be off, yes? You wait here?"

The last part seemed to have been more of an order than a suggestion, as Giraud turned around on his heels and disappeared into the house. Jehan was left behind at the spring, listening to the trickle of water and the thumping of his heart in his chest. He had the same ugly feeling he had had on the crossing of Beronsac, right before Giraud had kissed him.

Was there any way this whole affair would not end up in a terrible disaster? If there was one, he couldn't see it.

Jehan sat down on the upturned bucket and watched the ripples on the surface of the water basin. He could hear Giraud rummage throughout the house, could hear Segui grumble and hammer in the workshop. Yes, this probably would end in nothing but tears, but he was determined to see it through nonetheless. With a soundless sigh, Jehan burrowed his toes into the moss on the ground, careful not to uproot the water violets that were growing in between.

Instead of circling the same problem in his head again and again, Jehan tried to remember what he knew about Raëlle, the ancient witch that lived alone in a tower on the cliffs beyond Castelfort. It wasn't particularly much, but his grandmother had told him those stories often enough to give him at least a rough idea. How much of her stories had actually been lessons, he wondered? To the other children, they had always been fairy tales, nothing more, if good and scary ones. But Jehan had always known those creatures were as real as anyone else around the table. He had learned how to treat the Little Folk through her tales, that much was sure. To leave little gifts for the *lutins* wherever possible, but never to acknowledge them or even expect gratitude. To ignore the *nains* where possible, and only ask their help with labour when in genuine need. To stay away from noble fae as much as possible, and to treat them with the utmost respect if unavoidable. So, pretty much like human nobles, to be honest.

"He'll be right with you!"

Jehan looked up, and found Giraud's mother looking down at him from one of the first floor windows. Her round face was not as apple-cheeked as usual, but Marette seemed genuinely pleased nonetheless.

"Madame Forgeron," he greeted her with a sketched bow. "Please excuse the intrusion."

"Oh Jehan, please." She waved away his concerns with a soft laugh. "If at all, I have to apologise for my son being so scatterbrained he forgot that he promised to help you today after work."

"Well..." Jehan smiled at her. At least Giraud had picked the same white lie as he had, so hopefully their stories would match. "Thank you for allowing him to come."

"Oh, he'll have to sort that out with Segui, you know? I am not going to meddle in their business. By the way – I heard your grandmother isn't well. You send her my regards and our best wishes when you see her next time, will you?"

"Of course I will, Madame."

From somewhere in the back of the house, Giraud shouted a muffled question, and Marette turned around to answer.

"It should be up on the wardrobe in your room," she yelled into the house. "Where it belongs!"

Jehan couldn't make out Giraud's reply, but he could see Marette chuckle and shake her head.

"I'll help him find his stuff," she told Jehan, "or it'll take ages before you can do anything useful. Just don't let my boy get you in some sort of trouble, he's supposed to help you, after all."

She gave him a friendly wave and disappeared into the house with a slightly hobbled gait.

Muffled bits of her argument with Giraud reached the backyard every now and then, and it seemed to Jehan like the most loving and caring argument he had heard in a long while. It made him miss his own parents, and for a while, Jehan was lost in silent memories of family dinners full of laughter and silly games.

Something rumbled in the dark of the house, and a heartbeat later, Giraud came tumbling out into the backyard like a trout trying to escape a weir.

"Sorry for taking this long," he explained under his breath, smiling and presenting several bundles under his arm. "I had to pack a few things."

He wore his white shirt again, and his suede pants, Jehan noted, and high, fashionably cuffed boots. On his head at a jaunty angle, he wore a matching brown felt hat with green rooster feathers, and he looked every bit the young, dashing hero. Giraud's family had never lacked for money, and it seemed he had spent at least some part of his allowance on his clothes. At least, that was before a curse had started wreaking havoc on their business and health.

"Mama even threw in a few provisions, said I shouldn't expect you to feed me when I offered – " Giraud cocked his head. "Are you alright?"

"No, I am fine." Caught staring, that was, but hopefully not blushing again. "It's just ... those clothes suit you. You look very handsome."

"Oh." For half a moment, Giraud seemed taken aback. Then, a fine smile grew on his face, as if they were sharing a naughty secret, and he cast down his eyes in a rare, shy expression. "Thank you."

"Now that was one compliment easily given." Jehan rose from his bucket, righted his straw hat and walked over to Giraud. "Anything I should be carrying?"

"Actually – you can hold all of these. I have an idea." Without waiting for a reply, Giraud dumped the pile of stuff he had been carrying into Jehan's arms.

Somehow, 'I have an idea' sounded a lot more threatening and ominous than it should have. But as for now, Jehan merely nodded and followed his companion into the workshop. The bundles were heavy, and at least one sounded suspiciously like long, slender blades of metal grating against each other, even though it was too short to contain a proper sword.

"Papa?!" Giraud yelled over the din of the hammer. "Papa, can we have the horses?!"

The hammering stopped. From his vantage point behind Giraud, Jehan could see the smith cock his head pretty much in the same manner as his son and give him a suspicious look.

"I promised Jehan to help with his new fishing weir, and it's a long way there and back again," Giraud lied without even blinking. "I'd be back much sooner this way."

"Are the swords ready and packed?"

"In their box on the table in the back yard."

Jehan knew Giraud had put on his most winning smile, and he could see the effect on *Maître* Segui. His stern frown lasted only for a heartbeat before a wry smile broke through and he nodded indulgently.

"Thank you, Papa!" Already, Giraud was out of the workshop and off towards the small shed that housed the smith's horses.

"Just make sure you don't get into trouble!" Segui yelled after him. "And make sure they're both back tomorrow morning, and properly fed!"

"Thank you, *Maître* Forgeron," Jehan said while tiptoeing his way back out of the workshop. "I'll make sure the horses are fed when we bring them back."

"My son occasionally forgets such details," Segui added, still smiling. "A reminder or two would be greatly appreciated."

Jehan nodded in agreement and left the smith to his work. The horses were in their small shed next to the workshop, an older grey gelding that was mostly used to pull the smith's cart, and a younger, fawn-coloured one for errands. Giraud was already taking out the saddles for both of them, and he grinned at Jehan across the horses' backs.

"That should make things a lot easier, don't you think?" Jehan's apprehension must have been clearly visible on his face, for Giraud asked: "You can ride, can you?"

"I have ridden a donkey a few times," Jehan answered truthfully, "never a horse. Is it much different?"

"Not really, no." Giraud's eyes sparkled. "More skittish, obviously, and a lot taller. You'll get used to it in no time. I'll take Trajan, here, and you'll get old Grise. I promise he won't bite you."

"I am rather sure of it." For a moment, Jehan silently watched as Giraud put the well-worn saddles onto the horses and made sure their bridles were on properly. "You really are looking forward to this, aren't you?"

Again, Giraud looked up across the animals, his eyes bright like the green feathers on his hat. "Don't you?"

"There's quite a few ways this could end up in trouble."

"And quite a few that could make it worth the risk, am I right?"

"Maybe." Jehan shrugged. "You were right to ask me to help, and maybe there is a way to get the – I mean, to help your parents. But I don't exactly feel comfortable, you know?"

"But you know how it is in the stories." Giraud came over and relieved Jehan of the first two bundles he had been carrying. "It's always a disaster while you're in the middle of it. But once it's over, it becomes an adventure, and just another great story to tell."

"You and I apparently have been told very different stories. With very different endings, at that."

Giraud chuckled softly. "Apparently." He took the last bag out of Jehan's hands, looked inside and pondered it's contents for a moment. Then he shrugged, grinned and slung it over his shoulder. "Ready to find out what kind of story this is going to be?"

"Not really."

Giraud laughed out loud and handed him the reins to his horse.

"Then let's go."

***

They arrived at the crossing of Beronsac a short while later, and Giraud reigned in his horse, slowing down to a leisurely trot.

"This way, I assume?" He pointed straight on, towards the lesser travelled road that followed the right side of the river.

Jehan nodded. Usually, everyone used the old bridge of Beronsac to cross to the left side of the river, and continue towards Castelfort. The road ahead was little used except for a few merchants on the long way to Bergerac, who considered saving the detour via Castelfort worth the risk of brigands or wolves.

Giraud cast a glance over his shoulder, as if trying to make sure no-one was watching them. "You think we can pause here for a moment?"

"I guess. What for?"

"You asked me to join you as your guard. But unarmed, I'll be of little use, won't I?"

"I thought we decided against a sword..."

"I said I would think about it." Again, Giraud laughed out loud. "Oh come on, I don't want to get into trouble any more than you do. But I also happen to know a little about the laws and what I am allowed to carry and what not. I won't do anything *Capitaine* LaForge would object to."

Jehan severely doubted the part about Giraud not wanting to get into trouble, but he didn't say a word. Instead, he just followed him until they were around the nose of the cliff and sheltered from view of anyone would might have been on the road behind them. There, they found a nice, shady spot underneath a small copse of young oaks and dismounted.

With the grin still playing around the corners of his mouth, Giraud unpacked the suspicious bundle, producing a short leather jerkin and a pair of solid gloves that he put on with obvious relish. Next, he unrolled a leather baldric that he slung over his head, and a heavy belt he put around his waist. Lastly, he took up a long knife in a leather sheath that he fastened to his belt, and a worn-looking hammer to hang to his baldric. He put his hat back on and flicked it into the proper angle.

"So – how do I look?"

"Impressive." Which was kind of an understatement, once again. He looked radiant, even despite the odd hammer. "But are you sure that knife isn't going to get us into trouble? It does look an awful lot like a sword to me."

"Oh, absolutely not." He pulled the blade out of its sheath and laid the dagger's cross-guard against his wrist so the tip of the blade came to rest just above his elbow. "See? No longer than my forearm, so it's obviously just a hunting knife."

"If you say so."

"Indeed I do." He spun the blade around a few times, flipped it to his left hand and repeated the manoeuvre before he sheathed it again. "It's mostly for parrying anyway, and as long as we're not up against muskets, it should be deterrent enough."

"It definitely looks rather impressive." Still, that odd hammer tugged on Jehan's mind. "Why the hammer? You surely could have taken another 'hunting knife'."

"Oh, that?" He drew the hammer from it's sling on the baldric and whirled it around a few times with the same, elegant ease as the dagger before. Only this time, Giraud's grin had a decidedly wicked edge. "It's a cheap, old smith's hammer, the one I started training with as a kid. One can deal a nice bit of damage, but unless you go for the head, it's very hard to kill someone."

"Smart."

"Yeah." Giraud's smile grew vicious. "Unless you're fae, of course, then it'll hurt real bad."

The unexpected vitriol in his voice startled Jehan, and it took him a moment to realise what he had actually said. Finally, the dull gleam of the hammer made grim sense.

"Cast iron?"

Giraud nodded, his usually irrepressible smile gone from his face. "As a smith's hammer, this thing is crap. But as a weapon against them..."

For a heartbeat, Jehan didn't know what to say. Cast iron was hard and brittle and unforgiving – so hard the subtle magic of the fae withered and died around it. It was rather commonly known that the fae despised the metal, but there were only very few people who knew that they also feared it, and with very good reason. You could hit and bash and even stab one of the fae, and they would feel pain and fury, but they would also recover from almost any wound inflicted on them. Like the dreams and stories they were made of, they were almost impossible to kill. But wounds caused by cold iron, those were different, and healed less eagerly on a fae than normal wounds would on an average human.

Bringing a weapon of cold iron into a fight with the fae was a cruel and determined thing to do, and spoke volumes about Giraud's intentions. Something Jehan had never before suspected in him.

"I didn't know you've got history with the Fair Folk."

"Not much of a history, really." With a pointed gesture, Giraud shoved the hammer back into its sling, and his smile went up again like a mask. "Mostly a history of them not being there when needed."

There had to be a lot more to this particular story, but Jehan had a feeling that it wouldn't be wise to press. Another lesson he had learned as a child from watching his grandmother do her job while hiding under the kitchen table – they all would tell you, eventually, if you gave them time and made sure they and their secrets were safe with you.

"I am sorry," he said, giving the one answer that was always right when only being given a hint of a problem.

Giraud shrugged, re-enforcing his smile. "Shall we continue? I'd like to get past Castelfort as quickly as possible."

He was up on his horse again before Jehan could answer.

***

They passed Castelfort about half an hour later. Every time the forest opened up a little, they could see the crenellated fortifications of the keep on the cliffs across the river.

They were riding at a gentle trot, and Jehan found his mind wandering. Just a little further, he would have to start looking out for the cliffs of Petit Houx to his right, and then for two old trees that marked the path leading up to Raëlle's tower. But they would have to clear at least this one river bend before they –

Giraud reigned in his horse without warning, and Jehan's grey gelding halted so abruptly that he had a hard time keeping himself in the saddle.

"What's wrong?" Jehan asked, startled. But when he led his horse around, he immediately saw that a large tree had fallen across the road, effectively blocking most of it. "Crap. Should we dismount and lead the horses around the – "

A rustle in the undergrowth to his right startled Jehan, and he turned around just in time to see two cloaked figures crawl out of the shrubs. They wore dirty cloaks and hats the colour of dry leaves, and had their neckerchiefs pulled up over their noses so only their eyes were visible.

Brigands.

Jehan froze. He had never been ambushed before, and he had never thought it would happen here, within spitting distance of Castelfort. But the way they were brandishing their clubs left little doubt about their intentions.

A similar rustle to his left announced two more bandits, and almost simultaneously, a fifth cloaked figure climbed onto the fallen tree that blocked their way. Judging by the fact that this one had a nasty looking dagger and a red neckerchief over his face, Jehan assumed that this would be the leader of the brigands.

"Your money, or your lives!" the brigand with the red mask yelled at them. "Choose wisely."

Jehan felt his heart pound in his chest. This was exactly the reason why one kept to one's own turf whenever possible. Less than an hour out of town, and already he was being robbed. Not that he had any coin on his person, but the horses and Giraud's weapons would be worth a nice little something.

"Messieurs." Giraud's voice was calm, but surprisingly loud and clear. "I beg you to reconsider. If you let us go now, I assure you we won't harm any of you."

"Ha!" the leader of the brigands spat. "And how would you accomplish that, pray tell?"

"I am a trained fighter," Giraud replied evenly, spinning his 'hunting knife' around just like he had done earlier. "And you and your merry men, Monsieur, are nothing but peasants."

How could he? Jehan for a heartbeat was tempted to say something rash, but then he noticed the reaction of the brigands from the corner of his eyes. All of them hesitated, as if suddenly realising that they were up against a much greater opponent than they had planned. Maybe there were advantages to travelling with someone who looked like a dashing young hero that went beyond having something nice to look at.

"I assure you, Monsieur, don't allow our simple clothes to lead you astray – my men are trained warriors, and have killed many a traveller who spoke as rashly as – "

With a motion so quick Jehan almost missed it, Giraud leaned towards the closest brigand and grabbed the tip of his club. With a deft motion, he pulled both the club and the man towards him, then kicked the poor guy smack in the face. The bandit yelled in pain and stumbled back, landing on his back.

"They don't seem like trained warriors to me." Cold venom was dripping from Giraud's voice, and it was just as credible as his usual light-hearted kindness. He took the club he had gained and set it down onto his lap. "I repeat my offer. Leave now, and you won't be harmed. Well, no more than you have already been."

This time, the brigand leader hesitated visibly.

"So what is it going to be?" Giraud asked again. "Will you protect your health? Or your reputation as bumbling fools?"

"Watch your tongue!" The bandit leader barked, but he sounded rather angry than aggressive. "You seem to forget that you are still outnumbered."

Giraud cocked his head, making the feathers on his hat bob in the air. "Haven't I beaten you up once already, on the Saint John's day market?" he asked, the earlier bravado in his voice replaced by genuine annoyance. "You're from Castelfort, aren't you?"

"What?" Suddenly, the leader's voice sounded a lot younger. "No. We're brigands, former mercenaries in the service of Baron – "

"Oh cut the crap." Giraud slid off his horse. In the same motion, he had dropped the club and drawn his hammer. "You're bored boys, and I have no time for your games. So who's going to be first?"

He looked at the surrounding 'brigands' with a clear challenge, chin out, eyes cold.

"Isn't – isn't he that smith from La Morangiasse?" one of the bandits to the left asked, causing a stir among his fellows.

"The one and only." Again, Giraud flipped the hammer into the air, catching it without looking. He took a few steps forward and eyed their opponents. "Still so courageous?"

On Jehan's left, the one bandit Giraud had kicked into the dirt mumbled something unintelligible and crawled back onto his feet. He spat some blood and disappeared back into the forest, leaving his comrades to stare at his back in bewilderment.

"Come back, you arsehole!" the leader yelled, but his words seemed to get lost among the trees.

"Shit, Marton, this isn't what we planned," another one added. "I'm not getting my arms broken for this. I'm out."

That one had been standing to Jehan's right, and now walked across the road keeping a respectful distance from Giraud, even tipping his hat politely as he passed him, and disappeared into the forest as well. Jehan listened to his footsteps in the dry undergrowth disappear into the distance.

Still, Giraud had his weapons drawn, his expression as calm and grim as before.

"Don't test my patience," he growled, "it's not one of my strongest traits."

For a few heartbeats more, he and the bandit leader stared at each other in silence. Finally, the red-masked guy turned around and left his vantage point on the fallen tree so quickly his cape fluttered behind him.

"Men!" he yelled, "we retreat!"

The two remaining 'men' gave an audible sigh of relief. With another set of polite nods in the direction of Giraud, they slunk back into the forest to their left, now genuinely looking like a set of scolded boys.

When their footsteps had vanished into the general rustle of the forest, Giraud sheathed his weapons and gave a relieved sigh himself. He turned around to Jehan, his face still dead serious.

"Are you alright?"

"Yes." Suddenly as elated as he had been scared just a moment ago, Jehan realised that Giraud seemed even more attractive now, if that was at all possible. But his sombre expression didn't fit with the relief Jehan felt so deeply it tingled in his toes, so he asked: "What's wrong? You did great, that was ... really something."

"It was too close." But Jehan's compliment brought a tiny smile back to his face nonetheless. "Thank you, though."

"What to you mean, too close?"

"I am good at posturing, but not so good at fighting." Giraud mounted again and gave Jehan a tight smile. "I don't know if I could have done something against all five of them, at least not without seriously hurting someone."

"They didn't seem to have such qualms."

That one brought the familiar gleam back to Giraud's eyes. Damn, but he was pretty when he smiled.

"They were fools, and needed to be taught a lesson, but nothing more than that, really." He shrugged. "We were lucky I recognised him from last year."

"Indeed." Hardly able to suppress his smirk, Jehan asked: "Do you beat up many people when you're at the market?"

Giraud gave him a half-smile, looking somewhat guilty. "Less than you may think, more than I should have. I try to limit myself to one brawl per evening, though."

He spurred his horse into a slow step and carefully led it around the tree on the road. Apparently, they weren't the first ones to pass this way since the tree had fallen, and there was a narrow but passable path to the left. Trajan twitched nervously a few times when his flanks scratched against some of the branches, but Jehan's gelding seemed perfectly content to do nothing but trot after his companion.

"What I really don't understand," Giraud said, "is all this enmity between our town and Castelfort, you know? There is – we could do so much more if the youths from both towns would stop hating each others' guts and instead banded together. We'd have a lot fewer problems in this area, then."

"Well, that would be nice, for sure. But it's nothing new that our towns don't like each other, and given our history, I think that's more than understandable."

"Is it?"

They were trotting alongside each other by now, a bit faster than before to make up lost time, but still leisurely enough to have a comfortable conversation.

"Of course." A sidelong glance to Giraud told him that the situation was not so clear to him, after all. "You know, after what happened in the war?" Still nothing but polite cluelessness in Giraud's face. "Really? But you must have heard the stories."

"I have heard plenty of stories about us beating up the boys from Castelfort and the other way round, but there was never anything in it that sounded like a reason. And it definitely had nothing to do with the war, either."

Jehan had already opened his mouth to say something snappy, but caught himself in the last moment. Yes, he had always been aware that his grandmother's stories about monsters and fairies had been different. Of course – her stories had been real, whereas everyone else was just telling fairy tales. But what if she had cloaked a lot of other knowledge in those tales?

"As far as I know, it started in the Great War, when England and France were fighting for this land for over a hundred years."

Giraud's eyes went wide. "That really happened?"

"I have no reason to believe otherwise," Jehan replied. The more he looked at it, the more he came to the conclusion that grandma had force-fed him and his siblings knowledge, and without them even noticing. "As far as I know, before that war, this entire area was ruled by the Marquis of Beronsac, a staunch defender of France."

"The ruins..." Almost instinctively, Giraud glanced back over his shoulder.

"Yep, those. Beronsac held off the English for many years, but eventually fell. It was so badly damaged that the castle was abandoned, and the Marquis fled to his secondary keep – Castelfort – leaving their harbour town to the English."

"Beronsac had a harbour?"

"La Morangiasse, you dullard." Jehan laughed at Giraud's genuinely delighted expression when the details in his mind suddenly clicked together. "See? We were on different sides of the Hundred-years-war, our two towns, and even though it's been over for many years, the scars are still there."

"Oh, man." He seemed genuinely impressed. "La Morangiasse was English?"

"For a while, yes. Both our town and Castelfort and everything along the river changed hands several times. It's not called the Hundred-years-war for nothing, you know? But while both La Morangiasse and Castelfort have been owned by both the French and the English eventually, they never were on the same side for long."

"What a mess." Giraud shook his head. "I am just surprised that it's still noticeable after all this time. That war – how long ago was it?"

"Oh, not sure..." In his head, Jehan tried to string the stories about their country's past in a proper line. "But at least two-hundred years, I guess. A long time."

"Most people can only hold a grudge until they are sober again. And you really think it's because of that war?"

"Villages have a longer memory than people."

Giraud harrumphed some agreement, and for a while, the rode alongside each other in silence.

Every now and then, the forest opened onto the river flowing to their left, its lazy water dark at the foot of the cliffs on the other side. Several times, Jehan was tempted to suggest a short break and a dip in the river, but he kept his mouth shut. After seeing Raëlle, perhaps. And then, maybe not with Giraud around. He really didn't need another incident like that one on the bridge, did he?

It took him only a swift glance at his companion to remember that while he maybe didn't need another such incident, he pretty much would like one.

Chapter Four - The Cliffs of Petit Houx

"Over there, those trees!" Jehan pointed to their right, where behind a swath of low grass, two gnarled chestnut trees stood in the afternoon sun. "That should be it."

Giraud clicked at his horse and led it into the meadow towards the trees. As before, Jehan's horse followed without him needing to do much at all.

It was early afternoon, by now, and except for that one incident with the 'brigands' near Castelfort, their trip had been pretty uneventful so far. A fact that Jehan was unreservedly grateful for. But he knew that there would be enough challenges still to come, and those would be his to sort out. The ancient Raëlle wasn't particularly fond of visitors, and most of the tales that involved her were about the various nasty ways she had dispatched trespassers on her grounds.

Jehan forced a smile onto his face. He just hoped he'd find a way to talk to her before she became too upset by their presence.

Giraud passed the gap between the two chestnut trees and turned his horse around. "Where to now?"

There was nothing but a bit more meadow in front of him, and a rather dense looking thicket of holly and young oaks. Behind those, the cliffs of Petit Houx rose up steeply into the sky, covered with similarly dense and thorny growth. It all looked suitably uninviting.

"There's got to be something like a path here, leading up the cliffs." He followed Giraud past the two old trees, and stopped his horse when a familiar sensation tingled in his nose. Magic, subtle and old, hung over the place, something very tricky and hard to grasp. Different from the kind of work his grandmother did, but not entirely alien to him.

"Jehan? Hey, are you alright?" Giraud led his horse a few steps towards him. "Jehan?!"

"Huh?" With a startled look, he realised that he had lost himself entirely in the place's enchantment. "There's magic here. It's the right place."

"Really? It feels ... pretty much not magic to me. Actually, it pretty much feels like we're in the wrong place."

Jehan smiled widely. "Exactly."

He slipped off his horse, landing a little less elegantly than he had expected, and left Giraud to ponder his reply for a moment. It took him three delightful heartbeats until he puzzled it together, and Jehan could see his excited expression even without looking. With measured steps, he walked along the border of the holly thicket, looking for a path inside. Thorny leaves littered the ground, and he cursed himself again for not thinking about taking at least his sandals with him this morning. But then again, this morning, his plans for today had still looked decidedly different.

"Can you see anything?" Giraud asked. He had dismounted as well, and taken up the reins of both their horses.

"Nothing yet, but give me a moment." As old as this holly was, and in a place this saturated with magic, there was a good chance there'd be someone here willing to help. Jehan closed his eyes and gently touched the tip of a holly branch. "*Agrifol*?" he whispered, "*Agrifol*, are you there?"

A rustle inside the thicket answered him, but nothing more.

"Of course, you do not know me. But we have brought gifts." Smiling, Jehan withdrew his hand. "Giraud, can you please hand me the waterskin?"

"Sure." He turned around and began to rummage through one of the saddlebags. "But Mama has also packed us a bottle of wine, so if you want to eat a bite, we could open that, too."

"No, thank you," Jehan replied with a fine smile. "It's not for me."

Giraud handed him the water with a puzzled expression, but didn't say anything. It felt odd to Jehan to be doing things like this when not utterly alone, but then again – it was nice, too. Also, it felt good being competent at something, especially after that scene with the 'brigands', where he had been reduced to standing around, gaping in shock and feeling silly.

Like in the marketplace in La Morangiasse, Jehan poured a little of the water onto the holly roots, for good measure doing so in several places.

"For you, *Agrifol*." Another rustle of leathery leaves answered him, and he felt the clear tingle of a presence somewhere among the branches, watching him with pleasant surprise. Of course, there wouldn't be many people coming here, and even fewer would be willing to chat with a shrub and even bring gifts. "*Agrifol*, we come as friends, and we seek a way up the cliffs to visit the ancient Raëlle. Can you show us a path? Please?"

From the corner of his eyes, Jehan could see Giraud watching him with genuine fascination. He shot him a smile, and got an impressed nod in return. When Jehan looked at the wall of leaves in front of him again, something to his right caught his attention – and sure enough, the branches there didn't entwine as he had thought, but merely overlapped neatly, leaving a narrow passage between them. Maybe it had been there the entire time, and he just hadn't looked at it from the right angle. But then again, who could tell?

"Thank you," he whispered, adding a brief yet polite bow. "Over there, Giraud!"

This time, it was Jehan who didn't wait for a reply. Curiosity was tingling all over his neck and made his feet restless. Deep in the back of his mind, there was also a tiny voice reminding him sternly that curiosity had killed more than just the cat, but today, he chose to ignore that. The impressed smile he had seen on Giraud's face had tickled something inside of him he had never felt before, even though he couldn't name it. But he was very sure that he wanted to see that expression again.

The path through the holly was a narrow, scratchy affair, but obviously meant for exactly that purpose. And Jehan even had the distinct feeling that the branches were making an extra effort to bend out of his way – the entire thicket hummed with a sense of welcoming that was delightfully at odds with the spell that hung over the place. Once through the initial wall of greenery, it widened into an open clearing at the foot of a dry creek bed that came down from the cliff. Looked at from the right angle, it looked pretty much like a rough path.

"Should I bring the horses?" Giraud asked, still outside the thicket. "This doesn't look wide enough, and Papa's going to have my hide if I bring back the horses all scratched up."

Jehan looked back. From here, the path didn't look that narrow at all. "Bring them in, there's enough space once you're through."

"If you say so..." Giraud took his time calming his horse and leading it inside, while Jehan used the moment to get a feeling for the place. There was still gentle and old magic in the air, but it felt different than on the outside.

He wondered if this was Raëlle's work, the enchantment on the glade. It probably was. He closed his eyes, trying to get a feeling, a taste of her, trying to guess at what kind of woman she was. Her magic was more mellow than what his grandmother did, without any sharp angles or harsh orders. It felt a lot more natural, many-faceted, complex. Not friendlier, not even remotely – this was neutral to the point that it would help or harm with equal lack of concern.

What that told him about the woman behind the spell, he had no idea.

"Oh, this is nice!" Giraud had finally pulled his horse onto the clearing and looked around. "Now I can feel it, too. Itches in the nose."

Jehan nodded. "It's stronger here, but still mostly harmless. This glade is enchanted to help conceal things inside – not so much as to make them invisible, but to make everyone consider them none of their business."

"Smart."

"Indeed. I think we can leave our horses here, no one will bother them."

"Good." Giraud turned and left, only to come back a moment later with the gelding in tow. "He was already half-way through himself, can you believe it? Seems being a little simple actually helps against magic."

Jehan chuckled. "Not really, no. Only against little tricks that gamble on people thinking themselves smarter than they actually are."

"Hm." He patted the horse amicably. "Well, old Grise here definitely is at no risk at all of overestimating his abilities."

They shared a smile, and Jehan once again found his heart beat a little faster when he realised Giraud honestly seemed to like him. Not just the simple, quiet fisherman, but the fisherman who talked to shrubs and actually got answers. He had always thought himself happy, leading a calm and solitary life. But now, sharing all of himself for the first time, he realised he wouldn't mind someone by his side.

"You know, what you did outside, there," Giraud suddenly said, "I could feel the magic. Your magic."

Jehan blinked, taken aback. Until now, all those things had been something entirely private, never to be shared with anyone. It had been drilled into him from the very first moment he had insisted about seeing things no one else could see. Now Giraud not only standing by, but feeling it in his very bones made him feel unexpectedly exposed. Had Giraud been analysing his magic the same way he had done with Raëlle's enchantment? And if – what had he found? Had he liked it?

"Well..." Jehan had to swallow, his throat suddenly dry. "It wasn't my fishing skills that made you ask me for help."

"No, it wasn't." Giraud looked to the side, as if not sure how to continue. He seemed shy, of all things. "Thank you for helping, and thank you for taking me along today. This really means a lot to me."

"Sure... I am glad you agreed to come. I wouldn't have made it past those 'brigands' unscathed, probably."

"Glad I could help." Again, Giraud gave him a shy smile that Jehan couldn't quite place. "I am just happy that there's someone else who's ... well, maybe not like me, but also not normal."

That was a sentiment Jehan could understand only too well. "I am happy, too."

Giraud's face lit up like the sun with a happy, radiant smile, and he crossed the few steps between them in a rush and flung his arms around Jehan in a tight embrace.

"It is so good to have a friend," Giraud whispered, "finally."

Well, there are some things I couldn't talk to you about, Jehan thought wistfully as he closed his arms around him. Like the fact that I enjoy your innocent hugs way too much, and the way I can feel your body rest against my own.

Giraud loosened his embrace, but didn't entirely let go of Jehan. He looked him straight in the face, his eyes narrowing. "You have that look again."

"What look?" All of a sudden, Jehan realised that they were in a secluded grove, skilfully enchanted to keep everything that happened inside well ignored. Very much unlike the open crossing of Beronsac. The options were ... tempting.

"You look hungry, but too polite to ask." Giraud bit his lower lip unconsciously. "Time for another down payment?"

"Ah..." Jehan felt the heat of a blush on his cheeks, and his pulse quicken. "No."

For a heartbeat, Giraud had the tiniest pout and looked as if he'd kiss him anyway. But then he just shrugged and put his usual smirk back on. "Well, Monsieur, suit yourself."

And with no more than a glance, he quit their embrace. Instead, he turned around and looked up at the cliff before them with his hands planted on his hips.

"So – this is the 'path' you have been speaking about?"

Jehan gave a soundless sigh. This was difficult in more ways than he had imagined. "Yep. At least, it's my best guess for the time being."

"Well then." Giraud looked over his shoulders and eyed the horses. "You think we should take our food?"

"I hope we'll be back before we need any of that..."

Both shared a long look, then Giraud smirked, took the bag containing their provisions, and took out two apples before he slung it over his shoulder. He threw Jehan one of the apples and heartily bit into the other. "Better safe than sorry."

"Very encouraging."

"That's me." He added a conciliatory smile. "Ready?"

"Not really."

Both had to chuckle at his deadpan reply.

"Let's go anyway," Giraud decided and turned to climb the rocks in front of them. "Can you do this without shoes?"

"Rocks are fine, I am used to those." Jehan pointed at the small shrubs that lined their path. "Those little bastards are what worries me, but we should be good unless we have to walk right over them."

The cliffs of Petit Houx were all but covered with the knee-high shrubs that had given them their name – petit houx, or butcher's broom. They looked pretty enough from afar with their tiny dark green leaves, almost like boxwood. But where boxwood had round and soft foliage, the leaves of butcher's broom were pointed and so stiff they could just as well have been made from metal. They were nasty to step upon, almost impossible to rout, and pretty much everywhere. But, even Jehan had to admit, they made for excellent brooms when you had to do heavy cleaning.

"Yeah, well," Giraud offered after he had made a few metres' progress up the hill. "New riding boots maybe weren't the best choice, either." He lifted one of his feet, showing the hard and relatively smooth sole of his boots.

"We'll just take it slow and careful, then." Jehan followed him up the cliff, finding his footing here as easily as he did among the rocks that lined the river. He turned around and offered Giraud a hand in assistance. "You can take the lead again in case we have to pass through the forest."

Giraud took the offered hand, and together, they ascended step by step, following the ravine upwards. Once Jehan had found his rhythm, it became easier, and soon enough, he could all but walk along at the same speed he would have climbed some of the steeper stairs in La Morangiasse. Every now and then, he helped Giraud over another steep rock, and eventually, they reached the top of the cliffs without incident.

When Jehan turned around on the very last ledge to offer his hand to Giraud again, he almost stumbled when he caught the view that spread out in front of him. The top of the cliffs reached out of the forest, and he had an unobstructed view all across the entire valley. Roughly a hundred feet below, the vast river had turned into a glittering ribbon that curled through the landscape, lined by fields and meadows, wedged in between the cliffs on either side. In the distance to his right, he could make out the ramparts of Castelfort on their own cliff, banners fluttering lazily from the towers. Faintly, the church bells from Castelfort tolled all across the valley. He could make out the the bridge of Beronsac as a pale line across the river, straight ahead, and the dark, ragged shapes of the ruins on top of the cliffs above that. All beyond was lost in a dull green sea of trees.

"My, will you look at that..." Giraud asked, breathing heavily and yet smiling. "Now, that view alone is almost worth the trouble, isn't it?"

"Almost." Jehan had the distinct feeling that this hadn't been the hardest part of their way, yet. But he felt too happy to give any comment that would have reduced the elation they both felt, looking upon their home from this vantage point. "Do you see the dead river arm a little above the bridge of Beronsac?"

Giraud squinted into the afternoon sun. "I can see water glittering in the forest, if that's what you mean."

"Close enough. Almost halfway between where that water ends and the river begins again, there's my hut."

He squinted harder. "I can't see anything."

"Oaf," Jehan laughed and punched his companion playfully on the shoulder. "Of course not. But it *is* there."

"Must be nice to have a place of your own."

"It keeps nosy visitors at bay, yes. And it's nice to have no-one around wondering why I speak with the empty air all the time."

"Maybe I ought to come and visit you every now and then, after all."

"Hmm." Jehan nodded vague consent. Surprisingly, he found that he wouldn't mind this particular visitor. "I would like that."

"So then, let's see where to find that witch." Giraud turned around and scanned the forest behind them. There was a narrow path visible at the end of the ravine, following the side of the seasonal brook that ran between the trees, but it dissolved among the undergrowth after a few steps. Giraud turned to Jehan. "Any suggestions?"

Jehan looked at the treeline in the faint hope that he'd see a tower from here, but of course, there was nothing. "My best guess would be to head uphill, and look around there. The path wouldn't make sense if her tower weren't somewhere nearby, and there isn't exactly much space to hide a building up here."

Giraud looked doubtful, but didn't say a word. Instead, he turned to face the forest again and strode off, compensating his lack of a plan with doubled enthusiasm. Jehan followed him as fast as he could. Next time he ventured out in any business not concerning fish, he'd bring his shoes, he silently swore to himself. After all, he owned two perfectly nice pairs – one pair of sandals for longer walks, and even a set of really comfortable boots for winter. Of course, in their chest at home, they were of no use to him at all.

And the butcher's broom around here seemed to be of a particularly prickly variety.

"Curses!" it burst out of Giraud when something invisible swiped his hat off his head. "I don't like this forest."

"What happened?"

"Spiderwebs, I guess." He picked up his hat again and dusted it off. "But these are the strongest I have ever had the misfortune to run into. I swear, I even heard the last one snap, thick as it was."

Jehan looked around. At first glance, the forest didn't look different than any others in the valley. But Giraud was right, something was off. Spiders had woven their nets among the trees, but the threads were so thick they glittered in the dappled sunlight even from far away. The ground was loose and riddled with holes, the undergrowth tangled and prickly. Moss hung from the trees' branches in thick grey tufts, and everything that wasn't growing was covered in muted green lichens. This wasn't a place for humans, that much was sure.

The dense canopy of leaves made it hard to tell where the sunlight was coming from, and overall, it was almost impossible to get a bearing here.

Something about that last thought started to itch in Jehan's mind, and he gestured Giraud to wait. He never lost his bearings. It was one of the few things that he had always been sure of in his life. Maybe he didn't exactly know where he was at any given moment in time, but there hadn't been a single moment in his life where he had not been able to immediately point in the direction of the river.

He looked around again, closed his eyes, and all but burst out laughing.

"Oh what a wicked witch!" it burst out of him, in equal parts impressed and annoyed with himself for not noticing earlier. "We can't find her tower this way. The forest won't let us."

"The forest?" Distracted, Giraud swatted at some flying insect in the air. "Can't you bribe it? Like, the way you did with the holly?"

"I am afraid not." Jehan grimaced and knelt down to have a look at the plants growing at his feet. "The holly was a single plant, and one I knew the name of. This forest... I don't know how to call it. I have no name for this area, and I am not crazy enough to ask all forests of the entire world at once."

Giraud was about to say something clueless, but then he slapped himself on his neck, apparently flattening a gadfly that had landed there. "Damn this place," he mumbled. "I admit, I am useless in that regard. If you need something beaten up, I am your man, but until then, I'll be over here, leaving you to do the thinking. Or whatever it is you think needs doing."

Jehan cast him another wry smile and nodded. Around his scratched feet, the ground was dry and loose, mostly fallen leaves and crumbs of dirt, looking like they had been ploughed through by boars many times. But under the loose layer, he found soil, still light and loose, but damp enough to hold life, smelling faintly of mushrooms and mould. He dug a little deeper and sure enough, his fingers found what he had been looking for. With a few deft movements, he uncovered a white root that ran just below the earth, no thicker than an earthworm, flexible like a rope, but so firmly attached to the ground it could just as well be an iron bar. A few inches further, he found another one, and there would be more wherever he looked.

Butcher's broom didn't grow like most other plants by dropping seeds, at least not as its preferred method. Instead, they cast out a network of tough roots from which new plants sprouted all over the place. Most of the times, all those little shrubs remained connected to each other, so when looking at an entire forest full of petit houx, there was a good chance one was looking at a single plant.

And right now, that was what Jehan was counting on.

"*Fragon*, I know you can hear me," he whispered, twanging the exposed root like the string of a harp. "Come on, you little ruffian, wake up!"

A gust of wind suddenly breathed through the forest, shaking dust and leaves from the trees and upsetting the heavy silence.

"Dammit," Giraud cursed behind him. "Whatever it is you are doing, hurry up. These gnats are eating me alive here."

"Wake up, little monster, wake up," Jehan all but chanted. "Wake up, *Fragon*, we have business to discuss – *aïe!*"

A sharp pain blossomed in his left heel – Jehan looked down and found a tiny shoot right next to it, nothing more than three tiny, needle-sharp leaves on a single stem. And yet, it managed to look positively belligerent to Jehan.

"So there you are," he said, turning around to have a proper look at the little nuisance. "All right, here is the deal. We need to get through this forest, and find Raëlle. I can't break the enchantment on the forest, but you can lead us to her, can't you? You're everywhere here, surely you know where she lives."

Of course, the little three-leafed sprig didn't reply. Nonetheless, Jehan had the clear impression of someone crossing their arms in front of their chest.

"Why bother?" Jehan smiled. "Because everyone ignores you, and calls you a weed. And yet you are one of the largest and oldest plants in the entire forest. I know how mighty you are. And I know you can't be bothered for a sip of water, like all the other ones. You are a warrior, you need something stronger."

Curiosity welled up from that tiny plant on the ground, so intense and bubbling it made Jehan almost chuckle.

"In exchange for your help, I will give you something no one has ever given you before – a drop of my own blood, freely given. That is more than anyone can claim."

The shrubs around him suddenly rustled with excitement, very gently, almost making it sound like a shiver of anticipation. But there was no sensation of agreement coming from the little sprite at his feet, only calculation, and demand.

"What?" Jehan exclaimed, only mildly exaggerating his surprise. "One drop is not enough? I see, *Maître Fragon*, you are driving a hard bargain. So, what do you say – two drops?"

Again, the shrubs around him shivered eerily, but still he didn't feel that tingle of agreement.

"Don't get greedy," he reminded the sprite. "I am polite, and very generous. I respect your position. But I am human, don't forget that. I have other methods at my disposal should you prove ungallant." With those words, he pointedly pulled at one of the exposed roots until he heard it plop out of the ground further along in the soil. "But we both don't want to go there, do we?"

Now, the sentiment he got from the little shoot was defiant, rather stroppy than anything else. There was a reason he usually tried not to barter favours with this kind of plant.

"Do I really have to say it out loud? That one word that puts the fear of God even into you?" he snarled at the plant. Just for emphasis, he patted his satchel. "I have my tinderbox right here, don't you ever think I won't use it."

Wordlessly, he mouthed 'Fire!', and almost instantly felt a placating sensation welling up from all around.

"So do we have an agreement?"

This time, he got a clear sentiment of acquiescence, if only grudgingly so.

"Perfect. We are very much looking forward to working together with you, *Maître Fragon*." With a polite nod, Jehan pulled a small knife out of his satchel, and nicked the side of his finger. Very carefully, he placed a single, fat drop of his blood onto the tiny shoot at his feet. "One drop now, and another one after you have led us to Raëlle."

Again, grudging acquiescence, followed by a pointed rustle of a small shrub a few paces away, as if a rabbit or another animal had stirred inside.

"What was that?" Giraud asked, almost ready to draw his knife.

"That, my dear, is our guide through this enchanted forest." With a wide smile, Jehan rose back to his feet and walked in the direction of the rustling shrub. The sound died immediately, only to reappear from another shrub another few paces further into the forest. "Thank you, *Maître Fragon*, this will work nicely." He turned around to Giraud, who eyed both him and the plants on the ground with eyes full of wonderment. "Would you mind following us, young *Maître* Forgeron? It's this way, if you please."

Giraud was so fascinated he didn't even react to Jehan's mockery, and followed him silently.

The rustling shrubs lead them through the forest with many turns and stops, but at least it was a path free of impassable thickets of butcher's broom. They made good progress, and after a while, Jehan had the feeling they were approaching something like a large clearing. He was just about to point it out to Giraud when suddenly, something small and hard hit his temple.

"*Aïe!*" he yelled, ducking instinctively. "What the hell..."

Another something smacked into the ground at his feet and bounced on the loose earth. A little pebble, half the size of his thumb. A heartbeat later, another one.

"Someone's attacking us!" Behind him, Giraud ducked as well, scanning the trees for their attackers. "Can you see them?"

Jehan took cover next to a large butchers' broom shrub and knelt down to offer as small a target as possible. Every now and then, new pebbles were flung at them from above, too small to do any real damage, but big enough to leave bruises – if they hit.

"They're in the trees..." Giraud remarked, pretty much stating the obvious.

An angry buzz right next to him warned Jehan, and only in the last moment he managed to throw himself to the side, barely avoiding a club aiming for his face.

"What the hell ...?!"

It took him another heartbeat to realise that he had been attacked by a *lutin* who had sneaked up on him from the side.

A tiny, fierce creature, barely taller than the shrubs on the ground, wielding some sort of buzzing stick at him with grim expression. Jehan's eyes went wide when he saw the large hornet that had been tied to the end of the stick, as large as a man's thumb and rightfully furious.

If he had been hit by that, those pebbles would have been the least of their problems.

Giraud seemed to have come to the same conclusion, for he jumped up and yelled:

"Watch out! I've got this!"

With a few long strides, he covered the distance between himself and the *lutin*, and kicked the tiny creature with all his strength. The brave *lutin* got hurled of his little dirty feet and flew through the air like a bundle of wailing rags.

A heartbeat later, Giraud had both his weapons out, feet wide apart, ready to take on anything and anyone who'd dare to stand against him. From throughout the surrounding forest, an indignant murmur arose. The pebbles stopped flying, and for a moment, the entire place seemed to hold its breath.

The silence was broken by another furious buzz to their left when two more hornet-armed *lutins* dropped their camouflage and stared at them with unveiled hostility. Another rustle of dry leaves, and more of the little creatures appeared on their right. More and more of them appeared among the branches of the trees above them, each of their caps a speck of dull red among the dusty green leaves.

"We are not afraid," snarled one of them, right ahead of Jehan. "We fight until death."

His voice was thin and coarse, as if rarely used, but it still conveyed a mix of determination and fear that chilled Jehan.

"Giraud," he urged, "put that hammer down..."

"What? They can hardly do us any damage, and we can pick them off one by – "

"Now!"

Giraud blinked at the unexpected command, hesitated for a moment longer, then hung the hammer back onto his baldric.

A sigh of relief went through the entire forest.

Jehan raised his hands defensively and nodded to the *lutin* who had spoken earlier.

"We surrender."

"What, no! What are you – "

Finally, Giraud caught the look in Jehan's eyes and shut his mouth. They weren't fighting village boys here, but creatures of magic. Rules were a little different, and this was Jehan's area of expertise. Quietly, he also sheathed his knife, but not without throwing Jehan a doubtful look.

"We surrender," Jehan reaffirmed. "You have bested us."

The *lutin* in charge puffed out his chest and nodded, only to stand around a little lost at what to do with this unexpected victory.

"You and your men have cleverly outmanoeuvred us, and your arms are most effective and ingenious," Jehan continued. "You have clearly fulfilled your orders to protect this place, and have brought great honour to your mistress."

Under this barrage of praise, the *lutin* captain began to look mildly uncomfortable.

"We bow to your superior might," Jehan said and rose from his cover, only to bend down in the most courteous bow he could come up with, almost like a knight of old would kneel in front of his king. "Giraud, bow down!" he added in an urgent whisper.

Again, Giraud cast him an incredulous glance, but then followed his example. Only his genuflection looked properly dramatic and elegant. Of course.

The *lutins* in the forest around them muttered among themselves, proud and curious at the same time, but none of them spoke up. After an appropriate time had passed, Jehan rose and addressed the *lutin* captain.

"Now that we have sorted this out, will you let us continue on our voyage?" Jehan asked.

Another murmur rose among the *lutins*, this time more confused than anything. A wicked smile played around the corner of Jehan's lips, but he managed to swallow it.

"We mean no harm to your mistress, we come as friends," he continued. "Here, if you allow me, I have gifts."

He reached for his satchel, and the sudden motion caused another stir among the little warriors around them. Very slowly, he reached inside, searching for a moment until he found the last of the dried figs he had packed this morning. He had originally planned on eating those himself, as they were one of his favourites. But that would only make them more precious to the *lutins*, and that was what they needed more right now.

A few steps ahead, he found a sufficiently large, flat stone on the ground, and he walked over to clean it from leaves and dirt. He draped the figs individually on the cleanest leaves he could find and arranged them on the makeshift table before he backed away again.

"Captain, our present for you and your men."

With obvious curiosity, the *lutins* approached the dried fruits, at first poking them cautiously, before the captain took heart and bit off a tiny piece. His already large eyes widened even more when he realised how sweet the figs were, and he took a second, hearty bite, chewing loudly.

"Very generous presents, those." He nodded vigorously. "Sweet words and sweeter presents."

"I am very happy our gifts please you," Jehan replied. "May we continue on our way, now?"

For a heartbeat, the captain seemed undecided, but then he just stuffed his face with the remaining fig. Still chewing, he waved them on, while his little troopers gathered around the two other figs, apparently arguing who would get which part of the delicacy.

Jehan gestured Giraud to get up and follow him, hoping to get some distance between them and the *lutins* before they could change their minds.

"How'd you know they'd let us pass?" Giraud asked as soon as he was close enough to whisper.

"I guessed." Ahead of them, a butcher's broom shrub rustled pointedly, and Jehan turned his steps in that direction. "*Lutins* are fierce and wild, but they do not fight unless provoked. Yet these here were willing to face cold iron to protect Raëlle, so I guessed they might have taken an oath to protect her."

"I still could have taken them out," Giraud mumbled.

"I don't think so..." Jehan waited for the next shrub to signal them their path before he continued. "They are small and simple creatures, but their honour is strong. Stronger than most among the fae. Trying to uphold an oath would probably make them a lot more powerful than they seem."

"Damned fairies..."

Jehan swallowed any remark he would have had. Through the trees in front of them, he saw that they were indeed approaching a clearing, something that looked like a wide path and a hedge, and maybe a low roof behind that. He followed their leafy guides through three more turns nonetheless, hoping to avoid whatever last traps Raëlle had planted at the border of her forest.

Finally, they stepped out onto the path, relieved to have made it this far. It followed a huge hedge of wild roses, and behind it, there was indeed a house with a low slate roof.

The shrub at Jehan's feet rustled insistently.

"Oh, don't you think I have forgotten my payment, *Maître* Fragon." With a smile, Jehan took out his knife again and pricked another finger. This time, he placed two drops of blood onto the prickly leaves. "A second drop as agreed, and a third one in gratitude. Thank you, *Maître* Fragon, for your invaluable assistance."

"What the hell do you think you are doing there?" a woman's deep voice suddenly cut through the air. "And how did you get here?"

Both Jehan and Giraud all but jumped around. Behind them, a woman had appeared on the path, hands on her hips, staring at them balefully. Her hair was short and wild, but whatever threatening aura she possessed was severely hampered by the dirty apron she wore.

"I am just paying my debts," Jehan replied sheepishly, stowing away his knife before it could be misinterpreted. Luckily, Giraud hadn't drawn his weapons yet.

"One drop would have been payment," she grumbled. "Two drops looks like you're trying to bribe my front yard."

Jehan's sheepish grin grew another notch. "Are you Raëlle?"

"No...?"

"We come seeking your help."

"I am not in the business of helping people." She literally snarled at them. "Especially not men. Get lost. Leave me in peace."

"My grandmother sent us! She said you'd be willing to help."

"And why the hell should I care?"

"She said you knew each other – she's the midwife of La Morangiasse."

"Iolande?" She spat on the ground. "What's that conniving old hag up to? Can't she take care of her own business any longer?"

"No, she can't. She ... she isn't well."

Despite her coarse manners, Raëlle seemed to understand only too well what Jehan hinted at, and her gruff stance deflated into something a little less hostile.

"Aw, crap. I am sorry." She took a deep breath and wiped her hands on her apron. "Seems it's going to be one of those days. Come on in, boys. I'll hear you out."

She turned around and disappeared around the rose hedge with long, stomping strides. Jehan and Giraud exchanged an excited look and followed on her heels.

Chapter Five - In the Garden of Raëlle

In hindsight, Jehan couldn't say what he had expected a witch's garden to look like. The only thing he was sure of was that for the life of him he hadn't thought to find a lush orchard behind the wall of wild roses that Raëlle led them through.

After the scraggly growth that covered the cliffside and the dry and dusty forest, the exuberant, messy pile of green and flowers felt almost overwhelming. Jehan's eyes kept jumping here and there, always finding something new to marvel at – carrots as high as his knees, beetroots that looked black as Giraud's face after a day at the forge. Hollyhocks lined the gravel path leading to the house, and their slender stems reached well above Jehan's head. Nothing here grew in orderly rows or clearly defined beds, with no difference made between plant and weed. And yet everything seemed glowingly healthy, vibrant, happy.

"You sit down here," their host ordered, pointing at a weather-worn wooden table under a gnarled tree. "I'll be right back."

Without looking at them, she disappeared inside the house and started rummaging about. It seemed as ramshackle and uneven as the entire garden, but also well-kept and surprisingly cosy. There were small trees growing from the cracks in the slate tiles of the roof, the window blinds were all sagging and he couldn't spot a right angle on the entire building. It wasn't a palace, but not small either, sure enough a nice place for a woman all on her own out here.

Jehan and Giraud took off their hats and sat down on the simple benches that faced the table, still both looking around at the unexpected abundance. Deeper into the garden, where the rose hedge got more and more intermingled with blackthorn, he could spot an apple tree so laden with fruit its branches had to be supported with sticks. The tree they were sitting under, though, was unknown to Jehan, and he eyed it with fascination. The fruits looked like apples, pretty much, round and red and gold. But where apples had a little dimple on the bottom, these had a little crown sitting opposite their stems. Some of them seemed about to burst, tiny cracks showing something deep red and glossy inside.

"Do you think she's the right one?" Giraud whispered, leaning towards Jehan.

"What?" It took Jehan a moment to understand what he was talking about. "Raëlle?"

He nodded. "She doesn't look ancient to me. And really, this is a house, not a tower."

"You know how stories work." He shrugged and pointed at the far end of the building. "Maybe that dovecote has become a tower over time, growing with each telling of the tale."

Giraud seemed anything but convinced. So when Raëlle came out again, carrying a tray, he looked at her with narrow eyes.

"What?" she barked. "You must have seen an ugly woman before, boy, haven't you?"

"I..." Giraud had the decency to blush. "I didn't mean to – "

Raëlle gave him a dismissive gesture, clearly not intent on dwelling on the thought. Instead, she put down her tray and handed each of them a clay mug. A simple cloth bundle turned out to contain a pile of small, yellow peaches so ripe their scent all but jumped at them. Next, she cast a look towards the entrance of the house and gave an annoyed grunt. Looking up to Giraud, she said:

"Would you mind fetching us a fresh bucket of water? There's a bucket next to the door, and the well is down there in the garden, right next to the apple tree."

Giraud craned his head and nodded when he spotted the bucket. But he didn't leave without casting a questioning glance to Jehan, something that was both flattering and mildly patronising to him – what did Giraud think, that he couldn't talk to a woman on his own?

At least, he left without a word after Jehan nodded.

"So, Iolande," Raëlle suddenly started once Giraud was out of earshot. "How bad is it?"

Jehan sighed. "We don't think she has much time left."

With a grim set to her jaw, she nodded and picked up a little corked jar from the table. From that, she produced a few thick, dried leaves that she crushed in her hand and into the large clay pitcher she had brought out together with all the rest.

Jehan took a closer look at her. Raëlle wasn't ugly, just very plain, and it was obvious that she didn't care much for her looks. Her face was sunburnt and her heavy hands had dirt in the cracks of their calluses. She wore a simple tunic over what looked like a narrow skirt of rough linen, but

Jehan had the suspicion they were rather wide trousers. It was easy to believe that she and his prim grandmother had been of different opinions on many things.

"And you are her successor?" Raëlle asked out of the blue.

"What?!" That old story again. "No, no, I am just... I am merely helping a friend."

Her eyes pointedly wandered into the direction Giraud had disappeared to, but she didn't comment. Instead, she crumbled another handful of leaves into the pitcher. "So, if it's not you, who's going to take up her work?"

"My sister-in-law, Alienee, is the new midwife in La Morangiasse."

She frowned at that answer, but didn't comment either. Thankfully, that was the moment Giraud returned, carrying a dripping bucket of water.

"Here, Madame." He put it down next to Raëlle, gave her a brief nod and sat down again, looking from Jehan to her and back again expectantly. An odd silence spread between them, while she picked up the bucket and carefully filled the pitcher with water. Jehan seized the moment and used his tunic's sleeve to clean his mug of dust and a few dead flies. Apparently, she didn't have many visitors, indeed. When he looked up again, he realised he had forgotten something rather important.

"God, where are my manners," he offered. "Madame Raëlle, this is Giraud, the son of Segui, the smith in La Morangiasse."

She looked up and gave Giraud a curious glance, judging him like a particularly interesting insect, maybe. Giraud merely nodded and smiled politely.

"And I am Jehan. You already know my family, I assume."

At this, Raëlle nodded calmly. With a deft motion, she mixed the contents of the pitcher and put it down again.

"Aren't you hungry?" She pointed at the peaches while she sat down herself. "Boys your age are always hungry, aren't you?"

"Thank you." Jehan picked up one of the peaches and took a bite, trying not to get juice all over his chin. Chewing, he added: "We came here to ask you for your help."

"You already said so," she replied wryly. "I guess you are aware that my help doesn't come for free, are you?"

Jehan nodded. "Of course. What do you want?"

"That depends entirely on your problem."

"It's my parents," Giraud started, "someone cursed them."

"Someone?" Raëlle asked with an odd tone. "And you want me to lift that curse?"

"We'd be happy to learn who cursed them," Jehan interjected. "And I don't think I am strong enough to lift that curse – nor do I think anyone should attempt that. I'd like to know who, so I can barter with them to lift it."

"Hmm..." She seemed vaguely approving. "So you just want a name?"

"For starters, yes." Jehan gave her what he hoped was his most winning smile. "Any advice would be highly appreciated, too."

A laugh bubbled out of Raëlle, a snorting, rumbling sound that was as unrefined and honest as the rest of her. "Now look at that. A man your age, not thinking he knows everything. Your grandmother seems to have taught you some things, after all."

"She surely tried. I don't think I was a good student, though."

Still smiling, Raëlle nodded. "I think I can help you."

"So what do you demand?"

"Let me see." She picked up the pitcher and poured each of them a mug of the brew – deep purple, a colour so intense it made Jehan blink. "That's one nasty big hornet's nest you're poking there, so if I am meddling, that's not going to be cheap. On the other hand, you want all the trouble for yourself, and just a name from me – I won't have to ask for your firstborn here." She chuckled again at the stunned expression both Jehan and Giraud gave her. "Oh don't you look at me like that. It won't be something – "

"Eugh!" Giraud suddenly exclaimed and shoved away his mug with a disgusted, horrified expression. "Spider!"

Startled, Raëlle took the mug from his hands, her eyes widening when she looked inside. "Oh no, no, darling! Oh I am so sorry!" With a tenderness that her callused hands didn't suggest, she carefully reached inside the mug. When she pulled out her meaty fingers, a thick black spider clung to them much like a wet kitten being pulled out of the well. "Oh I am so sorry, I really should have looked... Come on, darling, let's get you dry..."

Softly muttering to the spider in her hand, Raëlle disappeared inside her house.

Giraud's shaky smile did nothing to hide his confusion. "All the Saints. What just happened?"

"You scared her favourite spider with your ugly mug, that is." Jehan chuckled. "And now she's gone, taking care of the poor thing until it feels better."

He huffed indignantly. "I swear to God it was trying to crawl up my nose."

"I believe you were just as startled as the spider." Jehan took a sip from his drink, surprisingly dry and sour, with a fragrance somewhere between roses and raspberries. "Please don't hold it against her."

"Neither the spider nor the witch," Giraud promised. He picked up his mug again, carefully scanned it for other unexpected inhabitants, but then took a sip without further hesitation. "Oh, this is nice."

Jehan agreed. "I have no idea what this is... It's some kind of tea, but I have never even heard of such a plant..." Curious, he picked up the jar and smelled at the dry leaves inside. Sour and dusty, but unmistakably aromatic. How odd.

"What do you think she'll ask from us?"

"Huh?" Jehan looked up. "No idea. I don't think she'll ask something outrageous, as she said. But you don't do this kind of things for free, so she'll want something."

"Like a kiss?"

"Yes." Jehan was pretty sure he was blushing again. "Though I don't think it'll be a kiss in her case. She doesn't strike me as – "

Raëlle reappeared in the doorframe, straightening her apron. She looked a little more composed, now, yet when she sat down again, she looked at both of them with a certain unease. Jehan wasn't sure, but it felt to him as if she was genuinely embarrassed about the spider incident and didn't know what to say. Not many visitors, definitely.

"You were talking about your price," he offered. "Have you thought of something?"

Her relieved look told Jehan that he had guessed right. Raëlle nodded and forced herself to smile. "Just a little something. You help me so I can help you." She pointed at a corner of the garden near the dovecote. "I've got a pile of firewood there that needs chopping and stacking. It's rare enough that I got strong hands up here, so that would help me a lot more than any firstborn." Her eyes sparkled with glee at the last remark.

"You want us to chop your firewood?" Giraud remarked. "Now that is ... a lot less weird than I feared."

"You can have a look at it," Raëlle offered, "and maybe even start while I go through the details with your friend here."

Giraud looked at Jehan to see if he agreed before he nodded. "Sure, I can do that. Anything special I should look out for?"

Raëlle shook her head. "Axe should be in the chopping block, and I think it's obvious where the chopped logs should go."

Giraud rose and tipped his hat. "Then I'll leave you to it." He left, apparently not too disappointed he'd miss out on the remainder of the discussion.

Both Raëlle and Jehan followed him with their eyes as he walked down the narrow path to the wood pile and assessed the situation with his hands on his hips. When he took off his baldric and jerkin, Jehan couldn't suppress a smile. How could a mere human make everything he did look so ... advantageous?

"That Giraud, what is he to you?" Raëlle asked. There was no insinuation in her question, but her tone indicated that the time for small talk was definitely over.

But, what was Giraud to him, indeed? How to answer that question when he didn't even have a decent answer himself?

"I am not sure," he replied honestly. "He's a friend, and his parents deserved none of this, as far as I can tell. So when he asked me for help, I agreed."

"Just a friend?"

"Yes." Jehan sighed inwardly. Yes, just a friend, and that a part of him longed for more was part of the problem.

"Hm." Raëlle just made an unintelligible sound, still entirely without judgement. She took a long, audible gulp from her own mug, thinking.

The sharp crack of an axe hitting a log of wood jolted through the quiet air, followed by the familiar sound of two smaller pieces tumbling to the ground. Both Raëlle and Jehan looked over to Giraud, who was already attacking the next log in front of him with single-minded fervour.

"How much do you know about him?" Raëlle asked without taking her eyes of Giraud.

"Just the usual, I guess." Jehan shrugged. He wasn't sure, but he had the distinct feeling Raëlle enjoyed the view just as much as he did. "He's a few years younger than I am, he's talented and popular and can charm water out of a rock."

"And?"

"And... He's not the the smith's bodily son, but the son of Segui's sister." Jehan frowned. "Do you think his real father has something to do with all this?"

"So he hasn't told you." Raëlle turned her look back to Jehan, her eyes cool and unreadable.

"Apparently not." He took a deep breath. "I guessed he didn't tell me everything. And I didn't want to push. But you do know who his father is, by the sound of it."

"Me? Oh yes. Can't you see the similarity?"

"Err... No."

"Well, once you know, you will." She leaned back, taking another sip from her mug, and returned to watching Giraud chopping wood.

"And will you tell me?"

"After you're done with the wood. Not before." She smiled, absent-mindedly.

In the back of Jehan's mind, he was still chewing on the bit of information Raëlle had given him. He leaned back, nursing his drink, and wondered what he had overlooked. He went through a list of people in La Morangiasse who could be potential suspects – there were enough married men in the right age, and enough of them were sufficiently unfaithful to their wives. But apart from his grandmother, there was no one in the entire town who'd have anything near the power to cast a curse as it had befallen Segui and Marette.

So – who then?

A glance to Raëlle confirmed that she was deeply lost in watching Giraud – admittedly, something Jehan could effortlessly relate to. He had taken off his shirt, and now chopped wood wearing nothing but his suede pants, his high boots, and a faint sheen of sweat. A wistful sigh escaped him, and he wouldn't have even noticed if Raëlle hadn't given him that look again.

"What?" he asked, a little more defiant than he had wanted to.

Her mouth worked and for a moment, it looked as if she were struggling to find the words. "That boy is trouble, you know that, yes?"

"And since when do you care?" he snapped at her, immediately regretting his words. "I am sorry. I ... I am just not used to ... talking. About those things."

Raëlle's face crunched into an expression of genuine understanding. "You're doing a lot better than myself when I was your age." She reached out as if to touch his hand, but then pulled back immediately. "People like us are few and far in between. We need to watch out for each other."

There was no doubt in him that her words were entirely honest and heartfelt. Jehan wasn't sure how he had earned that honour, but he would do his best to deserve it.

"Thank you, again." He paused when Giraud took a break from chopping wood to wipe some sweat off his face. "Anything I can do for you? Watch out for?"

She gave him a warm smile. "Just don't go around telling everyone you've found me. These days, only a few people come here, and I like it that way."

"They probably wouldn't recognise you anyway," Jehan replied, tongue-in-cheek. "You look much too young."

Raëlle cast him a questioning glance, and it took her a moment to understand what he meant. Then, she snorted, smirking, and poured herself another mug of the drink. It was much darker now than before, almost like wine. "It's more of an office, you know? I think I am already the third woman living up here, and there may have been more."

"It's a good place, if you like it a little remote."

"Ah, well." She turned her eyes back to Giraud. "Occasionally, visitors aren't too bad, you know?"

Jehan shook his head and leaned back against the trunk of the gnarled tree that was shading their table. It was nice watching Giraud, for once not having to avert his gaze every time someone might be noticing. And he liked Raëlle. Under all her gruff exterior, he was pretty sure there was a rather vulnerable woman, caring and good-natured, easily wounded by the meaningless snide remarks that people flung at each other so carelessly. Just the way she had treated that spider would have made her the townsfolk's laughing stock for years to come.

"You think I shouldn't get too close to him, don't you?"

"If he were a normal boy, I'd question your sanity for even smiling at him. But in his case – you're begging for trouble." Again, she gave him that wry look. "Maybe women are just better at keeping their passions in check."

"How do you mean that – he's not a normal boy? I know he's got the sight, but this sounds like you know more than that."

Now she looked at him almost with the same exhausted note of disappointment as his grandmother. "Still haven't figured it out?"

Jehan must have glared at her in helpless anger, for Raëlle chuckled softly and returned to watching Giraud.

He barely managed not to bite his lower lip in concentration like a scolded school boy. So Giraud's father was still around, and he was at least part of the reason for the curse. The more often Jehan rolled those facts around in his mind, the more he came to the conclusion that whoever Jehan's bodily father was, he would have to be rich. Only people with too much time on their hands invented such games. Only rich people. Only … nobles.

An icy shiver ran down his spine.

That made a frightening lot of sense. If Giraud had a noble father, that would explain why he hadn't come forward when Giraud's mother died. It would also explain why Jehan had no idea who it might be – Jehan knew the people in town almost as well as his own family, but with anyone living behind the castle's walls, he'd barely ever exchanged a word.

What it did not explain was how said noble got to spin a curse so intricate, so vast and yet skilfully light-handed. Or why, by all the saints, they would chose to do so.

Jehan stared at Giraud's naked back as if that would provide an answer to that riddle.

Someone with those powers would have been noticed before. One didn't gain such skills from not using them. But there were no other gifted among the people in their castle, no sorcerers or supernaturals. If there had been, his grandmother would have known, and she would have warned him.

And there were no nobles in La Morangiasse he hadn't at least seen from afar. No other human nobles, that was.

Another wave of vertigo washed through Jehan. No wonder that everyone looked at him like the village idiot these days. He was daft, after all.

"One of the fae?" it burst out of him. "Giraud's father was *a noble fae*?"

"So there is some brain in your head."

Suddenly, it was all so very obvious. Giraud's ridiculous good looks? His uncanny sense for decorum and manners? His smile that could melt a rock? That charm that worked on friend and foe alike and made people want to believe his every word? No mere human should have that many talents.

But to the fae, those weren't talents, those were birthrights. And Giraud seemed to take much after his father, in that regard.

"Do you think he knows?"

"It is pretty obvious that he knows what his father is," she replied, vaguely pointing at Giraud. "I am rather sure he doesn't know *who* he is, even if they have met."

"So that's what he didn't tell me. He knew I would never have taken this on..." Jehan felt like slapping himself. Instead, he decided to drop his head onto the table in front of him. "Oh God, I am such a fool."

"Don't fret." She patted his head with genuine, if slightly awkward, friendship. "There may yet come something good out of this."

"How?" he mumbled.

She paused for a heartbeat, and Jehan was rather sure she was smiling.

"There is something about the two of you. Something..." She gestured with her hands, struggling to find the right word. "You feel like two fitting parts of a greater whole. This might turn into a disaster, yes. But maybe, between the two of you, you have a chance of fixing this."

Jehan sat up straight again and took a deep breath. Giraud was a lot more cunning than he had given him credit for. He was an idiot for not making the connections earlier. And this entire thing was a mess.

And yet.

There was an unfamiliar emotion in his chest, something unwieldy, and something he didn't want to go away either. Longing? Desire? Wistfulness? Was it even possible to miss something that one had never experienced?

Across the garden, Giraud slammed his axe into the chopping block with a determined motion and wiped the dust off his hands, looking very pleased with himself. He started throwing the logs aside, roughly to where they should be stacked. The afternoon air filled with the swift clack, clack, clack of tumbling firewood.

But what if Giraud didn't feel the same? What if that kiss had just been in jest, just a boy's misguided way of having fun? Thoughtless, innocent, completely unaware of the possibility that Jehan might read more into it? Like a puppy humping the leg of a chair? The image made him flinch with embarrassment.

Besides, even if, there was no way they could build a life together. Giraud would eventually marry, and Jehan would live his life in his hut nicely away from other people, just like he had planned.

Maybe there were even laws against two men loving each other. Loving each other in the biblical sense, that was. *Père* Ancel sure would think it sinful – though, what didn't he consider a sin?

And yet. Again.

Raëlle had made a life for herself out here on the cliff. A life well away from prying eyes, where she could walk around in trousers, without a husband, caring for nothing but her garden and her little friends. She didn't seem unhappy, did she?

Down the garden, Giraud had started stacking the chopped wood neatly along the side of the house. Now that the quiet of the surrounding forest returned, Jehan could hear him softly hum a song, something about drinking and women on his knees and drinking some more.

"It seems you'll be leaving soon," Raëlle remarked. "If you follow the path in front of my house, it'll lead you back to the cliff."

"What about the name?"

"You could just ask Giraud about his father, couldn't you?" This time, her expression remained entirely unreadable to Jehan. "But either way, the name will come to you in the forest."

"I think we paid for a name, not another riddle."

"And a name you'll get." She gave him a sympathetic smile. "I have my reasons. Please."

He just cast her an exhausted glance. There was no doubt that she just wanted to be helpful, but right now he really was fed up with secrets and riddles and promises of more problems lurking around every corner. He was a fisherman, a simple worker, and he liked his life as it was. Or rather, as it had been.

He felt like dropping his head onto the table again.

Down in the garden, Giraud apparently considered his work done and put his shirt and jerkin back on. He slung the baldric over his shoulder, picked up his hat and came walking to their small table.

"I think I am done," he declared. His face was flushed, his hair matted, but he looked radiantly happy. "So, how's it been going here?"

"I think we were done as well," Raëlle answered with a sidelong glance at Jehan. "Here, have a last drink before you leave."

She poured him the last tea from the pitcher, dark and fragrant, and Giraud gratefully took the offered mug. He finished his drink in a few large gulps and grimaced.

"Whoa. Sour." He laughed at himself, and suddenly Jehan could all but see the fae on him. Now that he knew, it really was ridiculously obvious. "Good – so do we have a name, now?"

"Not yet," Jehan replied, "but we will once we leave."

Giraud raised his eyebrows but didn't say anything. Instead, he sketched a polite bow to Raëlle. "Madame Raëlle, it was a pleasure meeting you."

Raëlle in turn just snorted softly. "You guys." She smiled, somewhat sadly, and nodded as well. "I wish you all the best. Come visit me again once this is over."

"If we survive, we definitely will." Jehan eyed Giraud, who just looked back with innocent ignorance. "Thank you, again."

She shrugged, a small, shy smile on her face.

Jehan picked up his hat and rose as well. Giraud followed him, and together they left the garden in silence. They had barely passed the rose hedge when Giraud asked: "So – what did she say?"

"That you could have told me the answer all along."

"What?" Giraud picked up his steps until he was alongside Jehan and could look him in the eyes. "What do you mean? I don't know who cursed my parents."

"No? Telling me about your father would have been all I needed. And you could have done that, couldn't you?"

"I..." Giraud's instant excuse died in a mumble. "You wouldn't have helped me if you knew, would you?"

"We'll never know now, will we?" he snapped back. "Are you happy with tricking me into helping you against some fairy noble? Or was it more of an accident?"

"What?! This is my parents we're are talking about, the people I care about most. I couldn't risk you saying no just because it looked too risky for you."

"And you thought lying to me would get you any further?!"

Fuming, Jehan was at a loss for words, and Giraud didn't seem to feel any different.

They followed the path through the forest as Raëlle had told them to. It led them along a little ditch that would probably be a small creek in winter, and was thankfully empty of any thorny shrubs or belligerent *lutins*. They walked in icy silence until they reached the little clearing at the edge of the cliff. Already, the sun was hanging low on the horizon, and her golden light filled the valley below.

"So what now?" Giraud had a grim set to his jaw, but seemed determined to see this through.

"It's not as if I can leave your parent's hanging in this, can I?" There was a churning ball of conflicting emotions in Jehan's chest, but he was doing his best to keep it in check. "Who's it, then?"

"Who?"

"Your father. I do need a name if we're going to sort this out."

"I – I don't have a name."

Jehan turned to stare at him. "Please tell me you are kidding me. How the hell do you think this is going to work?!"

"How am I to know? I am not the witch, here!"

"You are a fucking half-fairy, for god's sake! How can you run around and not know your father's name?!"

"I couldn't care less," Giraud hissed. "All that asshole did was impregnate my mother and abandon her. He could just as well have pushed her off the cliff himself."

"Maybe she should just have kept her knees shut."

Giraud's fist came so fast Jehan couldn't even blink.

The first hit landed right next to his nose, the other one on his jawbone, and the impact made Jehan see stars and stumble back a few steps. Undergrowth tangled his feet and he fell over, Giraud following him in blind rage.

"*How dare you!*" Giraud jumped onto him, pushing Jehan to the ground. "*How dare you!*"

He continued hitting at Jehan, furious, unthinking, without aim or thought. Instinctively, Jehan raised his arms in defence, shielding himself from the worst blows, giving him a moment to get this wits back together. Giraud's face hovered above him, flushed and furious and streaked with tears of anger. So much pain behind his beautiful eyes, so much pain...

In a sudden moment of clarity, Jehan realised what he had to do.

He didn't know much magic when it came to humans, but a few lessons he had learned nonetheless.

"Stop it!" he ordered.

Giraud halted his assault with a sound very close to a loud sob, looking mostly lost and confused, his knuckles white.

With a swift motion, Jehan reached out and touched Giraud's chest, right in the middle, a bit above his heart. Anger, pain, fear, all those emotions could become just as toxic as any poison, but they were much harder to spot. At least, once identified, they could be cleansed a little more easily. Jehan felt Giraud's pain like a curled ball of fiery chains, something hot and searing, caustic, churning and immobile at the same time. He gritted his teeth and grabbed one of the rocks he was lying on. As soon as he felt the familiar calm of the earth in his mind, he reached out for Giraud's anger and pulled it into himself, guiding it like a flow of poisoned water, through his heart and out of him, into the earth beneath their feet where it dissipated like everything else.

Within a few heartbeats, Giraud's fury disappeared, leaving him shivering with exhaustion, his fists half-curled at his sides.

"I am so sorry," Jehan offered. "I should never have said that."

Giraud tried to answer, but all he got out was a choked sound. When Jehan realised he was fighting down tears, he acted without thinking. He sat up and pulled Giraud into his arms, cradling him against his shoulder.

"It's okay. Cry. Let it out." He pulled him closer, even though Giraud made some token effort to resist. He didn't let go. "You have all the right in the world to be angry. You have been hurt, and it still hurts."

Finally, Giraud slumped against his shoulder with a muffled sob.

"There." A moment ago, that boy had tried to beat the living daylights out of him, and now he lay crying in his arms. Was life always such an up and down when Giraud was concerned? With a shrug, Jehan started stroking Giraud's hair, cradling him. He smelled of sweat and dust, but also of smoke and white flowers. "We will sort this out. I promise."

It took Giraud quite a while to sort himself again. But Jehan didn't mind. He was sitting on a cliff with a beautiful view, with the prettiest boy in town in his arms, watching the sun set. From further downriver, he could hear another church bell ringing the full hour, and apart from his throbbing face, this was good. At least he was sufficiently sure his nose wasn't broken. He might sport a few funny bruises for the next days to come, but nothing more than that.

"Sorry." Giraud mumbled and sat up. "I shouldn't have hit you."

"Well, you had every reason to. I was an arsehole."

Giraud nodded vague agreement and sniffled loudly. His eyes were puffed and his hair in total disarray, but once again, he managed to look nothing but sweet and handsome.

"Damn, I am acting like a child," Giraud remarked, braving a smile. "Yelling, fighting, then crying. You must think I am a complete fool."

"I think living with the heart of a fae in the body of a human must be terribly hard at times." Jehan leaned forward and wiped a smudge off Giraud's face. "They are creatures of dreams and legends, and to have all those grand feelings in a simple mortal shell ... I think you are holding up commendably."

Giraud cocked his head, unconvinced. "What about my parents? Do you have any clue who we are looking for?"

Jehan shook his head. "Raëlle said the name 'would come to me in the forest', and I trust she believed so herself. But so far, nothing. Do you know what he looks like when he's not disguised as a human? Maybe that's something we can use."

"Uh – I think he has antlers, like a stag, maybe, you know?"

"That's all?"

"What? I could see he wasn't human, that was enough for me, honestly." Giraud gestured wildly, a grim set to his jaw. "I have seen that man only twice in my life, I think. We met on the road, one day when I was a kid, and once in Castelfort a few years ago, some evening after market day. We talked, we argued, he was condescending, I was stroppy. We're not exactly friends, you know?"

"Did you insult him?"

Giraud's hesitation made it clear there wouldn't be a credible 'no' from him. "I ... I called him a murderer?"

Jehan felt the strong urge to slap someone. "And you seriously wonder why he cursed your parents?"

"Well, he didn't seem that angry. He even asked me to join him, to live with him at the castle."

"And you rejected his offer?"

"Of course!" Giraud seemed genuinely offended by the thought. "He left Mother and me, and now expects me to come running as soon as he calls? Hell, my parents have been there for me all my life, and the very least I owe them is to take up father's business and care for them through their old age. My place is with them, and not with some wanton cockscomb!"

"At least now we can be pretty sure about his motive," Jehan replied with a sigh. "But that doesn't bring us any closer to a name..."

He leaned back onto his palms and allowed his eyes to wander through the forest. If Giraud was right and the man they were looking for had antlers in his real shape, that would mean he'd be some sort of forest fae. Not a dryad, of course. Maybe a sylph?

That last thought tickled in his mind like a fish nibbling at the end of his fishing rod. A sylph? No, they rarely mingle with other fae, and he had never heard of a sylph noble. So maybe something akin to a sylph?

Another cold wave of understanding rushed through Jehan as finally, the last pieces clicked together. It had to be that one. Anything else would not have been the biggest problem possible...

"What?" Giraud perked up. "Did you figure it out?"

"I... I have a strong suspicion, yes." He took a deep breath. It came out as a soft chuckle, even though he didn't feel amused at all. "Your father, let me guess – he was in the company of at least two guards when you met him, wasn't he?"

"There were two shady figures standing close by, if that is what you mean."

"Did they ever address him as 'my lord', or 'your highness'?"

"Not that I could remember." Again, Giraud cocked his head, curious. "They were very deferential, admittedly."

"Well, there is only one antlered fae in Castelfort that I know of, and I would wager a month's work that he's the one we are looking for."

"So?"

"His name is Silvanus, though he goes by Sylvain these days." Jehan smiled like a wolf. "Lord Silvanus, to be precise. Prince of Castelfort."

"Is ... that a problem?"

"Yes, that is a problem." Inwardly, Jehan rolled his eyes. How to explain something he barely had a clue of himself? "Lord Sylvain is the highest-ranking fae in Castelfort, and he rules over the fae of his domain just like our good Lady Givonne rules the fae of La Morangiasse. Creatures like him are even more bound by manners and customs than a human noble. Can you imagine what generous offer it must have been for him to ask you to join his court? You, a half-mortal bastard? And just how much you insulted him by rejecting it?"

Giraud crunched up his face. "Not really, no."

"Let's say he has all the reasons to get murderous."

"But – " His expression shifted from frustration to guilt to anger and back again in rapid succession. "Such scum, going after my parents then, instead of me."

"He's hitting you where it hurts you most. I can't see much fault in his strategy."

Giraud buried his face in his hands and took a moment to regain his composure. When he looked up at Jehan again, his face was filled with simmering rage.

"Oh that conniving tosser! Hasn't he done enough to hurt me and my family? Why is he doing this?"

"I am not entirely sure," Jehan replied truthfully. "But I have the suspicion he's not trying to harm you – he's trying to convince you."

"Convince me of what? That he's a heartless villain? He sure managed that."

"That you'd do better by his side." Jehan raised his hands in defence when he saw Giraud's eyes narrow threateningly. "I am not saying anything he does or did is right – I am just trying to say maybe he doesn't see himself as the villain here."

"He's fooling himself nicely, then."

"Be that as it may, but it could be our way to save your parents."

Giraud unruffled his feathers and looked vaguely curious.

"So he might be willing to meet with you, talk to you," Jehan continued. "He might even be willing to lift that curse when you apologise."

"What? Never! What should I apologise for? For wishing him the pox? For hoping that his codpiece catches fire? He can rot in hell for all I care – "

"Giraud, calm down!" Again, Jehan raised his hands, mildly surprised at the fact the Giraud actually stopped his barrage of swearwords. "I didn't say he deserves your apology, nor that you should actually mean it. But think about it – he is fae, as pure-blooded a noble as they come. If you come to him, offering him flamboyant regret, maybe penitence and some sort of token gratitude – he can't ignore that. He'll have to decide whether he'll want to be the good, forgiving father in this story, or the vengeful villain. And as much as I have heard about him so far, he really prefers to be the hero in his stories."

"I hate playing games." Giraud grumbled.

"That is just your human side talking." Jehan gave him a friendly nudge. "Question is – can you swallow your pride long enough to save your parents?"

"I am not worried about my pride." He took up the baldric with his hammer and weighed it in his hand. "I am rather afraid I'll want to bash his head in once he shows his face."

"That would firmly put you in the role of the villain here, and give him every right to hurt you and your loved ones."

Giraud snarled in frustration, but at least he put the hammer down. "Yeah, I know... I know how this works. I know our weakness."

This time, it was Jehan who cocked his head, curious. "Your ... weakness?"

"Well, you know how this is – " He smiled at him, almost apologetically. "Fae are creatures of dreams and legends, everything is a fairytale to them. So ... it is very hard not to act the knight in shining armour when there's a damsel in distress around."

Jehan nodded. Yes, that was the weakness of the fae – their penchant for stories forced them into one of only a handful of possible roles. But that didn't make them predictable, not even by far. "You could always chose to play the dragon and eat both the damsel and the knight," Jehan suggested.

"Probably." Giraud smiled, and finally something of his old, careless self returned. "Though I'd really prefer slaying dragons to eating princesses."

"No doubt about that." Jehan hesitated for a heartbeat. "But you are aware that from my point of view, you put yourself in the role of damsel in distress right now?"

Giraud looked genuinely taken aback, deeply amused and a little embarrassed.

"And as it turns out, you're even some sort of royalty," Jehan continued mercilessly. "You know what that means, don't you?"

Giraud laughed out loud and made a half-hearted attempt to kick Jehan, but none of that managed to hide the fact that it was now him who blushed.

"I never said I was particularly smart about this whole affair," Giraud declared. "And about the roles we play, that still remains to be seen. After all, you might turn out not to be my knight in shining armour, but a villainous sorcerer bent on doing me even more harm. Maybe this prince will have to rescue himself."

"Do you really believe that?"

Giraud's smile turned warm, and he cast down his eyes. "No," he replied softly and reached for Jehan's hand, giving it a grateful squeeze. His hand lingered a little longer than it had to, and it sent a tingle of excitement through Jehan.

Somewhat giddy, he realised that this might just have been Giraud's way of telling him he'd be interested in more than just a playful kiss between them. After all, in the end, the hero always got the princess. Or half-fae prince, in this case.

Unfortunately, the lives of humans didn't work along the lines of stories like those of the fae. The fate of humans was haphazard and fickle, at the best of times. But, maybe, there was enough magic between the two of them to make this work.

What a beautiful thought.

On the far side of the valley, the sun hung low in the sky, a fiery ball that tinged everything around red and orange. The ramparts of Castelfort were black crenellated rectangles on their cliff, the banners on top of the tower almost touching the sun.

"Are you ready to apologise to your father?"

"Right now?"

"Well, Castelfort is right over there, halfway on our way home. If we go now, we might make it back home only a few hours after nightfall, and have this sorted out for good by then."

Giraud seemed anything but convinced, but he nodded nonetheless. "You are right. We should at least try." He rose from the ground and offered his hand to Jehan. "It's not as if things could get any worse."

Jehan took the offered hand and pulled himself to his feet as well. "I only wish you hadn't said that."

"Do you think it'll go wrong?"

"Doesn't matter what I think, and wondering won't change anything. We go now and see how it turns out."

"Of course." Giraud picked up his hat from the ground, straightened out its feathers and put it back on. "I mean, what could possibly go wrong?"

Chapter Six - Moonlight Sprites and Garlic Soup

The sun had all but set behind the cliff when they passed the small bridge at the foot of Castelfort, and the sky was beginning to darken. Shops were closing up, and the scent of food hung heavily in the air.

Jehan and Giraud led their horses up the main street towards the castle and ignored the vaguely hostile glances that some of the townsfolk gave them. It wasn't unheard of for people from La Morangiasse to come here, nor the other way round, but this late in the day, their visit seemed to be something best to keep an eye on.

Similar to La Morangiasse, Castelfort had been built against the side of a cliff, as high up as possible to remain safe in case of another flooding. But unlike their home town, Castelfort sneaked up all the way to the cliff's top, where the castle sat on its rocky promontory like a heavily armoured lookout. Also unlike La Morangiasse, this town had two market places – one down at the river, for everyday goods, and another one up on the cliff in front of the castle's main gate, surrounded by a goldsmith, two tailors, a cabinetmaker and a perfumer.

Jehan had only been up there once before, on a delivery for the castle when a feast demanded so many crayfish that the fishers of Castelfort couldn't supply enough of them. The place had been daunting, with all those people in finery spilling from the castle and all that wealth on display. It was a world he had never been part of, and he had always been grateful for it. Going there now, with the clear intention of seeking an audience with the most powerful fae in town, made his neck itch with the strong desire to be anywhere else but here.

Giraud, on the other hand, didn't seem to have such concerns at all. While they rode up the main road towards the castle, he looked perfectly at ease, with his hat tipped back and his face smiling as if they were bringing gifts. Jehan knew him well enough by now to see that it was mostly a facade, a comfortable mask he wore to keep both the world around him and himself from noticing the chaotic emotions underneath. But he seemed determined to see this through, and willing to get this over with by peaceful means only, both of which Jehan counted as very good signs.

Also, it seemed that Giraud had a very clear idea of where he was going, another thing Jehan was deeply grateful for. It wasn't as if they would find Prince Silvanus at the castle gates, waiting for them. Jehan didn't know enough about the fae of Castelfort to have anyone he could ask for a favour, either. And actually passing into the realm of the fae and nosing around would be so impolite that he would only consider this as his very last option. Besides, Jehan wasn't too sure he could pull it off with Giraud in tow. So that left him only with the option to find someone or something they could beg or bribe or barter into delivering a message to the prince.

Jehan had a vague idea how to accomplish that, but from there on, it was all guesswork. His back itched uncomfortably with all these unknowns.

They followed the main road along several hairpin turns as it ascended to the castle, and Jehan watched in fascination as the houses grew narrower and higher with every bend. Here, the houses had scrollwork-covered lintels and painted beams. Gaudily painted shop signs hung so low he had to duck underneath some of them. People talked and laughed and shouted at every corner, in every building, all around them. The place was packed as tightly as fish in a basket, and stank of piss and manure. Maybe his hut in the forest didn't have stained-glass windows or brocade curtains, but Jehan wouldn't want to live in Castelfort for all the gold in the world.

When they finally arrived at the upper marketplace, the air freshened up a little, and Jehan breathed with relief. How could anyone think that this was in any way preferable to a nice, little place of his own in the middle of the forest?

"I'll make a short stop at *Maître* Burlain's," Giraud announced, pointing at the goldsmith. "So the townsfolk won't gossip too much. Will you watch the horses?"

"Sure." This was a place where you had to watch out for people stealing your horses? One more reason to get out of here as soon as possible.

They led their mounts across the square and dismounted in front of the goldsmith. Giraud handed him Trajan's reins and stepped inside, taking the few steps leading into the shop in one stride. Like all the other shops, it was closing up, but the apprentice called for *Maître* Burlain as soon as he recognised Giraud. Out on the square, Jehan couldn't make out much of their conversation, but apparently the goldsmith liked Giraud well and was willing to share his stocks of pewter, should they run out of it in *Maître* Segui's shop.

When their talk turned into pointless chatter, Jehan gave a soundless sigh and turned his attention back to the real reason for their visit. So how to find some way to get a message to the local fairy prince without turning absolutely unwelcome in the process? He let his eyes wander around the square, hoping for some inspiration. The horses were standing next to him, motionless except for an occasional flick of their tails. The grey gelding looked as if he were taking a little nap, while Trajan looked down on Jehan with a grim, watchful expression. Neither of them offered any help.

A group of guardsmen came out of the castle gates, chatting loudly and patting each other on the back. Apparently, there had been a promotion of some sorts, and they were now all off-duty and out to celebrate. The two guards manning the gate laughed with them and cheered them on before they turned back to lighting the large torches that illuminated either side of the gate. The church doors were closed, with rarely anyone going for prayer at this time of the day. A woman in a precious, peach-coloured dress rushed across the square, two small children in tow. In the dark gardens of the town, crickets began their nightly concert. On the far side of the square, just at the edge of the light cast by the gate torches, a musician unpacked his lute, settled on the ground and started playing. The gaudily coloured ribbons of his vest fluttered in the light breeze.

Right then, a soft whirring sound caught his ear, like the sound of dragonfly wings on a quiet afternoon. He perked up, trying to pinpoint where the buzz had come from, but with all the noise around, it wasn't easy. Somewhere to the left, he guessed, by the narrow passageway between the goldsmith and the 'Sanglier Ivre', the local tavern.

He cast a glance back over his shoulder – Giraud was still chatting with the local smith, and by the sound of it, he wasn't thinking of wrapping it up any time soon.

Jehan hesitated, but then took the horses and tied them to a rainpipe close to the goldsmith's shop entrance. For a moment, he wondered if he maybe should wait for Giraud, but another soft buzz to his left tickled his curiosity again. To hell with caution, he decided, he wanted this over sooner rather than later. With a gentle pat to Grise's flank, he left the horses behind and followed the sound of glittering wings around the corner.

The passageway was just wide enough for a man to walk through, and just a few steps long. Beyond that, it turned into a narrow path between high walls, with the goldsmith to one side and what seemed to be a walled garden to the other. The din of the square was muted here, the shadows darker, the air another bit fresher.

Jehan walked down the path, one hand trailing the wall, his eyes almost closed but all his other senses wide open. He could still hear the buzz of glassy wings, more than one now, and the faint tinkle of dripping water. Or was it laughter? It definitely wasn't the boisterous shouts coming from the tavern...

He could already see the alleyway open to another street in the distance when he realised he had walked past whatever it was that he was looking for. Jehan turned around and what he had thought to be just a shadow on the wall turned out to be a narrow, groined archway. He had to take off his hat before ducking through, but he knew he was at the right place as soon as he felt the faint scent of magic tickle his nose. The archway led to a tiny courtyard, wedged in between two walls and all but covered by the thick, black branches of an overhanging fig tree. In the dim light, it took Jehan's eyes a moment to adjust, but slowly, the vague shapes around him turned into two old stone benches to either side and a small, weathered fountain at the far end of the courtyard. The fountain was completely overgrown with moss, and feathery tufts of maidenhair fern grew along the walls and in the corners.

It was a beautiful, calm little place, almost forgotten by the people of Castelfort, but it was far from abandoned. With a wide smile, Jehan noticed a faint glimmer appearing at the edge of the fountain's pool, like a little dot of moonlight half hidden by a fern.

"Hey there, little one, don't be afraid," he whispered and sat down on one of the stone benches, slowly, not to scare anyone. "I am friendly."

Like a shy child, a tiny creature appeared from behind the fern, no larger than his hand. She looked like a slender, young woman, silver white both her skin and her waist-long hair, naked except for that silver glow around her, with silver-blue dragonfly wings on her back glittering like frozen moonlight.

"My, you are beautiful," Jehan said softly and offered a small bow by lowering his head. "Thank you for showing yourself to me, *Lunette*."

The tiny fae giggled like a girl, hiding her mouth behind her minute hand. The sound was barely audible, but still Jehan was sure it was a long time since anyone had paid her a compliment.

Another dot of moonlight appeared near the spout of the fountain, and two more in the dark corner behind the basin. Suddenly, the night was full of whispers, curious and playful.

The little *lunette* who had appeared first jumped into the air with surprising athleticism and zig-zagged through the air towards Jehan, very much like a glowing, silver dragonfly. He leaned back, laughing, as she zipped here and there, hovering in front of his face, flying in close to inspect his eyes, zapping around to touch his hair, then down onto the bench to look at his fingers in endless fascination. Meanwhile, more and more little silver dots had appeared, and soon, there was a veritable congregation of *lunettes* sitting on the basin's rim, watching him, chatting, some of them taking a bath, or arguing among each other. Every now and then, new fairies joined them, while others left with the zeal of urgent messengers.

Finally, the first moon sprite had finished her inspection and came back to hover in front of his face again.

"You're a witch," she declared firmly, her arms crossed in front of her chest. "But you are not a witch." She eyed him with narrow eyes, at least that was what Jehan made her diminutive expression out to be.

"Sorry that I am such a riddle."

"Oh no – don't be sorry. We love riddles!" Cheerful, tiny voices from the fountain chittered wide-spread agreement. "And you're much prettier than witches who are witches."

Again, she flew closer to his face to peer into his eyes, close enough that he could make out her tiny sharp teeth and the red glint in her eyes.

"So pretty!"

"Thank you, *Lunette*, you are too kind." He put on his most winning smile. "But I am still ugly compared to you."

"Of course you are," she chirped back without any insult. "You're human. But still pretty. Humans are always pretty when they are in love."

A very undignified sound escaped him, but Jehan caught himself before he could say anything stupid. Well, anything particularly more stupid than usually.

"You think I am in love?"

"Oh yes!" She did a pirouette in the air, happily clasping her hands. "It's still very small, but it's rather obvious. Is she pretty, too? Is she rich? Pliant? Talented? Can she cook? Can she sing? Why didn't you bring her?"

Suddenly, there was a whole group of *lunettes* hovering in front of him, all eager to hear a little bit of his story. Their eyes were so full of hope and excitement that, despite everything, he didn't manage to tell them a lie.

"Yes, he is very pretty."

At this disclosure, the courtyard filled with soft 'oohs' and 'aahs', and the entire swarm seemed to change its mood. Where they had been playful and chatty a moment ago, now they were calm and very attentive. Several of them settled on his knees, looking up to him with wide eyes. Seeing so many of them this close for the first time in his life, he realised that there were several among them with male bodies, lithe and muscular and just as moon-clad as the female ones.

"Oh, I don't know if I want to hear that story," the first *lunette* admitted. "They rarely have happy endings."

"I know." Jehan nodded gravely. "That's why I am trying not to fall in love."

"You can't not fall in love, you know that, don't you?" she asked, but answered her question herself immediately after. "Of course you know. Poor human."

"But I am on a quest to help him," Jehan offered on a whim. "I do not know if this will allow us to have a happily ever after, but it sure will help."

"Oh, a quest? Doomed lovers on a quest, oh, I love it already!" She spun in the air again, zipping left and right with excitement. "How can we help? Shall we slay a monster? Shall we scare a child or bite a dog? Braid a horses mane? We can make the milk go sour or the flames burn green, we can help in so many ways! We are fierce warriors, and many. Just tell me what has to be done."

At this whole-hearted and utterly valiant offer, Jehan could only smile warmly. "Thank you, that is so kind of you. I do not know if you can help us, or if I deserve such a deed. But yes, there is something you could do for the two of us."

"Speak, and we shall do what we can!" she proclaimed firmly, even managing to give him a deep bow in mid-air.

"Could you deliver a message for me?" Her face sagged with disappointment at the banality of his request. "The message is simple, but it might be very dangerous to deliver it."

At the promise of adventure, she perked up again. "Dangerous, you say? I am not afraid."

"Maybe you will be, when you hear who the message has to be delivered to."

She glanced at him sideways, her look doubtful. "I don't think so."

"Prince Sylvain."

Her eyes widened, but she didn't squeak and flee. "The prince?" she whispered.

"I am afraid, yes. But he is the only one who can help us."

"That is a big favour you ask, indeed." She looked over to her companions, and found her sentiment echoed in their faces. "The highborn don't much like us talking to them."

"Well, they sure wouldn't like me seeking them out, either. But I can understand how this is much to ask, and if it is too much indeed, I will not ask it."

"Oh..." She fluttered around nervously. "Oh, this is difficult. The prince is a stern man, you know?"

"But maybe he'll be kind once he hears the message you'll bear – that his son is here, and that he's willing to apologise."

Again, her eyes went wide with wonder. "You're the prince's bastard son?! Oh, no wonder you're so pretty!"

"No, Madame, not me." He gave her a conspiring smile. "But he's here in town with me. He is – he's that special someone, you know?"

He tapped his chest right above his heart, and the little *lunette* squealed with glee when she understood.

"Oh, oh, oh! Such a lovely story! So much wonder!" She flew a wide loop through the night air, hesitated for a moment and then threw herself against his chest, her arms spread wide in the oddest, tiniest bearhug he had ever received. "And you want me to be a part of your story! Thank you! You are such a wonderful man, no wonder that the princeling has fallen for you!"

"Yeah, well…" Jehan patted her back with a single finger, as cautiously as he could even though he knew he couldn't really harm her unless he'd cut her with an iron nail. "It's a little more complicated than that, I fear."

She looked up at him, frowning, at least that's what Jehan made of her expression by peering down his nose.

"What could possibly be difficult about this?!" She looked outraged, but also thinking very hard. "Good Lord, has he been ungallant towards you?"

"What?" Despite everything, Jehan had to smile at her fierce little heart, jumping from one conclusion to the next, whole-heartedly feeling whatever it was that struck her. "No, he has been nothing but gallant, and polite, and kind, and handsome. He even protected me from brigands, this very afternoon!"

She frowned at him, hard. "So he does love you?"

"I… " He broke off his explanation before he began, trying to sort the muddled thoughts in his head. "We're both human, remember? We don't always know what we feel."

"That is really stupid." She let go of his vest and returned to fluttering a few hands away from his face. "But he's only half human. That should help, shouldn't it?"

"I am afraid it only means he's got very strong feelings he isn't sure about."

"Oh, dandelions!" Even her cursing was cute. "You're not making things easier this way, you know that?"

"I know." He gave her a weary smile. "Will you help us anyway?"

"Of course I will." She flew a wide arc around the courtyard, as if trying to come up with the necessary courage. "So I am to tell the Prince you're here with his son, and he wants to apologise?"

Jehan nodded. "We will be here in town, I am sure he can find us. If you'd tell us his reaction, that would be nice, so we'll know we're not waiting in vain."

"I think I can do that..." She smiled impishly. "But you'll tell me the entire story once it's done, yes, will you?"

"Sure. If that's all you want, I'd be honoured to."

"Alright." She braced herself. "Then I'll be off, wish me luck!"

And with a loud buzz of her silver dragonfly wings, she shot up through the branches of the fig tree and into the night sky, veering off towards the castle before he lost sight of her. Quiet chatter of the remaining *lunettes* still filled the courtyard, pretty little things sitting here and there in small groups, laughing and doing whatever the little folk considered worth doing on a balmy summer evening. Jehan went on watching them for a little while longer, politely greeting the newcomers and returning their smiles.

It took him quite a while until he realised someone was calling his name. Giraud.

"I am over here!" he yelled, loud enough that most of the *lunettes* turned instantly invisible. "I am here, Giraud!"

He took his hat from the bench next to him, gently tapping it to make sure there were no invisible little creatures sitting inside. He ducked out of the courtyard and back into the narrow passage between the goldsmith and the garden of the *'Sanglier Ivre'*. Giraud stood in the small passageway that led back onto the marketplace, his face somewhere between relief and bewilderment.

"Where have you been?" he asked, looking Jehan up and down. "For a moment I wondered if they had maybe stolen you and left the horses, but then again, why would they leave the horses?" He hesitated and plucked at Jehan's tunic. "And why is there silver glowy stuff all over your chest?"

Jehan looked down, and indeed there was a faint silver smudge on his chest where Lunette had hugged him. He shrugged. The unexpected drawbacks of travelling with someone who could see that kind of thing as well.

"Ah well, you know? You're not the only one I am affectionate with."

Giraud blinked very slowly, clearly not sure what to make of this.

"Oh don't give me that look." Jehan laughed and pulled Giraud's hat down into his face. "I arranged to have a message delivered to the prince, that's all."

"Did you?" Giraud took off his hat, grinning. "So, what do we do now? Do we just wait?"

"I guess. We could go back to the marketplace, sit down at the fountain and eat some of the 'provisions' your mother gave us."

Giraud just grimaced in reply. There was a playful twinkle in his eyes, something that was at the same time worrisome and extremely attractive. "Yeah, I don't think so. I can have Mama's food every night of the week. Why don't we make good use of the occasion, and you allow me to spend a few of the *sous* I have and buy us a proper dinner? What do you say?"

"What's improper about a dinner of bread and cheese?"

"It's boring." As if that was all the explanation needed, Giraud grabbed Jehan's hand and pulled him back towards the marketplace. "The *'Sanglier Ivre'* has really good food, and it's the first time I am here with someone I really like, and I think it would be just the perfect way to spend an evening waiting."

They entered the dark passageway together, but two steps in, Giraud stopped and pushed Jehan deeper into the shadows and against the wall.

"What is it?" Jehan asked, alarmed. "Trouble?"

"Maybe." There was something in the timbre of Giraud's voice that made it abundantly clear that he was the only dangerous thing here right now. "I might be doing something stupid again."

"Why? What are you -?"

Giraud took Jehan's head in both hands and pulled him down to his face, kissing him right onto the lips. Gently, sensuously, curious and a little insolent. Just a stolen kiss in a dark corner, like so many countless kisses stolen in villages all over the country tonight. Only this one was happening here, right now, and Jehan didn't know how he had ended up in all this. Kissing the prettiest boy in town, meddling in magical affairs way beyond his means, and not giving a damn.

He slung his arms around Giraud and kissed him back, for a short while just losing himself in the sensation, so different from their first kiss on the bridge. Then, Giraud had been surprised, but now there was a hint of fire, a taste of something wild in their embrace. It drew in Jehan's thoughts one by one, his emotions, until he stopped worrying about their quest, about getting caught and most importantly about whether Giraud knew what he was doing. He simply allowed the moment to be everything.

A loud noise from the marketplace brought them back to reality. With a slightly embarrassed sound, Giraud let go of Jehan, but even in the darkness of the passageway Jehan could still see his eyes sparkle.

"So – am I in trouble now?" Giraud asked impishly.

Jehan needed a moment to gather a coherent thought, and immediately the folly of doing this, here, of all places, washed over him.

"I just hope no one saw us." He eyed the marketplace over his shoulder, but it seemed no one had taken notice of the two of them. "You can't do that in public! You might get away once by telling one of your stories, but people will talk. And you know how that ends."

"Damn, you're such a spoilsport. Tell me you didn't enjoy it, too!"

"I..." He let his head drop back against the wall. "I wish I could live in that moment forever. I am just afraid of what comes later, you now?"

Giraud hesitated for a heartbeat, his boyish enthusiasm somewhat doused. His hand still rested on Jehan's chest, a finger playing with the hem of his tunic. When he answered, his words were very soft, as if trying not to dispel the moment they shared.

"Can't you just lose yourself in the here and now? Why do we have to worry about what comes of this?"

"Because I want more than just this moment." The words were out of Jehan's mouth before he could think of it, and they surprised him. But it was true, nonetheless. "I ... You make me do things I would never have dared without you. Being around you is exhausting, wonderful, exciting, and I want you at my side for as long as I can hold on to you. But that also means not risking everything for a thoughtless kiss."

"I like thoughtless kisses." Giraud sighed, his finger plucking at Jehan's tunic aimlessly. "You are right, of course, as always."

"I am sorry?"

He laughed, bright silver mirth tinged with sadness. "There are no stories about the likes of us, are there?"

Of course that's what a fae would think of first. Even a half-fae. "None that I know of."

"Well, what a luck that we are heroes of our own right, then, isn't it?" Like a thief, Giraud stole another quick kiss from Jehan. "We will write our own story then."

There was so much conviction in Giraud's voice that Jehan felt himself agreeing. Yes, maybe among the two of them, they indeed had enough magic to shape their own fate. To write a new kind of story. One that had a prince instead of a princess, and a fisherman instead of a knight. The thought brought a smile to his face, and when Giraud took up his hand again and pulled him towards the marketplace, he found himself filled with wonder at the prospect.

Which, of course, was lost entirely on Giraud.

"I have been at the *'Sanglier'* a few times, when Papa was here negotiating some deal," he started babbling while he dragged him towards the tavern. "And I still remember the food there. You'll love it, I promise."

Without waiting for any kind of response from Jehan, he untied their horses and led all of them to the entrance of the *'Sanglier Ivre'*. The tavern had a wide, double winged door with ornate wrought-iron hinges that opened to the market, golden light shining within, laughter spilling out like water from a fountain. A boy was sitting on the steps, maybe eight or nine years old, and he jumped to his feet when he saw them approaching.

"Messieurs," he greeted them eagerly. "Are you going to stay at the *'Sanglier'*? I could take your horses, if you'd permit, Messieurs."

"You have a stable here?" Giraud asked, already handing him the reigns. "Could you make sure they are fed and watered properly? They've had a long day." He slipped him a coin, and the boy nodded even more enthusiastically.

"I'll make sure they'll be happy and shiny, Messieurs. I promise!" With something that looked somewhere between a stumble and a bow, the boy took off with the horses and disappeared around the house's corner.

"And you are sure he didn't just steal our horses?"

"He looked trustworthy to me," Giraud replied with a shrug. "Either way, we'll only find out once we leave this hospitable place and he doesn't show up again. Though I doubt a place like the *'Sanglier'* will have thieves loitering on their doorsteps."

Jehan was tempted to reply that thieves would loiter exactly on the doorsteps of places such as this one – at least, here it had people with enough money that thievery would turn into a profitable business. But he swallowed his remarks when he realised that Giraud was already half up the stairs and waiting for him.

So Jehan just shrugged, smiled and followed him.

Inside, the place looked like pretty much every tavern Jehan had ever been to, which admittedly weren't many. A large room crammed with sturdy tables and benches, a large fireplace in the back with only a small fire burning tonight, and a counter to his left, near the door, where a sturdy woman filled pitchers with wine from the barrels stacked along the wall behind her. Though this was the cleanest tavern he had been to, with proper hardwood floor instead of straw on packed dirt. There were also a lot more candles than he was used to from the *'Plume d'Or'* in La Morangiasse, and the folks here dressed a lot better. Unsurprising for a place so close to the castle, but still.

"Eh, what do you want?" The sturdy woman had left her place behind her counter, three pitchers of wine in each hand, and eyed them distrustfully. Particularly Jehan with his bare feet seemed to draw her ire.

"My friend and I are looking for a good place to eat, and this one comes with the highest recommendations." Giraud sounded like he had rehearsed that line the entire afternoon. "I still remember you have the best snail soup I have ever eaten."

That apparently didn't make them any more welcome here than before.

"We are pretty packed already."

"Just a light supper, and then we'll be off." Giraud smiled, and for the first time, her gruff expression wavered. "And it's not as if we can't pay." A coin appeared in his hand as if by magic, and found its way onto the counter. An entire *sou*, if Jehan had seen it right. And the lady in front of them hadn't missed it, either.

"My, Messieurs, why didn't you say so? Of course I have a table for you." She grinned and gestured them to follow her. "See that table in the back, boys? That one's yours, sit down, and I'll be with you in a moment."

Right beside the fireplace, there was a smaller table pushed against the wall, empty, but with a good view of the entire guestroom.

Giraud thanked her and sketched a polite bow before taking off his hat. They made their way past the other tables, thankfully with none of the other patrons paying them much attention. Talk here was pretty much the same as in the *'Plume d'Or'* – gossip, bragging, bits of news and occasionally a little bit of real conversation. It felt rather comforting.

Giraud dropped his hat onto their table and eyed it for a moment. Then, with a deft motion, he pulled it away from the wall, revealing a second bench underneath.

"Come on, I think I'll prefer sitting with my back to the wall," he explained with a grin. "Had enough surprises today already."

Now that was a sentiment Jehan could get wholeheartedly behind. He slipped behind their table, setting down his straw hat as well. Giraud followed him and had barely settled down when the sturdy woman reappeared at their table, two earthenware bowls in her hands.

"This one is on the house," she said with a wry grin. When she put them down, they were filled to the brim with pale, steaming soup, small dark shapes drifting between flecks of herbs and chunks of torn bread.

"Snail soup." Giraud hummed, sharing a conspiring grin with their hostess. "So you're not entirely immune to flattery."

"Ain't flattery if it's true," she returned with conviction. "This is damn good stuff, after all." She fished two wooden spoons from her apron and smiled at them with almost motherly indulgence. "So boys, what else can I bring you?"

Giraud measured the soup in front of him with his eyes. "More bread, and some wine. Good wine, for a good ending to a long day. And more food – what do you have today?"

"Hare stew, mostly. Some pheasant, leftover from yesterday." She looked them up and down again. "But you get that at home often enough, don't you?"

Hare stew did sound rather familiar to Jehan, so he looked to Giraud for a decision. The soup in front of them smelled delicious, he had to admit. Maybe hare stew wouldn't be a bad idea...

"I don't know," Giraud said ponderously, his fingers playing with another *sou* coin. "If I remember correctly, your kitchen does more interesting things than that..."

Her eyes went narrow for a heartbeat, then she burst into deep, happy laughter. "Oh I see. Well, as long as you can pay, I'll see what the kitchen can come up with on such a short notice, but I promise I'll make it worth your while."

Giraud flicked her the coin, and she caught it with expert ease.

"So – I'll get you bread and wine, and while you finish the soup, I'll have some duck gizzards warmed up."

"Duck gizzards?" Jehan asked incredulously. His kitchen experience was strictly limited to scaling fishes or shelling crayfish, but gizzards didn't sound like something he'd expect to pay good money for in a place like this.

"Yes." Giraud nodded to their hostess and once she had scuffled off towards the kitchen, he turned his attention back to Jehan. "Just wait and see. I am pretty sure you'll like it."

"If you say so..."

With a smirk, Giraud turned his attention to the soup in front of him, and enticed by the scent, Jehan did the same. The first spoonful was too hot to taste much, but it was good, and his stomach greeted the food with an audible rumble. Indeed, it was high time he'd got something proper to eat.

He dug in with a vengeance, and after a few more spoons, he had to admit that this was better than most things he had ever eaten. Besides the garlic, he could make out rosemary, and bay leaf, but apart from that, he had no idea what he was actually eating. Was there wine in the soup? Chestnut flour? At least the snails that studded his bowl were totally ordinary snails. Only, not as sandy as the ones Alienee made, which was really nice.

He cast a sideways glance at Giraud, and found him looking back with a happy smile on his face.

"Good?" Giraud asked.

Jehan nodded vigorously, grinning around a mouthful of soup. Giraud's smile brightened another notch, and just for a moment, Jehan forgot where they were. Damn, but he was one handsome fellow.

He stuffed his face with more food before he could blush again, or do something even more stupid than that. Thankfully, that was also the moment their hostess returned with a bottle of wine, two earthenware cups and a wooden bowl of bread. She laughed softly when she spotted their already half-empty bowls, apparently very pleased with her customers.

"Here you go, boys." With a tiny, sharp knife that she pulled from her apron, she quickly removed the bottle's wax seal and uncorked it with equal ease. She poured them a first cup each, pale gold and clear. "It's not one of the really expensive ones, but a good one, and one you can buy a second bottle of without ruining yourself. It should be a good choice."

Jehan took his goblet, curiously sniffing before the first sip. It smelled … smooth. Like wine, yes, but not as … sharp. More like flowers, or ripe fruit. He blinked in surprise. Maybe this bottle of wine cost a lot more than he would ever consider spending on an entire week's food, but maybe it was worth it. Well, probably not really worth it, but still. He took as sip and felt another smile spread on his face. Maybe worth it, after all.

"Good?" the hostess asked, nodding to herself when she could read the answer on their faces. "I'll be back with more food in a moment."

Jehan took another sip and took his time to enjoy all the various tastes he could make out. Good stuff.

From the corner of his eyes, he noticed Giraud looking at him again, that wide, happy smile plastered all over his face.

"What?"

"You like it. Makes me happy that I can invite you to a treat."

Jehan gave him a wry look. "I can't say I feel comfortable paying this much money for food. And I don't even want to know what this bottle of wine is going to cost you. But it's very nice..."

"Well, then I'll consider every single *sou* well spent." Giraud looked very pleased with himself, an expression that suited him rather well.

"I am not sure I like you spending money on me, either."

"No?" He made a show of looking Jehan up and down. "You do look like you're enjoying yourself nicely, though. And besides, it's my money, free to spend on what and who I want."

Normally, something like that would have made Jehan nervous to no end. But as it was so often the case with Giraud, he knew he meant it just the way he had said it – as a compliment, generous and caring, with no strings attached. Even though it made him nervous, but in a different way. How had the little *lunette* put it so aptly? You can't not fall in love. Especially if the other half of the game was so intently ignoring any shred of common sense...

Jehan forced his eyes away and took a sip of his wine instead, his lips still tingling with the memory of that kiss they had shared outside. Yes, he wanted Giraud to fall in love with him. No, he didn't want all the trouble that came with it. Yes, he wanted to figure out a way for them to be together. No, he had no idea of how to achieve that – Lord, he didn't know how a happy life for the two of them would look like in the best of circumstances.

What was he even doing here?

Across the inn, at a table packed tightly with arguing young men, someone was staring at them. He stared so balefully that he pulled Jehan out of his restless thoughts and caused him to look closer. Tousled dark hair, a wispy moustache, and a large birthmark over the right side of his face. No, not a birthmark, Jehan corrected himself instantly. A large bruise, fresh and still more red than black and blue. A bruise that looked an awful lot like the shape of a boot. Giraud's riding boot, to be precise.

Urgently, Jehan tugged Giraud's sleeve, who looked up from the last dregs of his snail soup.

"Huh?"

"Over there." Jehan pointed out the staring patron. "Isn't that the guys we ... met? On the road to Petit Houx?"

Giraud looked closer, squinting, but they didn't need to wonder any longer. The guy at the other table jumped up and yelled: "It's them! It's those arseholes from La Morangiasse!"

Now his friends turned around and glared at them balefully, too. There were more of them than this afternoon, Jehan noticed with a sinking feeling. And there were several other patrons around who had stopped their conversation and stared at them. Instinctively, Jehan shuffled back, further into the corner he was sitting in. Suddenly, sitting with his back to the wall didn't feel all that comforting.

Of course, Giraud had no such petty feelings.

"Pardon me, Messieurs?" He didn't shout, but his voice carried across the inn like a thrown bottle, cool and precise. "Have we met before?"

"You fucking arseholes!" the bruised would-be brigand snarled. "Of course you do, look what you did to my face!"

"My apologies, Messieurs. We are genuinely sorry that you ended up in a quarrel today. But it wasn't with us, I am afraid. I am sure that I would remember if we had met, and close enough for me to do anything to you. We are just guests here, in this fine establishment, and wish to eat and drink just like all the other patrons here. I hope that is not too much to ask."

Even with the sound of his heart beating in his throat, Jehan noticed how the mood in the inn shifted in their favour. Now that he knew Giraud wasn't entirely human, he could hardly understand how he had overlooked it all the time. With a few sentences, Giraud had painted them as calm and civilised guests, and all the ire directed at them as nothing but a misunderstanding. And most people here seemed to miraculously agree with him.

"But it was you!" their accuser made another attempt, but his voice had gained a notably defiant edge. "I could never forget that smug mug of yours, you -"

"Shut up, Pons, or I'll do worse to your face!" Suddenly standing right behind him, the sturdy innkeeper woman slapped him across his neck. "Now sit down and stop making a fool of yourself. No fighting in my house."

For a moment, it seemed like 'Pons' would rather jump across the table and attack them, but a sharp knock on the table caught his attention.

"Sit down." A clear voice, almost as well trained as Giraud's. It wasn't hard to recognise the leader of the brigands, wearing his red neckerchief around his neck now instead over his face. What had they called him? Marton? Whatever his name was, Pons dropped onto his arse like a puppet with its strings cut. He kept staring at Giraud like a madman, though.

"Good boys," the hostess commended, and patted the one closest to her on the shoulder. "So nice to see we can all just get along here, isn't it?"

She waited for a moment longer as if daring them to say anything against her. When nothing happened except a few pairs of shuffling feet and lowered gazes, she nodded silently and came over to Jehan and Giraud in their corner. This time, she carried a large wooden bowl, filled with leafy greens and a mound of dark red pieces of meat.

"Sorry for the ruckus," she said, gesturing at the 'brigands'. "Those boys are louts, just ignore them."

"No offence taken, Madame." Giraud sounded utterly at ease, and Jehan let out a breath he hadn't even noticed he had been holding. "Thank you."

She shrugged. "I am just a businesswoman. You're paying well, they don't." With a glance at their empty bowls, she added: "And you're good eaters."

"Well, good food makes it easy." Giraud gave her one of his sunrise smiles, and she chuckled in response.

"Flatterer." Her professional attitude wavered for a heartbeat, and when she leaned forward onto their table, her tone was serious. "Those louts aren't to be trifled with, they have a mean streak. I'd leave before them, if I were you, and maybe not through the main door. Come see me when you're finished, and I'll let you out through the kitchen."

"Thank you, Madame. We'll try to think of something to repay you."

"Just pay your food, and get back home safely, then I'll be happy," she said and shared a conspiring look with Giraud.

How could he have ever thought him a mere human, Jehan wondered. He was winding her around his little finger, and she loved every bit of it. Was it the same between them? Was his infatuation with Giraud nothing but the irresistible pull of Giraud's birthright magic? The image of Giraud's mother on the edge of a cliff came to his mind, unbidden and utterly unwelcome. Would he end up like her? Was it that kind of story Giraud was destined to live?

To fall in love, to break a heart? To leave Jehan, shamed and shunned by everyone, with no other choice but to throw himself off a cliff? The thought sent shivers down his spine.

Jehan hardly noticed how Giraud pulled out his purse and slipped a neat stack of coins to the innkeep.

"Here," he said, echoing her conspiring tone. "In case we need to leave in a hurry."

She cast a glance at the coins and took them with a soft smile. "I wish there were more boys like you two," she said, half parting already. "We need a few more kind souls."

"Enjoy your gizzards," she added, loud enough to be overheard by the closest tables. "Let me know if you need anything else."

Giraud raised his goblet and nodded, smiling as if he had no worries in the world. He turned around to Jehan, still beaming.

"Now that went a lot better than I expected."

"Really? I would have done perfectly fine without meeting those ... fine young men again."

Giraud shrugged and picked a piece of meat from the bowl with his fingers. "All bark, no bite. I wouldn't worry too much about them."

"But I do worry. I can't fight like you, and if they – "

Something buzzed along his ear, and instinctively Jehan tried to brush it away – only to meet a certain resistance in the air, followed by a tiny, outraged shout. A heartbeat later, he felt minute hands grab his ear so tightly he grimaced in pain.

"Oh, he's coming, he's coming!" Lunette's voice, soft and yet urgent, and so close to his ear she was uncomfortably loud. Was she out of breath? "The Prince is coming!"

"He is? Here? And when?"

"Oh, he's coming!" Lunette repeated, her voice all but tilting with urgency.

"Right now?!"

But instead of a reply, Jehan only got the buzz of little dragonfly wings and a gust of wind when she left.

Giraud cocked his head and needed a moment to understand what was going on. His eyes widened when he finally got it.

"What is it?" he asked. "He's coming, isn't he?"

"Yep." Jehan took the bottle of wine and filled his cup to the brim. "He's on his way. Too late to turn back, now."

And he finished his wine in a single, long gulp.

Chapter Seven - The Drunken Boar

Even though Jehan couldn't catch a glimpse of his true fae nature beyond his mortal guise, there was absolutely no doubt to the identity of Prince Sylvain when he entered the '*Sanglier Ivre*'. He was the man all eyes turned to the moment he stepped inside the inn.

Prince Sylvain looked just like any other human noble, on first glance, dressed in a dark green waistcoat that looked at the same time tastefully modest and yet ridiculously expensive. That was, he looked like a strikingly handsome, assertive human noble, bearing himself with the air of a seasoned soldier and leader of men. There was not even the hint of a doubt that he was a man to treat with utmost respect.

"My son!" he exclaimed with a grand gesture as soon as he spotted them. "My son, come to my heart!"

And there was no doubt as to who he was calling his son – now all eyes in the room turned to Giraud, who managed to look at least somewhat impressed.

Prince Sylvain crossed the room in a few long strides and hugged Giraud, his joy and pride rolling off him in waves, causing the guests to hoot and holler in celebration. They had no idea what was happening, but there was obviously a valiant noble of high standing, greeting his long-lost son – what was there not to celebrate? Jehan felt the urge to join them tug at his heart, but he managed to keep his elation down to a smile. This was a prince of the fae they were dealing with, and mere mortals were caught in their stories as easily as a moth in the flame of a candle.

The prince let go of Giraud and held him at arm's length, looking him up and down, every inch the proud father. And just as Raëlle had promised, their kinship could hardly be more obvious. Both had the same luxurious dark wavy hair, the same green eyes, the same straight nose and high cheekbones. But where Giraud was lithe and wiry in both body and mind, his father seemed muscular, heavy, wilful. Prince Sylvain had laughing wrinkles in the corners of his eyes, and the thought that Giraud might one day age into such a handsome specimen made Jehan's pulse quicken inappropriately.

"I have just received your message, son," the Prince opened the conversation, "and I am so happy to see you here, finally."

"Yes." Giraud's enthusiasm seemed somewhat moderate in comparison. "We need to talk."

"And talk we will, my son!" He jovially slapped Giraud's shoulder. "Anytime you want."

Somewhere in the back of his mind, something nagged Jehan to pry his attention away from the men in front of him. Something was not feeling right, here, but he would never figure it out if he remained transfixed by their glamour as he was.

"What about we sit down here and share a bottle of good wine?" Jehan offered out of the blue. He poured some wine into his cup and offered it to Prince Sylvain. "Here. Be our guest."

The Prince blinked, at first at Jehan, then at the offered wine. "And who would you be, Monsieur?"

"This is my friend Jehan," Giraud replied evenly. "He's here with me."

"Oh." Sylvain bowed briefly, barely more than a nod of his head. "*Maître* Jehan, what a pleasure to make your acquaintance."

Jehan's bow was significantly deeper, despite still sitting rather awkwardly on his bench in the corner. "Your Highness."

At that, Sylvain's smile gained a knowing edge, something about the sparkle in his eyes that told Jehan they were both aware of each other's special talents.

"It is good to see my son has friends." Sylvain took the offered cup and took a sip of wine. "Educated friends, with manners at that."

A sigh of relief almost escaped Jehan. Sylvain had accepted their invitation, so at least he wasn't planning on harming them outright. Fae were bound by the laws of hospitality even more than humans, and Jehan took it as a good sign that the Prince had barely hesitated.

"So – what about we sit down?" Giraud suggested and dropped back onto his bench before Sylvain had a chance to react. "I came here to apologise, and to ask for your forgiveness."

Much to Jehan's confusion, the Prince burst into heartfelt laughter. He sat down on the bench on the other side of the table, still laughing, shaking his head. "No need to be so formal, son. You don't come empty handed, and I think this is the nicest apology anyone has ever made the effort of bringing to my attention."

"Is it?"

Giraud managed to make his question sound politely surprised instead of completely flabbergasted. All the
Saints, had they overlooked something? Why was Sylvain
so jolly? Jehan had a terribly bad feeling about this.

"Oh, absolutely!" Nothing seemed to be able to dim
the Prince's mood. "I think it was a brilliant way of showing your allegiance."

"I tried to do my best," Giraud replied, mostly credible. "Happy to please."

Not his best lie, but right now, Jehan was happy with
everything they had. What the hell was the Prince talking
about? Allegiance to whom? Shown by what?

Glancing over Sylvain's shoulder, Jehan could make
out two figures in the shadows near the counter, one tall
and bulky, the other one slender and restless. He couldn't
sense any other magic in the entire room past the gleaming and glittering ego of Prince Sylvain, but he didn't
need his otherworldly gifts to be pretty sure that these
were the personal guards of the Prince, judging by the
way they kept a constant eye on him.

"I have rarely laughed so hard in years," Sylvain continued, still chuckling. He took his wine and was just about
to give a toast when he realised Jehan had not cup to raise
with him. Barely looking over his shoulder, he waved for
service, and the inkeeper came running as if she had just
been waiting for him to call. Well, maybe she even had.
"More wine, good woman, and more cups. This night
calls for celebration!"

She nodded, curtsied deeply, and scuttled off, all her former self-assured manner wiped away, bent into shape by
the subtle magic of a fairy prince expecting her to be nothing
but a moving prop on the stage of his grand adventure.

More and more, Jehan felt his hackles rise. He hardly
knew the man, but it was enough to be sure he didn't particularly like him.

"So tell me, my son, what exactly are your plans now?" the Prince asked once they each had a cup of wine in front of them.

"That's in good parts what I came here to find out." Giraud gave him a polite smile that got mirrored almost exactly in his father's features. "But first of all, I am here to ask you to lift that curse you put on my parents."

"Curse?" Sylvain blinked in genuine consternation. "I beg your pardon, but I really don't pay much attention to the may-fly affairs of mortals. They were cursed?"

"Yes. You cursed them." Giraud's eyes grew narrow, and suddenly he looked a lot more like his father. Maybe those wrinkles in the corners of Sylvain's eyes didn't come from laughter, after all, but from squinting in anger, just like his son. Instantly, Jehan found his attractiveness much diminished.

"Oh I am sure I would remember that." For a moment, Sylvain seemed to consider the matter settled for good, but then realised that Giraud didn't fall in line like other mortals around him. "I did not curse those people."

Jehan felt the gentle persuasion underlining those words tug at his mind. Did the Prince even realise he was bending the thoughts of all people around him to his will? Or did he consider it just a part of the natural order?

"I don't care what you think you did or didn't do," Giraud replied calmly, but with iron determination. "I ask you to lift that curse. Will you grant me that favour?"

This time, Sylvain didn't try to gloss over his ignorance. He gestured briefly, and the slender man in the back of the inn left his place in the shadows and walked up to their table.

On him, Jehan instantly spotted his fae nature. He didn't have that sense of power rolling off him like the prince, but there was that unmistakeable sense of otherness, of not-quite-human that he couldn't hide. When Jehan squinted at him at just the right angle, he could have bet he saw red and white fur, tiny round eyes and ears and long whiskers. With his gangly body and shifty motions, he couldn't hide that he was more weasel than human, though none of the other patrons seemed to notice at all. Not even the two nasty-looking daggers he wore on his belt seemed to register. No one here noticed anything the Prince didn't deem noteworthy.

Sylvain gestured again and he and his weasel leaned their heads together, whispering. This close, Jehan should have been able to overhear at least a few words of what they said, but he couldn't make out anything. He wasn't particularly surprised, though. The laws of nature seemed to go out of their way to accommodate the whims of the fae, as usual.

"Seems you are right, there is a curse on your parents," Sylvain admitted when their conversation was over and his weasel retreated to the sidelines. "And as much as I would like to grant you that favour you ask for, this is one of the very few things even I cannot facilitate."

"No?" There was an alarming note of threat in Giraud's voice. "Why not?"

"Because, my dear son, this curse has been crafted by someone who in many ways is my equal in power and standing. And I will not go meddling in her domain."

"So you'll just let them die? You abandon me like that? Again?" Giraud seemed close to jump across the table at his father.

"Giraud, maybe it's – " Jehan's attempt at calming the mood was outright ignored by both of them.

"I never 'abandoned' you," Sylvain spat back. "I looked out for you, more than any human child could ask for. I made sure you lived a charmed existence, even despite all those ill choices you made."

"Of course you would consider sticking with family an ill choice."

"Watch your words, you ungrateful fool." For a heart-beat, Sylvain's focus on his mask slipped, and his voice rolled like thunder echoing in the valley. Like the afterimage of a lightning bolt, Jehan now saw antlers over his head in ghostly shapes, leaves on his shoulders and storm in his hair.

This was an old creature, Jehan realised, much older than he had expected. Way older than the ways of magic he had been taught. This was a creature who had been young when magic still meant blood and death and darkness. What in the name of God had he gotten himself into?

"Don't threaten me," Giraud hissed. "I came here in good faith."

"You came here to beg." Again, Sylvain's voice rolled like thunder, and the room seemed to darken around him. And, like the good sheep they were, none of the human patrons noticed anything. "You played with powers you didn't grasp, foolish like just another mortal," Sylvain continued, "and now you do not want to pay the price."

"I never asked to be part of this!"

"Then why did you insult my wife so gravely if not trying to gain a way back into my good graces and into my court?"

"I did what?!"

Giraud's utter cluelessness finally managed to get through to his father. His anger evened out as quickly as it had risen, and instead he was calm and cold when he replied.

"Insult the Lady Givonne, you did. On Saint John's night, six weeks ago." A cruel smirk played around the corner of his mouth. "You rebuked her advances, calling her old and painted like a whore. I haven't laughed so hard in many, many years."

There it was again, that rapidly sinking feeling as if having jumped off a cliff.

Giraud was still busy staring at his father in confusion, so at least he couldn't instantly do something stupid. But in Jehan's head, thoughts were racing like never before.

The Lady Givonne was the Lady of La Morangiasse, the highest ranking fae in the domain, just as Sylvain was in Castelfort. Jehan vaguely remembered hearing a tale in which the two of them were married, but that was ages ago. Both the story and him hearing of it. But if that was true, if Sylvain and Givonne were still married, then she had all the reason to hate Giraud's guts – after all, he was her estranged husband's bastard son, living in her domain. A living insult she had to face every day, and one she couldn't easily get rid of. Oh, how suddenly all this mess made sense, and what a terrible sense that was.

The vaguely guilty expression on Giraud's face told Jehan that he at least remembered saying something rash that night.

"What did you do?" Jehan asked. "What did you say to her?"

"I – not much, I can hardly remember." Giraud obviously tried hard to rake up any bits of memory he could get hold of. "There suddenly was that woman … of a certain age. Friendly, generous, we laughed and we danced around the fires. But then she wanted to get into my breeches, and I told her off."

At his place across the table, Prince Sylvain snarled with grim satisfaction.

"Can you remember the exact words?" Jehan asked again.

"I … not really. I think I told her I'd prefer someone younger, less … artificial."

"You called the most powerful fae of your home town an ageing, painted whore? And you wonder why your family is cursed?"

"I didn't know who she was!"

On the other side of the table, Sylvain broke into thigh-slapping laughter.

"Is this funny to you?" Giraud hissed at him. "Is my family's suffering really nothing but a laugh?"

"Oh you silly mortals, of course it is." Sylvain took another sip of his wine and leaned in. "What else should it be?"

"I am not a mere mortal. And through me, those 'short-lived' creatures are your family, too." Giraud glared at his father balefully, not withering under his gaze as probably all other people did. "But I should have known that you do not honour your family."

"Don't you ignorant little shit dare comment on my honour." Again, thunder rolled in Sylvain's voice, and the candles flickered. "You are no family of mine, not as long as you reject the very heritage I gave you."

"You have given me nothing but rejection so far."

"I have given you power!" Sylvain hurled the last word at Giraud so forcefully that Jehan could have sworn he saw crackling sparkles scuttle across the walls where it hit. "I have given you more chances than anyone else in this realm, and what have you done with it?! Nothing. Absolutely nothing."

Taken aback, Giraud blinked, and for once kept his mouth shut. But Sylvain didn't even think of letting the matter rest now.

"I have given you what other men would kill for, and all you do is cling to those mud-crawling humans who cleaned your ass when you were too small to do it yourself. You cling to them like a drowning man to a chest of gold. You weigh yourself down with cold iron to suppress what would set you free, and yet you come here and blame me for your misgivings?! Ask me to save those people who keep you bound to a life you don't belong to? If they were living in my domain, I'd have taken them out of their misery a long time ago already."

He rose to his feet, tall and commanding, surrounded by a faint image of his real self like a halo. He was cold as the winter storm that Jehan saw tugging at his hair, and unmoving as the cliffs that framed their valley. Was he wearing a storm-torn cloak over his shoulders? A gilded leather cuirass?

"Tell me, Giraud of La Morangiasse – why should I feel anything but embarrassed when I look at you?"

"Because unlike you," Giraud pressed out between his teeth, "I honour the ones I hold dear. Because unlike you, I have a heart. And whatever power you think you hold over my life, I don't give a damn."

"Fool." For a heartbeat, Sylvain hesitated, looking at Giraud and Jehan carefully. "Unless you reject those mortals you call your parents, and as long as you insist on wearing that insulting necklace, do not seek me out ever again. You are no longer welcome here."

He turned around on his heel, the ghostly cloak on his shoulders fluttering dramatically. But those surreal images around him faded with every step he took away from them, until he once again was nothing but a handsome human noble in a green coat. His guards had taken up position at his sides, and they cast them dark looks over their shoulders.

At the far end of the guestroom, Sylvain stopped in his stride, right next to the table with the would-be brigands. The boys hadn't noticed anything of the wild exchange that had happened at their table, and were drinking and arguing and laughing just like all other patrons in this place. Though now, they shut up one by one as they noticed the noble standing at the head of their table, curious to learn what he was going to say. Sylvain waited until he had their undivided attention before he spoke up.

"The entire evening, those two back there in the corner have done nothing but brag about how they beat you up like little children. How you cried like girls and ran, screaming for your mothers. If I were you, strong and courageous sons of this beautiful town, I'd teach them a lesson they'd never forget."

What a nasty way of not attacking them directly, but still harming them as much as he could without breaking the laws of hospitality, one had to give him that.

"I knew it!" Pons yelled and jumped onto his bench. "I will make them pay for this!"

Marton was instantly up on his feet as well, glaring at them. "We tried to keep this civilised, but this has been one insult too many!"

Once again, Jehan found himself trying to shuffle deeper into his corner. Which, of course, was entirely useless, but for a heartbeat, he focused on the vain hope that he would be able to just melt into the masonry.

The brigands rose to their feet, slow and determined, and the nearest uninvolved patrons made sure to get out of their way. No one in their right mind thought about interfering. After all, those bastards from La Morangiasse needed to be taught a lesson, didn't they?

With all eyes on the brewing brawl, Sylvain seized the moment to slip out of the inn, but not without casting a last, bitter smirk at Giraud and Jehan. His guards kept lingering around the exit, though, probably to make sure no one left too early.

"Grab your hat!" Giraud whispered urgently. "Ready?"

Pretty much in reflex, Jehan grabbed his hat. "Ready for what?!"

Instead of an answer, Giraud put his own hat back on and grinned, a devil-may-care sparkle in his eyes. "Ready to follow me?"

"No...?"

Giraud laughed and grabbed Jehan by his wrist. Without looking back, he shoved away the table they had been sitting at and jumped to his feet, dragging Jehan with him.

He let go of Jehan's wrist and dashed across the aisle where he jumped onto the table on the other side. The men sitting around the table hollered in surprise, but were too surprised to do anything useful beyond that. Giraud ducked, held on to his hat and ran up to the window at the far end of the table. Like a human cannon ball, he shattered both sash and glass and disappeared in the darkness behind.

Now, the first of the brigands realised their prey was on the run, and came rushing after Jehan. Which made the decision rather easy for him. With a polite nod to the stunned patrons, he hopped onto the table as well, held on to his hat and jumped after Giraud.

The night air was surprisingly cool after the stale air of the inn, and there was a surprising lot of it – Jehan had enough time to realise that the fall was a lot longer than he had expected before he crashed onto the ground. He had forgotten the few steps leading up from the market place into the '*Sanglier Ivre*', and that it meant they were jumping out of a window a little more than nine feet above the ground.

Groaning, he heaved himself back up onto his feet. Nothing broken, and nothing sprained, though his left side would probably sport a nice array of bruises the next day. His palms and knees burned from scrapes, but he didn't waste time looking. All wounds would still be there tomorrow – now he had to make sure they would remain the only one.

"Here, Jehan, over here!" In the darkness, Jehan needed a moment to spot Giraud, already back on his feet, standing at the far end of the inn, towards the road that lead downhill and out of town – and towards the stables, where their horses should be.

Jehan gave him a brief wave and hobbled in his direction. His left hip smarted more than it should, he'd have to have a proper look at that tomorrow when the sun was up again.

Jehan had barely passed the main entrance of the inn when a whole gaggle of young men burst out of the door and spilled out onto the marketplace. Yelling and arguing among themselves, they needed a moment to realise that it was Jehan who limped right across their field of vision. But not much more than that.

Less than two heartbeats later, one of the Castelfort boys tackled Jehan with all the force his burly body could offer, and the two of them crashed onto the cobblestone street. This time, Jehan landed on his back, and felt the air being forced out of his lungs by that ox of a man.

"I've got him!" the guy on top of him yelled. "I've got one of them!"

Shouts and grunts answered him, and the mob spread in search of Giraud. Jehan's assailant fought off his feeble attempts to free himself and grabbed him by the wrists, much like a grown-up would restrain a child in a temper tantrum. Fear pounded through Jehan's veins and clouded his mind. What if Giraud fled without him? He'd never get out of here alive. Already, others were gathering around them, laughing at him, kicking him without any real force.

"Not so courageous anymore, now, are you?" Pons' spiteful voice cut through the torrent of fear that held Jehan in his grip. "Let's see how much fun you'll have when I kick you in the face."

Suddenly, there was an angry buzz of dragonfly wings in the air, and the brute sitting on top of Jehan yelled in pain.

"Whoa!" he yelled, letting go of Jehan's hands and holding his face. "What was that?!"

Blood welled up from the corner of his eye, coming from a tiny wound that looked like claw marks no wider than an earthworm.

"Ow!" he bellowed again, this time holding his ear. "What is that? Stop it!"

At the sight of the blood on his face, the fear in Jehan finally subsided, replaced by an icy cold. This wasn't about doing right any longer. This was about survival.

Swift as a snake, he grabbed the brute's hand and bit down hard on his fingers until he felt bones grind under his teeth and warm blood fill his mouth. Instantly, the guy slammed his free fist into the side of Jehan's head, filling his vision with stars.

"He bit me!" the brute growled. "Bit me like a girl!"

Mean snickering filled the night air, directed in equal measure at Jehan and the guy who was still pinning him down. But he didn't care. He had the man's blood now, and that was all he needed. Deep inside, Jehan felt magic thrum through his being, something old and feral and nothing he would have ever touched freely.

"Oi! Shitface!" he yelled, adding an awkward kick to the brute's back just for good measure. "Yes, you! Look at me!"

The brute looked down, startled, and for a heartbeat looked as if he was about to knock out Jehan for good. But then his eyes connected with Jehan's, truly looked at him, and his motions froze.

Yes, look at me, you animal, Jehan thought grimly. See my soul, see what I really am, and know yourself for the vermin you are. He bared his teeth, red with the man's blood, and he watched the guy blanch at the sight.

"What ... are you?" he whispered, suddenly nothing left of his earlier courage.

"Get off me," Jehan ordered, pushing with his mind as cruelly as the brute had earlier pushed him with his body. "*Get. Off. Me!*"

As if suddenly realising he was sitting on burning coals, the brute jumped off Jehan and staggered back.

"Whoa. Get back!" he shouted, warning his fellow mobsters, who reacted mostly confused. "He's got devil eyes!"

"What's wrong with you?" Pons again, staying back but stirring shit. "He's fighting like a girl, that's all."

There were five of them, now, standing in a wide circle around Jehan, as cautious as wine and company allowed them to be. A few more were loitering on the marketplace, and there were sounds of fighting coming from down the road, near the stables.

The thought of Giraud alone against these ruffians filled Jehan with a resolve he had never believed he could muster. With a few swift motions, he picked himself up from the ground. His heart beat loudly in his chest, echoing like thunder in his ears. Damn all these fools, he thought, and damn the consequences.

"What now?" Pons hissed from his spot behind the first row of onlookers. "You wanna fight us all?"

"Oh sweetheart," Jehan replied, surprising himself with how cold and even his voice sounded, "I don't have to fight you."

He looked down at his palms, and found dark blood glistening at the ball of this thumb. He closed his fist until there were fresh drops running down, and licked them off with relish.

"Your blood, my blood," he whispered barely audible, the words coming from a memory that was older than his life. "Your will, my will."

"Guys," Pons yelled, a note of fear in his voice. "Someone take that creepy dude down, how hard can that be?"

"Shitface, shut that fool up."

Jehan's order was softly spoken, but could just as well have been delivered with a shovel. The brute jerked as if Jehan had hit him with a club, his breath going heavy. With lurching motions, he turned towards Pons.

"What? No!" Pons stumbled a few paces back, his eyes filled with fear. He was a scrawny guy, and no match for the ox of a man currently walking up to him with murder in his eyes. "Gis, seriously you can't do that!"

But the brute didn't stop or even waver in his motions. His self was currently confined to a tiny corner of his mind, all else subsumed and controlled by Jehan. He raised a massive fist, ready to strike, but Pons didn't let it come to that. With a squeal, he ducked and ran away, fleeing across the marketplace down a narrow alley along the castle's walls. Gis took a few lumbering steps after him and came to a grinding halt. With Pons out of sight, Jehan didn't care any longer what happened to him, and so his puppet didn't care, either.

"Will you let me go now?" Jehan addressed the remaining bystanders. "Or do we have to do this a few more times?"

Two of them raised their hands, signalling a peaceful retreat, but the other two didn't look entirely convinced.

With that ox on a leash at his side, Jehan was rather sure he could take them down, but it would take much too long. Who knew how many Giraud was currently fighting off, and he really, really had to get him out of there before he caused some irreparable damage. Or got irreparably damaged.

Gis grunted and shook himself like a man trying to wake up after a long sleep.

His hold on him was already slipping, Jehan noted with alarm. It had been a crude little thing of magic, unprepared and wild, very effective, but dissolving with the same speed as the blood in his mouth. He gave the two remaining villagers a quick glance and decided that there weren't much options to ponder. His ox was too slow, and he couldn't take them on by himself.

"Your strength, my strength," he whispered under his breath. "Your skills, my skills."

And then, he pulled.

Across the marketplace, Gis crumbled into a heap like a half-empty sack of grain. At the same time, new energy flooded Jehan's body, washing over his aching limbs and filling him with confidence.

Not even deigning to look at the remaining 'brigands', he walked past them, towards the alleyway he had seen Giraud disappear in.

"No one said you could leave," one of them snarled.

Jehan didn't stop.

The lout put a heavy hand on Jehan's shoulder, and with a motion he had never before used in his life, Jehan grabbed that hand and turned around himself. Suddenly, he found the guy kneeling in front of him, pinned down by the twisted hand in Jehan's iron grip, yelling in pain.

"I do not need your permission to leave."

He let go of the man with a final shove to his arm and watched with satisfaction as he crumbled to the ground, nursing his wrist. Jehan turned to the alley again, not looking back. His borrowed strength and skills wouldn't last long.

But he didn't have to go far. Barely around the corner, he stumbled into a throng of cheering onlookers, blocking much of the road. They were standing around a brawling pile of men on the ground, and beyond them, at the bent of the road, Jehan saw that stable-boy peeking out of a gateway, their horses in tow. Not the worst sight he could have imagined. Now hopefully Giraud hadn't done anything really stupid yet –

"He's got a sword!" someone closer to the brawl yelled, followed by the clatter of metal on stones.

Instantly, the gawking throng tried to get a few steps further away from the brawl, shuffling and cursing. No one took particular notice of Jehan, thinking him just another onlooker, which suited him just fine. He seized the opportunity and pushed further towards the actual fight, barely registering how people bumped against him and looked him up and down with surprise when he didn't budge.

On the ground, he found Giraud buried under three other men. They were trying to pin him down, to restrain him, but he was fighting like a cornered badger, and hissing pretty much the same way. His face was bruised and bleeding, his pretty hat nowhere to be seen, but so far, he appeared to be more infuriated than wounded. Jehan gave a silent prayer of relief and waded into the fight.

Not particularly caring where he stepped, he treated the bodies on the ground like a nest of eels – looking more dangerous than they were, as long as one made sure to have secure footing. He waited until the writhing mass of bodies washed one of them up in a useful way, then he bent down, grabbed the guy by his belt and the scruff of his neck and hauled him off the ground like a sack of coals. He used the momentum to hurl him a few feet away, satisfied when he landed at the feet of the onlookers with a startled groan. Not wasting any time, he grabbed a second assailant in pretty much the same manner and hurled him off, though this time it looked a lot less impressive. His unnatural strength was fading rapidly, and he maybe had one or two moments left before he was just his humble self again. Well, maybe not so humble, tonight.

"Get off him!" he ordered, startled at the deep bellow that came from his mouth. Apparently, he had stolen more than mere physical strength. To drive his point home, he kicked at the last of the assailants.

"What the hell – " The kicked man jumped up to his feet – only then Jehan noticed his red neckerchief and that cocky attitude. It was Marton, the self-style leader of the local 'brigands'. "You!" Without hesitation, he swung a heavy fist at Jehan.

He dodged the blow expertly, much to his own surprise, and instead delivered a nasty hook into the other man's kidney. Marton stumbled back, startled, furious. Howling with anger, he ran up to Jehan and tried to bowl him off his feet. Which didn't quite work as intended.

There was still some stolen strength and brawling skill left within Jehan, so he managed to grab Marton by his forearms and hurl him around with his own momentum. They both crashed down onto the cobblestone road, but with Jehan on top, one of his knees firmly planted on Marton's sternum. Jehan heard him gasp for air and momentarily give up any resistance.

"Jehan, you alright?" Giraud's voice, breathless.

He glanced over his shoulder and found him standing on his feet again, holding his side, his face bloodied but alive. Giraud's 'hunting knife' lay a few feet further down the road, thankfully clean and gleaming in the light falling from the surrounding windows. They were still surrounded by at least a dozen onlookers, but none of them showed any particular interest in starting a fight with them.

"Mostly fine," Jehan replied, a little short of breath himself. "You?"

"Great," he croaked.

"You don't look great."

"Pah. You should see the other guys."

"I'd rather not." Jehan got back onto his feet, feeling a little more wobbly than he would have liked. "We really should get going – *Aïe!*"

A sharp pain shot up from his ankle, and Jehan toppled to the ground, again slamming painfully onto the the cobblestones. From the corner of his eyes, he could see Marton jumping to his feet, red with fury and by no means calmed by his previous defeat. He had kicked Jehan against his ankle when his attention had been on Giraud. Unfortunately, Jehan had come to lie with his head downhill on the steep road, and struggled to get his bearing. It was enough for Marton to close the gap between them and deliver two hard kicks to Jehan's side, swift and vicious. The pain blotted the world around Jehan with red.

Giraud, who had gone to pick up his knife, jumped around and immediately was at Jehan's side. He shoved Marton away, causing both of them to stumble on the uneven ground. Instantly, they were at each other's throats again, shuffling and trying to land a decently aimed fist in the other's face. Jehan's eyes swam with blurry images, there was a metallic rattle in his ears and the smooth cobblestones felt even more slippery than usual. Why was it so hard to get back on his feet?

From the corner of his eyes, he watched Giraud and Marton exchange kicks and blows, vicious and definitely not just trying to settle an argument. Finally, he managed to get his feet back under him, and rushed in to help.

He tried to hit Marton, but all the borrowed skills had left him along with the guy's blood in his mouth. Indeed, it was mostly his own blood he tasted now, and a lot of it, too. So he did what came most naturally to him – he stepped between Marton's legs and shoved him downhill.

With a startled yell, Marton toppled over and fell flat on his face, the increasingly steep road causing him to roll over twice and land against the cornerstone of a house in a tangled heap. Giraud looked up at Jehan, blood in the corners of his mouth and running from his nose, but grinning.

"Damn. You fight like a girl."

Jehan just gave him a dark scowl and rushed down the road towards the gateway that led to the stables. Halfway down, he stopped to pick up Giraud's knife, and had almost reached the stable gate when a yelled command from behind stopped him dead in his tracks.

"Halt! In the name of Marquis Aliazar of Castelfort, stop right where you are!" The crowd of spectators got pushed aside by half a dozen of the local guards, armed and armoured, looking mightily pissed that some tavern brawl had ruined their lazy shift. So that metallic rattle in his ears hadn't been imaginary, after all. "Everyone turn around, and drop your weapons."

A few steps in front of him, Jehan saw the stable-boy safely retreat around his corner and out of sight of the guards. Smart boy.

"Watch out, he's got a sword!" someone yelled.

Jehan turned around, and of course found Pons standing right there among the first row of onlookers, a mean little smile on his bruised face.

"It's not a sword," Jehan growled. "It's a god-damn hunting knife."

Giraud, still standing halfway between Jehan and the guards, at least had the decency to look embarrassed.

"Drop that sword," the guard captain ordered, "or we will drop you."

Two of his men had light crossbows on them, and raised them now to take aim at Jehan. He closed his eyes, silently cursing himself for allowing Giraud to drag him onto this adventure. He was no hero. He was a fisherman, trying to live a peaceful life, and nothing else. This is what you got for meddling in affairs way above your concerns. The hunting knife fell from his hand and clattered on the ground, slipping downhill another few paces.

"Good. No one needs to get hurt." The guard captain sounded relieved. "Now come on, everyone, get lost. Fight's over, no one has been grievously hurt."

The first onlookers took that as a cue to disappear quietly into the night. But Pons couldn't let the matter rest.

"You can't let them go, captain!"

The guardsman dropped his shoulders and turned towards Pons. "And why, pray tell, can't I do so? Do you have any real crime to report?"

"Of course!"

The captain gesture for him to come forth with whatever crime Pons wanted to report, but for a long moment, the only sound to be heard was the chirping of the crickets in the night air.

"So do you have anything to report or not? We don't have all evening for this."

"Slander!" it burst out of Pons.

"Really? You're wasting my time cause you've been insulted?"

"It's true, captain."

Everyone turned around to see Marton back on his feet, wiping some blood from the corner of his mouth.

"You can ask anyone inside the '*Sanglier*', captain." He took a few steps up the road, closer to the guards. "These men are from La Morangiasse, and even though they talked ill about us all night, we tried to be good men and allowed them to have a meal in our midst. But they continued telling lies of cowardice and lawlessness, so brazen that even the nobles visiting the tavern felt slighted. We were just sending them out of town when things got out of hand."

The captain still didn't look particularly convinced. "You're Marton, right? If I remember correctly, there's a nice handful of brawls here in town that you have started, and it took a lot less than such a colourful story for you to use your fists."

"But it's true!" Pons hissed.

"Boys, grow up." The captain pushed back his helmet and scratched his forehead. "If I were to lock up every lout who's been insulting another here in town, we'd be – "

"Witchcraft!" Pons yelled.

"What?!" For a heartbeat, the captain looked as if he was about to slap Pons, but then he straightened up. "Say that again."

"Witchcraft," Pons repeated, with more conviction this time. He pointed an accusing finger at Jehan. "That one. He's in bed with the devil."

A scandalised murmur washed through the crowd, just as an icy cold wave of dread washed down Jehan's spine. No, he corrected himself, he had been wrong earlier. *This* was what he got for meddling.

"That is a grievous accusation," the captain said, carefully keeping an eye on all four men involved. "Do you have anything to back that up?"

"Oh, I have seen it all!" Pons took a step forward, visibly revelling in all the attention. "He jumped out of a window of the '*Sanglier*', and he sailed to the ground like an owl in the night. You know how high up those windows are, and look at him – nary a scratch!"

The captain eyed Jehan up and down. "He looks a bit the worse for wear to me..." he mumbled.

"But then, on the marketplace, when we had him restrained, he bewitched poor Gis."

"He did what?"

"Captain," Giraud tried to interfere. "This is all ridiculous. Witchcraft, in this day and age? It is years ago that we burned the last witch here. It's clearly just an attempt to – "

"Shut up!" the captain ordered with a sharp gesture. "I don't care for you louts beating each other up. But if a citizen of my town raises an accusation of witchcraft and sorcery, I will damn well listen carefully."

Giraud cast an alarmed glance to Jehan, and all he could do was shake his head, hoping he wouldn't try anything else and make things even worse. Though right now, he wasn't too sure how things could possibly get any worse than this.

"He bewitched Gis, captain, he scared him witless with nothing but a glare, and you know, Gis isn't a man easily scared."

The captain nodded pensively. "He's admittedly too stupid for that..."

"He had fire in his eyes!" a deep voice from the rear added in halting words. "He had eyes ... eyes like the devil himself."

A renewed murmur passed through the crowd, and this time it sounded rather scared than scandalised. The onlookers parted again, and Gis stepped onto the scene.

The scratchmark along his left eyes was puckered and bright red, and he held his right hand in a blood-soaked cloth, but apart from that, he seemed mostly unharmed. Gis stopped right next to the captain, and even though he was a good head taller than the man, he bowed deeply.

"Captain. That man. He is dangerous," he explained with the slow cadence of a man not used to so many words. "His eyes, like the devil."

Gis, quite obviously, was a simple creature, but now that simplicity worked seamlessly against Jehan. No one doubted that Gis was a humble and honest man, maybe even likeable, and that he was terrified to his marrow by what he had seen.

Even if the captain considered the entire story somewhat fishy, he was beginning believe there was something dark going on his town. With a brief gesture, he sent some of his men to take up position next to Jehan and Giraud, flanking them so that any thought of a late escape was crushed.

"Tell him," Pons urged him on, "Tell him what happened then!"

But Gis just lowered his gaze and shook his head in embarrassment. "No..."

"But you must!" Pons looked at the assembled crowd. "You don't want them to walk away free, do you?"

Again, Gis shook his head.

"Then tell the good captain what happened next."

"That man," Gis continued in his halting way, "he took my blood, when he bit me." He held up his hand to illustrate his words, shivering with distress. "And when he had my blood, he – "

Gis broke of, shuddering.

"What did he do?" the captain asked, and the entire crowd seemed to lean in and hold their breath just to make sure they wouldn't miss a single word.

"He – he ate my soul."

"Beg your pardon?"

"He was in my head!" Gis was so upset his voice almost tilted. "He was in my head, and he made me do things, things I never wanted! I don't hurt my friends, I would never, you must believe me, captain, please, I would never hurt them!"

The crowd leaned back with another unnerved murmur.

"I was there," Pons continued doing his worst. "I saw him bewitch that poor man, and he ordered him to kill me! It is only for his valiant struggle that I am still alive!"

"I am so sorry," Gis mumbled, still shivering. "I would never hurt my friends."

"I think I have heard enough," the captain decided, his face dark and troubled. "I don't know what has happened here, but it is clear that something did indeed happen." He turned and faced his men flanking Jehan and Giraud. "Lock those two up for the night, and make sure there's a priest close by. I won't have talk of witchcraft in my town."

"A wise decision, captain, one cannot be too careful with that kind of folk."

"Shut up, Marton," the captain snapped, "or I'll have to wonder who's framing who here tonight."

He turned around to leave, and the guards directly with him followed suit. The guards flanking Jehan grabbed him by the arms and shoved him up the road, while those standing next to Giraud did the same with their charge.

"You can't do that!" Giraud yelled. "You can't just believe those fairy tales!"

The guard to his right slapped him across the head. "Shut up or we will do so. You've caused enough of a stir for the night."

"No, I will not!" With a sudden jerk, Giraud pulled himself away from the guards and ran downhill, away from the crowd and towards Jehan and his guards.

Jehan barely managed to give him a pleading glance. What the hell was doing? If he ran now, everyone would believe them guilty of at least something. But already, Giraud was past him – dodging the guards on Jehan's either side by simply dropping onto the ground and sliding a few bumpy paces downhill.

"*Halt!*" someone yelled, accompanied by the ugly, grinding sound of a crossbow's ratchet locking up. "Halt right where you are, or I swear by God I will nail you to that wall!"

Down the road, Giraud stopped his flight at the foot of a tall fieldstone wall that marked the turn of the road. He raised his hands, slowly, and turned around. In the night shadows, Jehan could hardly make out his face, but he looked pained, anguished, terrified. What the hell was he going to do?

"Really now?" one guard of Giraud's escort mumbled in frustration. Together with his companion, they slowly walked down the street, careful not to slip on the steep decline in their heavy boots.

But apparently, Giraud hadn't planned to run, but only to gain a few heartbeats of time – he was fumbling around with his necklace, pulling and tearing as if trying to strangle himself with it. The words of Prince Sylvain came back to Jehan's mind – that insulting necklace that was weighing him down with cold iron... Involuntarily, Jehan hunched up his shoulders in dreadful anticipation of what was about to happen, even though he had no idea of what it was.

The faint click and tinkle of breaking metal probably was too faint for anyone else to hear, but to Jehan, it was deafening. Slowly, Giraud straightened up and took a deep breath, and with him, so did the entire street. Not only the people, but the houses around them and the horses in the stable and the trees and the very night sky seemed to draw a deep breath of fresh air. The tingle of magic was so strong Jehan felt his eyes water.

Down at the foot of the wall, Giraud still looked like before. Only, with every heartbeat, the wall behind him got smaller. No, Jehan corrected himself, it wasn't that the wall changed, it just became less relevant. As if Giraud gathered up every little bit of light around him, he commanded every bit of attention anyone in the street had to spare. He drew looks like a whirlpool drew water, just as his father had done in the tavern. All conversation came to a grinding halt, and even the guards who were on their way to pick up Giraud a second time halted in their steps.

Silence spread, filled with rapt attention for whatever it was that Giraud was about to say, and no one wanted to miss a single one of those words, magnificent as they would surely be. How could they not, coming from such a magnificent young noble? Maybe he was a prince, even?

Blinking in silent wonder, Jehan noticed that Giraud suddenly sported a hint of antlers above his brow, short and wilful, and where the summer breeze pulled his hair aside, tips of pointed ears were showing among his curls.

"Friends."

The word rolled up the street like a gust of wind and left a smile on every face. We were all friends here, weren't we?

"Please, do we really have to talk of dark deeds on such a beautiful summer night?"

His words weren't loud, but they were easily heard everywhere, and the murmur among the crowd was one of clear agreement.

Giraud took a few step uphill and nodded at the guards who had come to arrest him. With a polite inclination of his head, he walked past them, and they bowed deeply as if it were the most natural thing in the world. And to them, it actually was. Just like his father, Giraud enthralled humans to the point that their own will meant nothing in his presence.

He came up to Jehan and cast him a look that was filled with sorrow, a wordless, dreadful apology and silent prayer for forgiveness. But his words were as cold and condescending as any noble's, "Get your hands of my man."

Instantly, the guards holding Jehan let go of him as if he burned their fingers.

"My apologies, Milord," one of them mumbled, his eyes downcast.

Giraud dismissed him with a wave of his hand, and the man stepped away. Deeply fascinated, Jehan watched Giraud walk by and towards the guard captain. It was still the same Giraud as ever before, the one who stood at his market stall only a day ago, covered in soot. But now his fae nature was no longer hidden, no, it was bright as the full moon and glittering and blotting out everything else around. Were those white flowers in his hair?

"Good captain, please accept my sincerest apologies for the unrest we have brought to your beautiful town."

The captain mumbled something unintelligible, polite, vaguely dismissive.

"Rest assured I will compensate you for all the damage that might have been caused." The crowd murmured again at such a generous gesture. "But please, captain. Sorcery?" He chuckled, condescendingly, as if the notion itself was the sign of a feeble mind.

"But we all heard what Gis said," Marton interjected, his mind a little more resilient than most. "We can't just ignore that!"

Giraud's head snapped around, his eyes all but throwing sparks of fury. "No, we cannot ignore that," he hissed, "but maybe we shouldn't read too much into those words, should we?"

"What – what are you trying to say, milord?" Again, the guard captain proved he was among those who kept a relatively clear head even in the most unusual situation. "Do you say he was lying?"

"Poor Gis? No." Giraud stepped towards the group of remaining onlookers and grabbed Pons by his vest. "But this little rat, I tell you, *he* was lying."

"No, I wasn't – I tell you – "

"Silence!" Giraud ordered, and Pons all but choked on his words. "Good people of Castelfort, just look at him. He is short, and poor, and ugly, just look at his face!"

Mean sneers rose from Giraud's audience, agreeing with him.

"That pointed nose, that hunched gait – doesn't he even look a little like a rat?" Again, the crowd murmured their agreement, and Pons cringed at the humiliation. "Doesn't this miserable little man look like someone who'd say anything to bring down someone of undoubtedly better birth? Wouldn't he do anything just to harm me and my companion? Wouldn't he just lie?" He turned his attention to Pons directly, and the poor guy shrunk away from him in fear. "Didn't you just lie to harm us? Did you?"

"I ... "

"Speak the truth!" Giraud barked, and Pons ducked lower as if trying to dodge a blow.

"I lied," he whimpered, "I lied, I lied, I am sorry!"

"See?" Giraud faced the captain again. "I am sorry for this mess, but I am not tolerating such false accusations."

"Of course, milord. But – what about Gis?"

"Oh that poor man." Once more, Giraud scanned the crowd. "Gis, my good man, come over here, will you, please?"

Like an ox on a leash, Gis left his spot in the rear of the crowd and stood next to Giraud.

"I believe every word you said," Giraud told him. "You are a good man, and strong, and anyone who has your friendship can be proud of it."

Gis' face lit up like a child's at Christmas, praised by an important Lord such as Giraud.

"But really, captain, we are not talking about the brightest man in town here." Giraud looked Gis directly in the eyes. "Tell me, have you seen many devils before?"

"Milord?"

"Have you seen many devils before tonight? Do you meet with them regularly?"

"No...! No, Milord. I would never."

"So, how can you tell this man had the devil's eyes?"

"I ... " Confused, Gis looked down to his feet.

"Also, Gis, have you been drinking, tonight?"

"Yes, milord?"

"Wine?"

"Yes?"

"How much?"

"I ... " Gis looked around as if the answer was hiding in some corner. "I am not sure. Two pitchers? Three, maybe?"

"And it was Pons who told you about that devil you think you saw, wasn't it?"

Gis eyes went to Pons now, as if looking for clues, but Pons was still cringing and not saying anything. "I ... I'm not sure, milord? He might have?"

Giraud shook his head, his expression now one of sympathy and sorrow alike. "How lowly to use the childlike imagination and inebriation of a simple man to bolster one's own lies. I believe this clears up all of your questions, good captain?"

"Yes, milord," he confirmed with a nod.

"So me and my man, we are free to leave?"

"I think so, yes. Yes, milord."

"Free of any charges?"

"Yes, milord."

"Well, then, what a luck we could sort that out." Giraud tipped the rim of his imaginary hat. "Good night to you, captain."

In a gesture that looked like a dreadfully exact copy of his father, Giraud turned on his heel and strode off, downhill towards Jehan and the stables. All that was missing was the fae image of a fluttering cloak around his shoulders.

He passed Jehan without a glance and stopped at the stable gates, the scent of white oleander following him like a retinue. The stable boy rushed out to meet him, leading their horses by the reins, and held them so Giraud could mount leisurely. Only when he was up in his saddle, Jehan realised that he should follow him. One of the guards had picked up Giraud's knife and handed it to Jehan, very politely, hilt first, while another one brought them their hats. The man even had an apologetic smile at their trampled state for him. Jehan took all the items with according gratitude and turned to Grise. But at the last moment, he hesitated, took his foot back out of the stirrup and walked over to the fieldstone wall and searched through the weeds there for Giraud's necklace. He found it quickly enough, even though one link was broken and a part of it missing. He tucked it into his pocket and hurried to get onto his gelding.

Up on his horse, closer to Giraud, he saw his eyes were wide with dread, and his breath was going fast and shallow.

"I am so sorry," Giraud whispered. "So sorry for everything."

Jehan struggled with a reply, conflicting emotions clogging up his throat. But only for a heartbeat, then he shrugged it off. "Let's get out of here, quickly."

They spurred their horses and left without even so much as looking back, riding out of Castelfort as swiftly as the road allowed.

Chapter Eight - Drifting Among the Stars

They had barely reached the bridge of Beronsac when Giraud broke down.

Night had fallen completely by now, and an almost full moon hung brightly over the cliffs, illuminating the road and glittering on the lazy waves of the river to their left. They had been leading their horses in a swift canter since they had passed the gates of Castelfort, with Giraud going ahead. They both wanted to put as much distance between them and that town as quickly as it was possible without it looking like an escape. But as soon as the cliffs of Beronsac loomed on the horizon, promising safer ground, Giraud let his horse fall back until he was side by side with Jehan.

"I – I am so sorry," Giraud pressed out. "This is all my fault. I should never have dragged you into this, and..." His voice broke off, as if choked by tears of anger he was valiantly trying to suppress.

A swift glance to the side showed Jehan that Giraud indeed looked miserable, and despite everything, he couldn't make himself feel anything but worried. So he pulled his horse closer and grabbed Giraud by his baldric, forcing him to slow down until they both came to a halt.

"Hey," he said, placing a calming hand on Giraud's shoulder. "You didn't want anything that happened to you, either, and now -"

"Stop trying to defend me! It is all my fault, and now my parents are dying, and that Prince hates us, and you hate me, and – "

"Giraud! Shut up!" Jehan barked, and surprisingly enough, Giraud did as told.

Jehan used the moment of silence to wipe his face, cursing softly as the salt of his sweat burned in the scraps on his palm and the bruises on his face smarted. Next to him, Giraud was still breathing in jagged bursts, his legs twitching with nervous energy, making his horse just as jumpy.

"Nobody hates you. I don't hate you."

Now, Giraud's expression mellowed to something between gratitude, self-loathing and despair, something that Jehan only found marginally easier to stomach. Strong emotions he didn't know how to make sense of, indeed.

Good Lord, that boy was in no condition to be on his own, right now. The thought of dropping Giraud off at his parents' and leaving him out of sight for the better part of a night and maybe half a day tomorrow filled him with dread. There were just too many short-sighted, heroic things Giraud could attempt in that time. And he could still do a lot more harm to himself and his loved ones than he already had.

A look up at the stars told him that it was still well before midnight, and with a little bit of luck, things would look a lot clearer after a few hours of sleep. Also, maybe his own body would have stopped aching all over by then.

"Here's what we'll do," he said firmly, leaving no room for Giraud to voice any doubts. "We'll ride to my place now, get cleaned up and sleep. First thing tomorrow at dawn, you'll get the horses to your father's stable and work like the good journeyman blacksmith you are. Understood?"

Giraud frowned, sniffled, and nodded hesitantly.

"And I'll think about how to get the both of us out of that entire other mess."

Giraud blinked in disbelief. "You are still going to help me?"

"Oh, of course, you oaf." Jehan slapped him across the brim of his hat. "Now come on. My hut is barely a mile from here."

He tried to spur his horse into a light canter, but good old Grise didn't give him much more than a leisurely trot. He had done enough work for the day, clearly, which, in a way, was just as well. At least, Giraud fell in behind him without a word.

They didn't follow the road across the bridge and onto the side of La Morangiasse, but instead rode straight ahead onto a narrow path that followed this side of the river. It was barely wide enough for a horse, and not exactly even, but Jehan knew the area by heart and would have found his way even in pitch darkness. He had to dodge a few low-hanging branches, but apart from that, they could keep a good pace. Every now and then, the slender oaks to their left gave way to the river, dark and calm and entirely unperturbed by the events of the day. At least one thing that hadn't been shaken to the core.

They continued their silent ride through the forest for a while, until they came to the bend in the path that marked the beginning of the hill that Jehan called 'his'. Many years ago, the river had forked in two, here, flowing around a crescent shaped little island. Over time, the river had dug it's bed deeper to the west, towards La Morangiasse, and this old arm had had been cut off from the stream. These days, it was nothing but a narrow lake, only connected to the river by a single inlet farther upstream. Trees had covered the island, and no one had cared when Jehan had build his hut on the top of it.

Calmly, he slid off his horse and took Grise by the reins.

"We'll have to dismount for the last bit," he told Giraud, "The path is very narrow, and I don't want the horses to slip."

Giraud nodded and climbed off his horse with a lot less elegance and vigour than usually. He looked dreadfully tired.

"Come on, we're almost there."

Jehan led them across a narrow dyke of tamped dirt that served as bridge across to the former island, leaving the dead river arm on their right. From there, a simple footpath led farther uphill, the yellow rocks cleaned of soil and beginning to lose their roughness after being used as stepping stones countless times already.

Jehan's hut stood in a small clearing that covered most of the island's hilltop. Initially, he had cleared the trees to find more rocks for a decent fieldstone foundation. But he liked the small meadow that had grown, and he entertained the idea of maybe keeping a few chickens there eventually. The hut itself was a simple thing, barely four by four paces wide, a half-timbered box with yellow mud walls and a slightly lopsided, slate-covered roof. But it was large enough for a bed and a chest, a fireplace, a table and two chairs. And admittedly, that second chair had never seen any use other than to take up space. At least, until now, that was.

"Here we are," Jehan announced with more grandeur than he thought his retreat deserved, "welcome to my humble abode."

Giraud paused, and a tight little smile appeared on his face. "Thank you."

"As I said, you're welcome." Wordlessly, he took Trajan's reins off his hand and led the two animals to the chicken meadow. For a heartbeat, he stood there, feeling silly, but then he turned around. "Giraud, I have no clue how to care for the horses. We have to take the saddles off, don't we?"

This time, Giraud chuckled. "Yes, we do. Let me help."

"That's a great idea." Jehan handed the reins back to him. "I'll go and make sure we get something to eat in the meantime. I don't know about you, but getting only half a supper made me hungrier than not eating at all."

He took the saddlebag with the provisions from Trajan and carried it over to his hut while Giraud took care of the horses. He had never bothered to buy a lock for his door, after all, he didn't own anything worth stealing. The air inside was hot and stuffy from an entire day with the shutters closed, so Jehan swiftly decided against an indoors supper. There was a simple bench and a slightly wobbly table standing in front of the house, facing east, where Jehan took his breakfast and watched the sun rise every morning as long as the weather wasn't too foul. Both bench and table were little more than driftwood tied with old rope, but they were functional and the bench actually surprisingly comfortable. They would do nicely for tonight.

He took the provisions and the remaining half loaf of his own bread and put them outside. Inside the bag that Giraud's mother had packed for them, he found another chunk of bread, two chunks of cheese, a dried sausage and two boiled duck eggs. A carefully wrapped bundle revealed a small apricot tart, somewhat crumbled, but still a most delicious surprise. Together with the full bottle of wine she had packed them, this would more than make up for the half-finished dinner they had abandoned in Castelfort.

Satisfied with his preparations, Jehan fetched a knife and a corkscrew, and in the last moment decided to pick up his large stoneware pitcher, as well. He placed knife and corkscrew on the table, made sure Giraud was still busy brushing down the horses, and walked down the other footpath towards the river. Even though this was a view he had every night, the sight of moonlight dancing on the shallow river waves never failed to make him smile. The river might not care about the humans living on its shores, and it had taken a lot from Jehan, but it had also given him much.

With a happy little sigh, he stepped onto the large, flat stone that marked the end of his path and knelt down. Somewhere to his right, the loud slurp of a hunting catfish broke the silence, but only for a moment. Soon, the only sounds around him were the soft gargle of the river, the calls of the night birds and the rustle of little creatures on the forest floor. Even the incessant crickets had calmed down somewhat.

Jehan dipped his hands into the cool water and bit on his lip as it burned in his wounds. With calm, deliberate motions, he washed first his hands, then his arms and finally his face, the cool water soothing his bruises until he felt a little less frazzled. With his wet hands, he combed back his short hair. This would have to do for the moment.

Lastly, he picked up the pitcher from the ground and filled it with water from the river. He poured the water out and re-filled it again, three times the same motion, as he had done for as long as he could remember. His grandmother had always said this was how she had known he wasn't like other children, but she had never explained why.

That would be a long and difficult talk, with his grandmother, tomorrow, explaining to her what had happened and making a plan how to get out of it again. But he would face it, and get over it, and get this stinking pile of a mess sorted out. Hopefully.

Jehan turned back to his hut and, on a hunch, took a little detour to the small smoking hut he had set up a short way from his place. On the highest rack, there were still a few smoked trouts – too small and too dry to sell on the market – but maybe another nice addition to their late-night meal.

Back up on the hill, he found Giraud already sitting on the bench, fumbling with the bottle of wine. At least, he smiled when he looked up and saw Jehan approaching.

"I've taken some rope from that lean-to with all the nets," he said almost apologetically, "to tie the horses to a tree, I hope that is alright with you. It's unfamiliar territory, and I just wanted to make sure there weren't any ugly surprises."

"We've had enough of those, haven't we?" Jehan placed the pitcher and the trouts on the table and sat down next to Giraud. "Any wounds I should be looking after?"

Giraud looked down at his hands, his knuckles dark with scraps and bruises, almost black in the cool moonlight. "Nothing that won't heal on its own."

There it was again, that self-accusing note in Giraud's voice that made Jehan want to slap some sense into the boy. But instead, he took a deep breath, poured both of them some wine and raised his cup. "To adventures."

That earned him an unamused glare from Giraud, but at least he wasn't moping any longer. He raised his glass, and nodded. "This feels more like a disaster to me, so it serves me right. To adventure!"

Jehan smiled faintly. Adventure, indeed. He drank his wine and started to pull apart the bread, while Giraud busied himself cutting up the cheese. For a while, they ate in silence, munching peacefully, until they both felt less harried.

Sitting this close together, Jehan sensed Giraud's fae nature like a summer breeze around him, like sunlight falling through a canopy of leaves. It was dimmed, now that

Giraud was not consciously trying to impress everyone, but it was still unmistakably there. Each time he looked closely enough, he could see those antlers growing out of Giraud's forehead, with three tips and not quite a forearm's length, but it gave his face an entirely different cast. Together with the ghostly pointed ears that showed every now and then between his curls, it was a fascinating change.

But more than the antlers and ears, it was the the white oleander flowers that blossomed among his hair that caught his attention again and again. Their scent came together with the breeze, stronger one moment and almost gone another. Jehan had a hard time to do anything but stare at him.

When Giraud divided the last bit of wine between their glasses, he finally spoke up.

"I really didn't know who she was, that night, when I insulted Lady Givonne."

"You must have known she was fae, didn't you?"

"I..." With a deep sigh, Giraud leaned back against the hut. "I knew what she was, though not who. I just didn't care."

"Normally, I'd say that this is the kind of attitude that, one day, will make you pay dearly. But you already know that."

"Tell me about it." His mouth worked soundlessly for a moment, searching for words. "The problem is, I really don't want to care in those moments. I knew my words would hurt her, but she was getting on my nerves, and I just – lashed out. Can you imagine what would happen if I weren't wearing that necklace?" He shuddered again, focussing on the cup of wine in his hands. "I made that thing when I noticed my powers growing, and my temper, too. As long as I wear it, I am able to control myself, but if not... On that street in Castelfort, when those fools started talking about witchcraft – I just wanted to silence them. And it was so easy. Can you imagine how difficult it was not to push harder? Not to force that stupid rat to wet himself in front of the entire town? Or to humiliate that bumbling fool to tears? If I had really tried, I guess I could have made him jump off a cliff before sunrise."

"What luck you didn't."

"But that's what I am saying – I ... Sylvain said he gave me all that power." He looked up and right at Jehan. "I don't want any of that if it makes me become like him. Treating people like toys just because he can – I don't want to become that kind of person."

"Then don't."

Giraud gave a bitter, scoffing laugh. "I don't know if I can. Look, that scene in Castelfort – should I have kept my necklace on? Should I have allowed them to take you? Lock you up and maybe burn you at the stake for no other reason than the stupid lies of some bored boys?"

"Oh he wasn't lying." Almost laughing at Giraud's startled expression, Jehan added: "I didn't eat his soul. But I did take his blood and forced him to do my bidding. Just a bit of nasty, efficient blood magic."

"But ... you said..."

Jehan shrugged and took a deep breath. "I didn't care. You were in danger."

"You ... risked that for me?" Stunned, Giraud finished his wine and put down his cup with jittery fingers. His eyes were wide and dark, searching Jehan's face for something he couldn't name himself. "I don't think anyone's ever done anything that courageous for me. Or crazy. Thank you. That means a lot to me, you know that, yes?"

"You are welcome." Seeing Giraud's fingertips flutter nervously again, Jehan took his hands into his own and held them, gently, until the shivering started to subside.

"That's a fine mess I have put us all into."

"Indeed."

For a moment, they just sat there, holding hands, while Giraud tried to calm his nerves. Finally, Jehan rose and walked over to where Giraud had stacked their saddlebags on the steps to his hut. Somewhere among them, he found his satchel, and inside, the broken necklace Giraud had discarded. Next, he took a spool of thread from the window sill, the one that he usually fixed his nets with, and sat down next to his guest again. He cut off a length of thread and tied it to the broken link, holding up the necklace for Giraud.

"Here. This should help at least a little."

Giraud eyed the thing with apprehension, but nodded and turned around, holding up his hair. It was so odd to see that even when he didn't think about it, Giraud's hands never came near his antlers, and his grip neatly gathered up his half-length real hair as well as his longer fae curls. He put the chain back around his neck but hesitated when Giraud twitched awkwardly at the touch.

"Does it hurt you?"

"No... Yes. A little." With another sigh, Giraud let go of his hair. "It burns, but only a bit. I only notice it right when I put it on."

Jehan tied the necklace with a careful knot, adding a second loop just to be safe. When he withdrew his hands, he came to touch one of the oleander blossoms in his hair, and had to smile at the touch.

"At least now I know why you smell so good."

"Huh?" Giraud blinked at him over his shoulder, his mind slow with exhaustion both in his heart and his body. "Oh, those. They'll soon be gone, too."

"I could always smell them when you were around," Jehan confessed, a little sheepishly. "At least now it makes a lot more sense."

"Hmm." Giraud sagged against Jehan, leaning his head onto his shoulder. "Thank you. I really don't know what I would be doing without you."

Neither do I, Jehan was tempted to reply, but he managed to keep his mouth shut. Instead, he put his arm around Giraud and held him tight. The fae images around him were fading fast, and with a certain melancholy, he watched the white flower stars disappear from his hair one by one. At least, the physical contact seemed to do wonders in calming Giraud, his breathing becoming more and more even and his fingers finally stopped twitching.

Jehan became painfully aware of the fact that he had only one bed, and that offering to share it with Giraud might give an entirely wrong impression. At least, Jehan was pretty sure it would be the wrong impression.

The night was very mild, so maybe he could just offer the bed to Giraud and sleep under the stars? It wouldn't be the first time he did so, after all.

He was still gathering his courage to ask when Giraud gave a happy little sigh like a sleeping kitten and sagged off Jehan's shoulder, nestling his head in his lap as if he had done so a million times before.

Somewhat helpless to resist such innocent charm, Jehan gave a defeated smile and leaned back, gently stroking Giraud's curls. His antlers had fully disappeared by now, and of the flowers only the familiar scent remained.

He leaned back against the hut and allowed his eyes to wander over the river that glittered through the trees in front of him. The moon had almost completely wandered behind the horizon, but its light was still enough to make the rising face of the cliff on the other side of the river stand out among the dark forest like the Milky Way that filled the dark sky. But the beautiful sight didn't calm him the way it normally did. Tonight, the quiet and solitude only made his own thoughts feel all the louder, and they circled around in his head without aim or order.

Finally, when his feet started twitching nervously and he risked waking up Giraud, Jehan carefully extricated himself. He went inside, took the straw-filled pillow from his bed and tucked it under Giraud's head, trying to make him as comfortable as possible on the lumpy bench. It would do well enough for a single night, and Jehan really needed a walk to clear his head, or else he wouldn't sleep at all.

He strolled down the path towards the river, listening to the murmur of the water and the rustling of the leaves. With the moon now mostly gone, the stars were out all over the sky, and the milky way painted her familiar, twisted ribbon across the whole sky. Once he reached the riverbank, he turned right, stepping from stone to stone, and followed the edge of his island upstream.

On nights like this, he wished he could just jump into the water and let himself drift with the flow, watching the world pass by and not think about anything. He had done so a few times as a kid, travelling upstream until he felt uncomfortably far away from home and then allowing the river to carry him back. With his feet in the water, Jehan recalled that floating sensation, untethered and yet sheltered. Once this was sorted out, he wondered if it was time to do this again. Alas, not tonight, or any time soon. There was work to do, even if he had no idea at all on how to proceed.

Wistfully, he dug his toes into the soft mud between the rocks and remained there, like a tree growing on the water's edge, soaking up the starlight with his imaginary branches. He felt his mind sinking deeper into the earth, spreading and drawing strength, while his branches reached up to the sky and took in the stars' silver light like a cleansing rain. With every breath he took, the tension of the day drained out of him a little more, washed away by the river at his feet, leaving him calm and refreshed.

And aching.

More and more, the various scrapes and bruises he had sustained first from the scuffle with Giraud on the cliff of Petit Houx and later on their flight out of the '*Sanglier Ivre*' clamoured for his attention. So he gathered his dispersed mind, cursing under his breath when his first steps were barely more than a hobbled stagger. His left side, which he had landed on after jumping out of the window, smarted in particular, and when he lifted his tunic, the cluster of bruises was clearly visible in the starlight. He could even make out the pattern of the cobblestones he had fallen upon. He peeled down the waistband of his trousers and grimaced at the blood-smeared lacerations over his hipbone. Every single muscle in his body seemed to ache with the unusual exertion of fighting for his life, and demanded care of some kind or another.

Giraud most probably wasn't feeling any better, though at least he was sleeping soundly. He'd have to prepare a little something for both of them in morning, most importantly a story that Giraud could tell his parents. And something to make sure their wounds wouldn't get infected, something to assist the healing and disperse the bruises...

But not now. Now he had to take care of himself, else he wouldn't be in a condition to help anyone at all. Jehan picked up his walk along the river in careful steps. He paused when he reached the point that had been the tip of the island and checked upon the little charms he had set up on a chest-high rock there. It was nothing elaborate, nor particularly magical. It was just a handful of trinkets that looked special to him – a river pebble that looked like a smiling sun, a piece of driftwood in the shape of a fat fish, a shard of blue glass polished by the river. He thought of them as charms for good fortune, colouring the energy that flowed along with the river in hues that he liked. Seeing that everything was still unchanged, he left with a smile.

Following the bank further upstream, he came to the spot where the river had forked in two many years ago. Now only a low stretch of rocks remained, separating the river from its old arm. Beyond that, a narrow lake stretched deep into the forest, dark and still like a mirror. Jehan climbed over the rocks and stepped into the lake, smiling when he found the water warm with the day's heat. A swim in the river would have been refreshing, but also pretty exhausting, and he really had had enough of that today. Normally, the lake was too tepid for his taste, but tonight, this was a perfect place to take a long, leisurely swim, drift along for a while and relax all those muscles that screamed abuse.

Swiftly, he slipped out of his tunic and breeches and hung them over a low branch of one of the oaks lining the lake. He stepped into the water, careful not to stub a toe on one of the rocks, and slid in as soon as it was deep enough. At first, the water burned in his wounds, but as soon as he dove in and the water closed over his head, it was all but forgotten.

Yes, he had been born into his profession, but he considered himself lucky for having been dealt this kind of fate. He loved water, loved swimming, and he felt nothing but well protected when submerged.

He stayed under water as long as he could hold his breath, and returned to the surface only once he absolutely had to. The night air was cool compared to the water of the lake, smelling of dust and dry leaves, and it made him giddy. He closed his eyes and swam straight ahead, deeper into the forest, with long and measured strokes. The stars were framed by the trees to either side of the lake, like a painting of nothing but black and silver.

He swam on, feeling his body warm up and his muscles calm down with the gentle exertion. He was a good swimmer, and made few waves, but in the dead of night, even this gentle sound seemed loud to his ears. Jehan caught himself trying to swim soundlessly, silent like a fish, breaking the water as little as possible.

It was only after he had turned around before the dyke and swam halfway back around the former island when he noticed the faint ripples on the surface next to him, and the silver shadow underwater. Anyone else might have mistaken it for a reflection of the moon, but he knew that particularly curvy shape rather well by now. He stopped, drifting in one place for a moment, and watched the underwater moonlight circle him a few times.

"You know I can't talk underwater," he said with a soft chuckle. "Come out."

The water in front of him rippled, and a beautiful young woman emerged from the depth, her face round and pale as the moon, with hair as black as the night. Droplets of water glistened on her skin, and if one looked close enough, there was a faint pattern and rainbow sheen of scales on her cheeks.

"Greetings, *Limnada*. How are you tonight?" he asked.

"Why aren't you with your visitor?" Her eyes sparkled and for a moment, the pale blue tip of her tongue was visible when she bit her lips in fascination. "Why aren't you with him? In your house? In your bed?"

Of course that would be the first thing on her mind. But then, that was her nature. When he had met her for the first time, Jehan had worried that he had maybe built his hut near the lair of an *ondine*, and that she had no other desire than to lure him into her arms and drag him down forever. But as it turned out, Limnada was a nymph, and as sweet and harmless as they come. Her idea of privacy was pretty much non-existent, though, as were her manners. And her thoughts tended to revolve around one subject only.

"I am not sleeping with him because we're friends, not lovers," he replied, a little more breathy than he would have preferred. But speaking while swimming had its own challenges.

"I don't see how that's any hindrance."

"Of course you don't." He smiled at her. "Just take it as it is. We are friends, and friends don't do that."

She gave him a long, ponderous look, drifting a little aside. "Lots of humans do 'that', even when they are friends."

"And how would you know?"

"Oh, I watch them. When they think no one is watching, when they come to the river for a little ... fun."

Jehan rolled his eyes heavenward. Her view of the world was a little one-sided, but sweet in her odd innocence.

"Come on, let's find a place to sit," he offered, "You know I don't like speaking and swimming at the same time."

"Oh, of course," she said, nodding. It had taken him some time to make her see that with two legs instead of a fish tail, swimming was nice, but not exactly effortless. "What about the big one, over there? The one with the table?"

Her white hand reached out of the water and pointed to an overhanging tree. In the shadows underneath its branches, a square rock reached just a hand wide above the surface. Right next to it, Jehan knew there was another flat rock lying in the water, fully submerged, but close enough one could sit on it and use the other rock as a table.

"I'll race you," he quipped and immediately started in the direction she was pointing.

He managed two strokes before she gave a surprised yelp and disappeared into the water with a gentle slosh, only to emerge a scant moment later next to their target.

"First!" she shouted, happy and beaming. "Again!"

"Indeed." Two more strong strokes, and Jehan was with her, cautiously reaching ahead to make sure he didn't break a finger on a rock he hadn't anticipated. That would have been a most unnecessary complication.

Beside him, Limnada vigorously pulled herself onto the sitting rock, splashing and huffing. As elegantly as she moved underwater, she was happily lubberly on land. She could shape her body at will, but she very much preferred her lower body to be shaped like the tail of a fish, her scales silver and blue and faintly purple. She wrung out her hair and slung it back over her shoulder, letting the remaining water run down her curves in little rivulets. Jehan waited a moment until the waves had subsided before he pulled himself up next to her.

"But I did see that right, didn't I? That visitor you brought home with you is that sooty human from the village, the pretty one, isn't he?"

Jehan nodded silently.

"Oh, he is a fine one. I have watched him a few times."

"With women?" The question was out before he could stop himself.

"Oh no, mostly he's just washing all that soot off him, with the other humans from town. Very pretty." She cupped her hands and poured some water over the part of her tail that was above water now, to wash off an unsightly smear of mud. "Sometimes, he comes to my river all alone, and thinks no one is watching, too. You know how boys are when there is no one around, they – "

"Ah!" Jehan stopped her with a sharp gesture. "We talked about this. No crudeness, no personal details."

She raised him a mocking eyebrow, but didn't complain. "But you are interested in him, aren't you? Then why wouldn't you want to know?" She added a conspiring smile. "I can tell you he is rather delicious. That boy could take a dip in my pond any time he likes."

"Believe me, I know. But I am not sure he would be interested."

"Not sure he's interested in what I offer, either." Limnada looked up at Jehan with a quizzical smile. "Like you, he never stares at my breasts." For emphasis, she took both of them in her hands, giving them a little jiggle.

"Those are beautiful breasts," Jehan told her in all honesty.

"Of course they are!" She jiggled them again, laughing at her own silliness. "And even though it should go without saying – I like that I can talk to you and it's not always about ... 'that'. So when I saw you and the sooty one arriving together, I thought, maybe, you know...?"

Jehan wasn't particularly sure what she had thought, but he didn't want to ask, either. He was pretty sure he didn't want to hear her illustrative answer anyway. So instead, he just smiled and sighed.

"That doesn't sound as happy as you deserve," she quipped with a faint frown. "What's wrong, tadpole?"

"Oh my, where to begin..." Jehan leaned back and looked up to the stars. "Giraud is the bastard son of Prince Sylvain, for starters. And he has managed to terribly insult the good Lady Givonne. Who has in turn bitterly cursed Giraud's poor parents."

Limnada grimaced painfully. "*Macarelle!*"

"Indeed. But that's not the real problem."

"No?"

"The real problem is that I really like him." He chuckled at her clueless expression. "I like him, not as in – " he offered a very rude gesture that left very little to imagination, "but as in – " he put a hand onto his chest, beating like a fluttering heart. "You know?"

"Oh I see..."

"I might be doing stupid things for him, very stupid. There's already people in Castelfort who are quietly convinced I am in league with the devil."

"With whom?"

Jehan blinked at her for a few heartbeats, completely at a loss until he remembered that he was talking to a creature older than Christianity, and pretty much untouched by human beliefs. "The devil ... the ultimate evil."

"But you aren't. You would never!"

"I know that, you know that. But people will still happily burn me at the stake just to make sure."

"Burn you? At a stake? Like ... a salmon?" She shook her head in genuine bewilderment. "Humans are such weird creatures. If you lot weren't so pretty..."

Jehan shrugged. "All I am saying is that it was a difficult day."

She squinted at him, hesitant. "Was that your blood then that I tasted in the water? Did they hurt you, tadpole?"

"Only a little." He raised his hands so she would see his palms, freckled dark where he had scraped off his skin. "Prince Sylvain couldn't attack us outright, so he set up a little peasant mob to chase us out of town."

She took his hands gingerly in her own, touching the wounds so lightly he hardly noticed. "Is the sooty one also wounded? Giraud, you called him, didn't you?"

"Yes, Giraud. He's pretty much as black and blue as I am, but he's sleeping now."

"Good. Sleep heals almost everything..." Somewhat distracted, her gaze wandered up his left arm up to his shoulder, and then down his side until she stopped at his bruised hip. "This is ... barbarous! How could they do that to you?! I hope you slew a good many of them."

"I – no. I didn't slay anyone. And that's a good thing." He smiled at her doubtful expression. "There's a lot more of them than there are of me. All I want is to lead a peaceful life."

"Well, that dream's dead for sure, now that you meddle with princes and high ladies." She grabbed his chin and stared at his face, where first Giraud and then Gis had whacked him hard. "Oh, tadpole, they even damaged your face."

"It's all right, it'll heal."

She frowned at him, hard, her forehead wrinkled with umbrage. "You humans are a hardy lot, I'll give you that.

But this won't do, not at all." She pointed a webbed finger at him with authority. "You stay exactly where you are. I'll be right back." And without waiting for a reply, she slid off the stone and disappeared into the dark waters with barely a ripple.

Jehan closed his eyes and leaned back, resting his elbows on the 'table'. The air was getting cooler now, and he could feel a first, refreshing chill on his wet skin. He'd have to get back to his hut before the dew came down, and at least find some kind of blanket for Giraud. Or maybe he should wake him up and put him to bed...?

The silence of the forest submerged his tired thoughts and slowed them, his eyes gradually slipping shut. It had been a very long day indeed.

A sloshing wave announced Limnada's return, and immediately, Jehan was wide awake again. She heaved a dark, oozing shape out of the water and placed it next to Jehan before she hopped back onto her place on the stone. Smiling widely, she gathered up the strands of wet hair plastered to her face and daintily tucked them behind her ears.

"Can you help me clean them?" she asked, pointing at what looked like a pile of mud between them. "I really don't want to have all that muck between my teeth."

"Sure." He had absolutely no clue what she was talking about, but that was certainly no hindrance. "Just tell me what to do."

She scoffed softly and reached into the muddy mess between them. It turned out to be an old, half-rotten basked filled mostly with scum, a few algae, and several of the largest river mussels Jehan had ever seen. She pulled out one of the mussels and started cleaning it carefully in the water. With a shrug, he did the same.

After a few moments of meticulous scrubbing, she lifted her mussel up to eye level and stared at it intently.

"Nah, crap," she mumbled and flung the poor thing back into the lake. "Not that one."

Wordlessly, Jehan handed her his mussel, and it was inspected with the same precision. This time, she nodded, apparently satisfied, and placed the mussel behind her onto the table rock. They spend a while cleaning in silence, until she found a second shell that apparently met her strict criteria.

"Would you be a darling and throw the remaining ones back into the lake?" she asked. "Just give each of them their own corner, they're not the most social creatures."

"Sure."

He flung each one of them to a different spot around them, until he was stopped by a horrifying, grating, crunching noise from next to him. Halting in mid-motion, he looked over to his companion, and found her gnawing at the thick end of one of the 'good' mussels with very healthy teeth.

"What?" she asked. "Never seen a woman open a mussel?"

"I ... Oh, never mind."

Jehan continued distributing the surviving mussels into the lake and even washed the rotten basket, while next to him, Limnada gnawed and crunched and grumbled until the poor thing in her hands finally gave up. Smiling with satisfaction, she slurped the meat out of the shell and placed the remains back onto their table. The unsettling display happened pretty much unchanged with the second mussel, until that was opened and eaten, too.

Limnada bent down to the water and dabbed some remaining bits of shell from the corners of her mouth before she returned her attention back to Jehan.

"Now, here." She picked up one of the shells from the table and presented it to him. "I have left the best bit for you."

In the pale star light, the nacreous interior of the mussel looked precious and oddly immaculate considering the dark mud it had been dug out from. But there was one blemish – a knobbly pearl the size of a pea.

"A pearl. Thank you?"

She nodded, her smile widening a notch.

"I am sorry – what am I do do with this?"

"Now – eat it, of course! What else would you do?" She held out the shell for him. "It's a strong mussel, it'll help."

Jehan picked up the pearl and eyed it cautiously. Now that he was holding it, he felt the faint tickle of natural magic in his fingertips. "Help with what?"

Again, she squinted at him. "Healing, tadpole, just the healing. I know you wouldn't want help with anything else."

"How very considerate of you." He eyed the pearl in his hand, wondering if it wasn't maybe overly selfish using such magic to heal a few bruises. His grandmother needed every little bit of help she could get, now. On the other hand, if such simple things as river pearls could help her, she'd surely have sought those out many years ago. "Do I just swallow it?"

"Considering that human teeth aren't the best, I think that might be a wise choice."

With another shrug, Jehan put the pearl in his mouth and swallowed. It tingled gently on its way down, but otherwise, he didn't feel anything out of the ordinary.

"Thank you, *Limnada*." He smiled at her fondly. "You are too kind to me."

"Barely worth mentioning." She gestured towards the other shell on the table, holding another single pearl. "That one is for your sweetheart. He should eat it soon, they quickly lose their power once out of the shell."

"I will make sure he'll take his medicine. Anything I can do for you in return?"

"Oh please. You have been nothing but kind since we met, and never once tried to grab me or drag me on land – or stared at my breasts, for that matter. If at all, it is me paying my debts to you, here."

"Well, I am not going to argue with that." He eyed the pearl on the table for a long moment. If only all his problems could be solved that easily. "You don't happen to know a way to dissolve that curse Lady Givonne put on Giraud's parents?"

"Much to my regret, no. I have always tried to stay out of the affair of the Highborn, and it has served me well."

"Yeah. I have heard that counsel once or twice already today."

"At least the people you talk to have a shred of common sense." She put a cool hand on his thigh, patting him gently. "Don't you worry, tadpole. I am sure you will find a way."

"Are you?" He forced himself to smile. "I can't say I share your conviction."

"Oh, sure you will. Humans are nothing if not inventive, especially your kind. You'll find a way, figure out a solution, do something outrageously daring and inappropriate, and you'll save the day."

"Do you really think there is a way?"

"Absolutely. This is how the world turns – the creatures of the night do as they have always done, but the humans, they invent new ways. New stories, as your fae friend would say."

That indeed sounded oddly like the remark Giraud had flung at him, in that dark passageway in Castelfort, right after he had stolen another kiss from him. We are strong, maybe even strong enough to forge a story of our own.

He took Limnada's hand that was still resting on his thigh and gave it a friendly squeeze. They were both right, in a way. It was humans who upset the natural order of things. So far, he had always thought this to be a bad thing, a cause for unrest and pain. But right now, it also looked like an opportunity for genuine change. A change for the better.

"Maybe you are right."

"Of course I am right." She huffed in mock indignation, pouted and splashed a handful of water at him with her tail. "Nymphs are always right."

"Of course you are, Lady of the Lake." Jehan glanced up at the sky, but what few stars he could see weren't enough to give him a clear idea of the hour. Considering how tired he felt, it had to be late. "I think I should go now. After all, there's a fairy prince in my hut, waiting to be fed a pearl."

"Stop mocking me, you little newt." She smirked at him and nodded. "But yes, you should go. You'll need your sleep, after all you have big things ahead tomorrow."

"Do I?"

"Oh yes. You're going to change the course of your story."

Her smile didn't allow any doubts, so Jehan just nodded dutifully. He leaned over to her and placed a polite kiss on her cheek before dropping back into the lake.

"Then I wish you a good night," he said as good-bye, "and I'll come by and tell you how the story continued."

"Sleep tight, my friend!" she replied, slipped off the stone and disappeared under water. Her silver shadow circled a few more times close by before she disappeared for good.

Despite himself, Jehan had to smile. She was such a kind and caring creature. Crude, at times, and indecent, but full of genuine affection. He really would have to visit her once all this was over.

With long, deliberate strokes, he swam back to the inlet of the lake, and noticed with delight that his leg hurt a lot less. If that was due to the light exercise or to Limnada's magic, he couldn't tell, but he was grateful either way.

Back on land, he gathered up his clothes, but didn't bother putting them on again. He would only make them wet, and it wasn't as if anyone would see him here, anyway. So he sneaked through the forest entirely mooncladd, exhausted from the day but happy nonetheless, smirking each time he felt a gentle breeze touch his skin. It took him a while to find the spot where he and Limnada had been sitting from the shoreline, and another while to get from the footpath to the table, but he managed without stumbling in the dark. The second pearl still lay untouched in its shell, and Jehan picked up both reverentially. He gathered up his bundle and continued on his way around the lake until he reached the dyke. From there, it wasn't far to his hut, but he stopped when he was half-way up the hill.

What if Giraud wasn't sleeping? Or woke up when he approached?

Feeling somewhat embarrassed, Jehan carefully set down the shell with its precious content and dressed himself. At least, his walk through the forest had been long enough to dry him off mostly, leaving only his hair a little damp. But it was still a lot better than walking up on his guest entirely unclothed.

He picked the shell back up and walked up the remaining steps to his hut. Giraud was still lying on the bench, perfectly relaxed and at ease, wheezing ever so softly.

It was an image almost too dear to his heart to disturb Giraud. But he didn't want to waste Limnada's precious gift, either. So he knelt down next to his guest and gently nudged his shoulder.

"Hey, sweet prince, wake up."

Giraud opened his eyes and blinked at him, mildly embarrassed. "Oh. I fell asleep, didn't I? Sorry."

"It was a hard day, nothing to be sorry for." He took Giraud's cup from the table and poured him some water. "Here, I have a little present for you."

Giraud sat up and stretched, scrunching up his face with drowsiness. He squinted at the shell and the pearl it contained. "Not to sound ungrateful or anything – uh, what?"

"Silly." He took Giraud's hand and dropped the pearl into his palm. "It's a gift from a river nymph, a dear friend of mine. To help us heal."

His eyes went wide when he noticed the tingle of magic, noticeable even though his supernatural senses had to be dimmed now that he wore his necklace again.

"So what am I to do with it?"

"Just swallow it. Here, have some water."

Giraud smiled at him, and despite his messy hair and bruised face, it seemed to Jehan he had never been prettier.

"You sneaked off in the moonlight to barter healing spells with a nymph, eh?"

"That nymph and I are just friends, so get your mind out of the gutter. And I didn't sneak off. I just had to take a walk before I got so fidgety that I would have woken you up."

Giraud nodded, clearly not believing a single word. But he took the pearl and swallowed it, washing it down with his water.

"That felt ... really weird."

"We'll see if it does any more than that tomorrow. But until then – it's getting chilly out here, we should move inside."

Giraud seemed to consider another remark, but then just nodded sleepily. They were both too tired to exchange witty banter. Jehan was even too tired to worry about having only one bed for both of them by now. He just wanted to make sure they got a few good hours of sleep and didn't wake up any more frazzled than they already were. He picked up their various bags from the doorstep and walked inside, leaving the door open behind him for Giraud to follow. The air inside was significantly better by now, barely warmer than outside. He was just leaning the window blinds shut when Giraud stepped inside as well, the straw pillow under his arm.

"Hrm," he mumbled and looked around. With the shutters closed, the single room was merely a collection of dark shapes. "Where to?"

"Bed." Jehan pointed at the large shape in the back of the room. "If that is okay with you."

For a heartbeat, Giraud seemed insecure, but his face was too hard to make out. He didn't move, though.

Jehan walked around him and closed the door, then slipped into his bed. The straw inside his mattress rustled with mild protest when he shuffled closer to the wall instead of his usual spot.

"Come on, I won't bite."

Giraud hesitated for just another heartbeat, then came over and sat down on the side of the bed. He handed Jehan the pillow and slipped out of his boots and leather jerkin before he lay down as well. Jehan pulled the blanket over both of them, cursing softly when he realised it wouldn't cover much of him or Giraud if they insisted on keeping a polite distance between them. He was already half-decided to let Giraud have the entire blanket for himself, warm as it was anyway, when Giraud moved and all but tumbled into the comfortable dent in the middle of his bed. A faint wave of oleander scent reached Jehan, and he smiled despite himself.

Silently, he slung an arm across Giraud's chest and slipped closer to him, burying his nose in his hair.

Giraud remained entirely motionless for a few heartbeats, like a startled deer, half-ready to bolt and run. But when nothing else happened, he relaxed again. Soon, his breath was going softly and regular, his chest rising and falling underneath Jehan's hand.

"This is nice," Giraud mumbled all of a sudden and snuggled closer into Jehan's arm. "I could get used to this..."

Jehan knew it couldn't be. But just tonight, he allowed himself to wonder what life would be like, living with the man he loved, holding him in his arms each night when falling asleep. It was a beautiful dream.

Chapter Nine – A White Lady in Waiting

Ugs' house seemed deserted, except for the geese that came running to see if maybe Jehan was bringing some food. He wasn't, but that didn't keep them from checking again and again. They were worse than dogs in that regard.

"Hello? Anyone here?" he called out.

"Back here, behind the house!" A girl's voice – Marianne, if Jehan wasn't entirely mistaken. "I'm here!"

Jehan went around the house and found his niece sitting on a chair at the base of the house, in the dappled shade of the chestnut tree. She had another chair next to her, a small box full of threads and ribbons on it, and a piece of white cloth on her lap. Apparently, she was hemming another bonnet just like the one she wore.

Marianne smiled at him, but not as brightly as usual.

"Are you here to see Grandma?"

He nodded.

"Oh, good. Mama asked me to look after her, but I really can't go in there," she confessed. "I am so sorry, but it just gives me goosebumps every time I am alone with her."

"It is alright. I'll see if she needs anything."

"Thanks, uncle."

"Sure." Jehan looked around. "Where are all the others?"

"Papa is trying to catch some shads in the shallows upriver, with the boys." She gestured in the other direction towards La Morangiasse. "And Mama and the others are in town, helping with preparations for the miller's daughter's wedding next week. I am behind with my stupid sewing, so I had to stay."

"Spent too much time playing at being a knight, didn't you?"

Marianne tried to look indignant, but didn't manage to hide her guilty smile.

"I know your mother doesn't want me to say that – but really, I think you could make a tremendous knight one day."

Now her smile returned in full force. "I think so, too."

He answered her smile in like and turned towards the steps that led to the door. "Anything you need from inside?"

Marianne shook her head, though clearly grateful for the offer.

Jehan acknowledged her silent reply with a nod and walked up to the door. He knew he had to talk to his grandmother, but even now, he had no clue what he was going to say.

When he had woken up this morning, with Giraud still sleeping in his arms, he didn't want that moment ever to end. But it had already been embarrassingly late, the birds' morning chorus almost over, and so he had woken Giraud rather unceremoniously. As expected, he had been worried how late it already was and that Segui would be livid if he arrived after his father opened shop, and a thousand other things. Jehan had sent him to prepare the horses, and made a small pot of gruel for both of them. They had eaten in silence, and for most of the way to La Morangiasse, Giraud's worries had eaten up any chance of conversation.

At least, *Maître* Segui had been barely in his workshop when they arrived, so he hadn't grumbled too much. He had scolded his son for 'skirtchasing' the entire night and promised to make him work hard today, but apparently didn't think twice about his son's overnight absence. Also, Limnada's gift had literally worked like a charm – while still somewhat stiff and sore, both he and Giraud were mostly healed again, and if one didn't look too closely, no one would suspect they had been in a tavern brawl the night before.

Giraud had swiftly slipped into his working clothes and hurried to assist his father. There had been nothing left for Jehan to do but thank him for his assistance with the new weir, tip his hat, and leave.

Slowly, step by step, Jehan's feet had found the way back to his family's home, and even though he had no idea what to tell his grandmother, he knew he had to talk to her. She had always known what to do.

He gave himself a nudge and opened the door.

As usual, the single ground floor room was dim after the bright summer sunlight, and it took Jehan a moment to regain his sight. His grandmother's alcove was a dark recess in the far wall, and he could barely make out her minute shape underneath the blanket. There was already a chair standing close to her alcove, and Jehan imagined Alienee sitting there for the better part of the night, *looking* after her friend and mentor.

Jehan dropped his straw hat onto the family table and sat down next to his grandmother. Her bonnet had slipped, wispy white hair clinging to her face, damp with sweat. She had turned even paler, her cheeks were hollow, her breath shallow and swift like that of a bird.

"Grandma, can you hear me? It's me, Jehan."

She twitched, her lips moving, but she didn't open her eyes.

Should he try to wake her? Or should he rather let her sleep? Sleep was good, it would help her heal. With a grim frown, he forced himself to acknowledge the facts.

She wouldn't recover. Maybe she would miraculously get better, yes, but there was no recovery from old age.

"I am sorry grandmother." His words were soft, and even though he was not sure she even heard a single word he said, it just came tumbling out of him. "I am so sorry I never listened. I always wanted to be normal, to be like all the others. You were right, I was such a coward."

She twitched, faintly, her hand moving out from under the blanket as if trying to reach him. Jehan held his breath for a heartbeat, but nothing else happened. He took her hands in his own, gently holding her cool fingers. There was nothing left of her but skin and bones, a mere paper shell for the strong spirit inside.

"I should have listened," he confessed. "I should have let you teach me, teach me how to protect people, how to help my friends and family. But I thought, if I kept my head low, I wouldn't have to. Shows what a fool I have been all these years."

A soft shuffle on the other side of the room made Jehan look up. There was a faint white something on one of the many chairs around the table and at first, Jehan thought it was nothing but sunlight dancing in the air, or maybe a wisp of smoke. But the closer he looked, the more he realised that they weren't alone in the room.

He squinted, trying to make sense of what he saw, and when he did, a cold shiver ran down his spine. There was a woman sitting at their table, pale and translucent, as if woven from nothing but gossamer and moonlight. Her body was hard to make out, shapes shifting like mist over water. But her face and her hands were as defined as his own – slender fingers working soundlessly with a needle and a stitching frame, her face finely chiselled and noble, with cool eyes that judged him wordlessly.

A *Dame Blanche*, a White Lady.

They were powerful spirits, separate from the fae and the spirits of nature. They were neither ghosts nor demons, but what exactly they were, Jehan had no clue. What he knew, though, was that among many other things, the White Ladies were harbingers of death.

"Milady." Jehan inclined his head deeply, sketching a cautious and respectful bow.

She inclined her head in return, not as deeply, but still rather polite and graceful. When she looked up to Jehan again, she gave him a faint smile before she returned her attention to the needlework in her hands.

So that wasn't as bad as it could have been. Jehan took a deep breath. No wonder that Marianne felt uncomfortable inside, and that everyone else had found urgent work elsewhere. With a White Lady in the house, even someone as deaf to the supernatural as his brother Ugs would become nervous.

"You are here for my grandmother, aren't you?" Jehan asked, immediately realising how silly that question was. White Ladies were silent, never spoke a word, and yes, who else lay here, dying and important enough to warrant the calm attention of such a being? "Excuse me, of course you are." Naturally, the spirit didn't react. "Please be kind to her, will you?"

At this, the White Lady looked up at Jehan again, her eyes all but piercing him. But then she nodded, calm and reassuringly, with another of her faint smiles.

"Thank you, Milady."

Her gaze returned to her stitching frame, and Jehan's thoughts returned to his own problems. He had dearly hoped his grandmother would have been able to set him onto the right path of how to proceed with this whole mess he and Giraud were entangled in. But now it seemed he'd have to figure it out himself.

"I really should have listened," he repeated, though mostly to himself this time. "There is so much I do not know."

If he approached the Lady Givonne, asking her to lift her curse on Giraud's parents, her reaction would likely be pretty much in the same vein as the one of Prince Sylvain last night, only a lot less restrained. Sylvain wouldn't help them as the entire mess played into his hands, and Lady Givonne would only budge if she gained something worthy in exchange.

But the thought wasn't without merit, Jehan realised. Was there possibly anything that they could offer her in exchange for the lives of Segui and Marette? She had expressed rather personal interest in Giraud, but as fae went, that probably wasn't much of a bargaining chip. Also, that was a subject Jehan would prefer to breach only in the most dire circumstances, and he genuinely hoped they weren't that desperate yet.

So what else was there?

What little he knew about Prince Sylvain and Givonne came from a half-forgotten fairy tale, how once upon a time, the young ruler of this fief met a fair foreign maiden wandering on a flowering meadow and fell madly in love with her. But despite his best efforts, Jehan couldn't come up with much more. He remembered that she was headstrong and didn't agree to wed him easily, and that there had been quests and challenges for both until they found each other worthy. Most importantly, he remembered that it had been a story of love among equals, who had been genuinely happy, deeply in love and full of affection, and that the story had genuinely touched him.

What had happened to that love?

He perked up when his grandmother's hand twitched faintly.

"You think I got something there?" he asked, softly. "If it's something we can fix, maybe that would be a favour big enough to the Lady Givonne to rethink her actions..."

But how to figure out what they were looking for? It might be long in the past, and the village's best repository of fairy tales was lying in her cot next to him. If he found the right spirit, he might manage to barter for the proper piece of the story, but that would be like looking for a needle in a haystack, or hunting for one particular rabbit in the entire forest.

Jehan cocked his head.

There was a way of hunting down something that didn't want to be found. His grandmother had told that particular story often enough, and it had scared him sleepless each time. Old magic. Blood and sacrifices and more determination than he had ever thought himself able to come up with. But then again, last night in the marketplace of Castlefort, he had used blood magic as if he had never used anything else.

He felt his heart thump in his chest. Was he really thinking he'd be able to pull it off? Was he willing to live with the consequences?

On the other hand – would he be able to live with the consequences of not trying?

Jehan gently patted his grandmother's hand. "I should have learned a lot more from you. But I won't fret. I'll figure it out."

She shifted in her sleep and a smile ghosted over her cracked lips. "Good hunting," she whispered.

How could she – ? But then again, she had probably been waiting for him to grow up for a long time now.

"Thank you, grandma." He squeezed her hand as firmly as he dared. "Rest now. I'll be back tomorrow, and tell you how it went."

He tucked her hand back under the blanket and rose. His heart was still racing, but at least he had a plan now. A mad, daring plan, but something that had a chance of sorting this mess out. Jehan picked up his hat and sent a polite bow to the White Lady before he put it back on and left the house. After the cool, stuffy air inside, the warm morning felt like a blessing.

"Marianne?" He dashed down the stairs, taking two at a time. "Marianne, do you know if you still have grandma's old wolf pelt? The silver one, with the head still attached?"

"Good Lord, that horrible thing?" She sounded genuinely appalled.

"Exactly that one."

Marianne was still sitting in the same spot, hemming the same bonnet. Her expression was mildly disgusted, but intrigued. "Last time I saw that ugly thing, it was in a chest in the attic. What in all the Saints' names do you need it for?"

"Hunting," Jehan replied, laughing at her doubtful expression. "I'll go hunt a rabbit." And since he wouldn't be going alone, he'd need a second pelt on top of the one he already had.

Chapter Ten - Chasing the White Rabbit

Somewhat daunted, Jehan surveyed his work.

The rabbit hide in his hands was stuffed with rosemary and lavender, bound with simple string to resemble the former animal. It looked good, almost lifelike, if a little stiff. He smoothed the pale fur until it looked as natural as possible. With a soft sigh, he put the bait down onto the rest of the equipment he had gathered for tonight.

There were no laws governing this kind of magic, no set of rules he could safely adhere to. He just had to follow his intuition, and hope he'd be right. For the first time in his life, he would go and actually use the powers he had been given, forcing his will onto the natural order and hoping he'd manage to ride out the consequences.

Although – that wasn't exactly right. Two days ago, in the marketplace in Castelfort, he had done just that. And it had almost brought him to the pyre. He grimaced painfully at the memory.

But he wouldn't back out now. Marette and Segui didn't deserve any of this, and more would follow. There had to be someone in town making sure the creatures of the night didn't have free rein over the affairs of the mortals. And there was no one besides him who could possibly be up to the task.

Jehan looked up at the sky where the sun was already half-hidden behind the horizon, spilling a riot of colours in all directions. To his left, the pale disk of the moon was visible if one looked close enough. Round and full, the moon would guide them tonight. Hopefully.

He rolled up the cloth bundle at his feet and wondered what to do until Giraud arrived. The church bells of La Morangiasse had already rung the ninth hour of the evening, and he wasn't here. Giraud had promised to be here at sunset, but that could still leave Jehan with enough time to lose his nerve several times over. On the small table in front of his hut, he had assembled a light supper – two bowls of gruel and some cheese, nothing more. There was no good hunting on a full stomach, was there?

Prowling up and down in front of his hut didn't do anything to calm his nerves, either. So Jehan walked down to the river and washed his face and arms, the cool water returning some focus to the here and now. In his head, he went through the list of things he had gathered – the wolf pelts, the dagger, flint and firesteel, the rabbit skin, the bottle of herbed wine.

What if Giraud had forgotten any items? What if something had happened to him on the way here? What if Giraud had decided that all this was too dangerous and he wouldn't come tonight? What if –

With an annoyed grunt, Jehan turned on the spot, walked back to the waterfront and dipped his head into the river. The flowing water tugged at his hair, washed around him, gargled in his ears. He stayed underwater until he had to come up, gasping. Better, definitely better now.

"Jehan? Are you there?"

Giraud's voice, and apparently he was already at the hut. Jehan took a deep breath of relief. He had come, and now the wait was over.

"I'm down here!" he called back, his feet already dragging him onto the path uphill.

Giraud wore his 'adventuring' outfit again tonight – knee-high boots over deerskin trousers, a billowing white shirt and the matching hat with green rooster feathers. It made Jehan feel positively frumpy in his simple tunic and breeches. But if everything went as he had planned, where they were going tonight they wouldn't be wearing clothes, anyway.

"Already worried you might have gone without me," Giraud greeted him. "Keeping all the fun for yourself."

"Oh, like hell I would." Jehan pulled him into a close embrace and patted his back, genuinely pleased at seeing him. His now-familiar scent of smoke and oleander enveloped him like another, intangible embrace. "You dragged me into this, so I'll drag you along until the bitter end. Besides, I told you I might need someone who knows how to fight. Have you brought what I asked for?"

Giraud nodded eagerly and pulled out a small leather wrap. He unrolled it and showed Jehan three small slips of paper, each one with a different coat of arms drawn on them in elegant lines.

"Oh, they are good," Jehan remarked. "Did old Aldric make them?"

"Yep. He was a bit hesitant at first, but as you said – as soon as I showed any real interest, he was more than eager to help me out. He is really bored out of his mind since Comte Rainaud has that new scribe. Can you imagine I paid for these with nothing but a handful of candles?"

"I can actually imagine only too well." Jehan smiled at the thought. Aldric was the former court scribe of La

Morangiasse, but his eyesight had worsened measurably over the last few years. Candles sure were in short supply in his household.

"I haven't eaten anything since noon, as you asked. But I am starving now." Giraud eyed around Jehan's shoulder at the food on the table. "You think that is enough?"

"I think it would be even better if we had been fasting, but I am not that cruel." He invited Giraud to his table with a gesture and they both sat down. "We'll need hungry minds and bodies tonight. If this works out, we'll feast later."

"Well, I can guarantee a hungry body, that for sure." Giraud stirred his gruel with apprehension. "Segui is feeling rather under the weather, and despite her bad leg, Mama is making dove with grapes tonight..."

"I promise your sacrifice will be appropriately acknowledged."

Giraud only sighed wistfully at the thought of the dinner he was missing. Apparently, dove with grapes was one of his favourites. That Giraud was sitting here, instead of coming an hour later with a belly full of dove, made him go up another notch in Jehan's respect.

They wolfed down the cheese and gruel Jehan had set out in mere moments, and they took another few to scrape their bowls as clean as humanly possible.

"So." Giraud placed his empty bowl back onto the table. "What do we do now?"

Jehan looked up at the sky, where the sun had almost completely disappeared below the horizon. The sky was purple and dark blue, now, and in the west, the first stars were coming out. It was the hour called *entre chien et loup*, between dog and wolf, where the familiar became feral and unpredictable. It was time.

"We pack up and go."

"Go where?"

Jehan grinned. He was getting better at anticipating Giraud's questions. "Just a bit away from here. Just far enough so there are not so many man-made things in the area."

Giraud gave him a curious look, but didn't enquire further. Instead, he gathered up what remained of their supper and placed it onto the table inside the hut. Jehan went through his preparations one last time before he gathered up the blanket he had piled everything on and tied it into a neat bundle. He waited while Giraud made sure Trajan was comfortably tied to a tree on the chicken meadow and gestured him to follow.

They walked down Jehan's little hill, past the lake and deeper into the forest, away from the river and its people. Neither of them spoke, and while Jehan felt the risks of tonight's endeavours weigh heavily on his mind, he felt Giraud almost hum with excitement, probably biting his lips not to burst out into a barrage of questions. The image filled him with silent contentment though. At least one of them was looking forward to this, and it lifted his mood a bit more with every step.

It didn't take them long to reach the clearing Jehan had picked as their starting point. They were about half-way between the river and the cliff, and the forest here was dense and wild. Fallen trees lay on the ground like half-rotten reminders of a grander, long-forgotten age. In the forest's deep shade, moss grew on almost everything, thick green tufts on the ground, curly grey beards on the trees. The scent of decay hung heavily in the air, and the wildlife all around them seemed to watch their intrusion with bated breath.

In front of them, one of the ancient trees had fallen not so long ago, its roots reaching up like a wall now. The gaping hole its roots had left in the forest floor had filled with water, and a small pond had formed. Around it, where the old tree had suppressed all new growth, there was enough open space for their little ritual, and Jehan put down his bundle with a huff.

Even in the dim light, he could see Giraud was pursing his lips, smirking, bouncing on the balls of his feet.

"Alright. Before you burst with questions – Yes, magic. No, nothing indecent, though that probably depends pretty much on who you'd ask. No, I am not going to explain, but you'll see soon enough." He smiled at Giraud's eager expression. "Anything you need to get off your chest before we start?"

Giraud shook his head, wordlessly, his eyes sparkling.

"Well, then." Jehan opened his bundle and unpacked, carefully placing every single item onto the forest floor in a wide circle around him. "Your knife, and the drawings, please."

Still wordless, Giraud handed him the leather wrap with the drawings and presented an assortment of various blades from his bundle.

"You made all of these?"

He nodded, clearly taking pride in his craftsmanship.

Jehan searched through the options and smiled when he found the 'hunting knife' among them. But in the end, he picked a small, pointed blade barely longer than his hand. It had a slightly crooked back with hammer marks clearly visible on its sides, but its horn handle was bright and smooth and faintly discoloured from years of use.

"This one will do nicely."

"It's one of the very first I made," Giraud offered eagerly. "Actually the first one that was good enough to put a handle on."

Jehan nodded. He had already guessed something like this. He surveyed everything one last time and nodded to Giraud.

"Now it's time to get rid of everything man-made that we don't explicitly need."

"Like... my necklace?"

"Yes." Somehow, he had dreaded this moment, but now that it had come, he couldn't help but smirk. "And all your clothes."

Giraud blinked at him owlishly.

"Yes," Jehan confirmed. "All of them."

"You said we wouldn't do anything indecent..."

"You don't seem to think it indecent, swimming in the river, nude, with the entire town watching."

"That's ... different." He looked aside. "It's different when it's just the two of us and no one is watching."

Was he blushing? Compared to his usual swashbuckling nature, that seemed unexpectedly quaint. But Jehan's smile widened even another notch when he remembered what Limnada had said about boys feeling unobserved.

"Believe me, out here in the forest, you're never unwatched." With a cocky note, he added, "And besides, you know what they say – it's only a disaster while you're in it. Afterwards, it becomes an adventure."

Giraud grinned back at him, but didn't reply. Instead, he took off his necklace, fumbling a little with the string but still managing rather elegantly. Almost instantly, the light around him seemed to change again, shifting to his advantage, making him stand out from the forest's darker backdrop. The scent of oleander blossoms began to weave its way through the air, adding a strangely sensual quality to the night, almost like incense. Did it have some sort of meaning that one of the most poisonous flowers grew on him? Probably, but Jehan had no clue of what it was telling him. He only hoped that it wouldn't interfere with what he had planned for tonight. Those flowers were part of Giraud's innate magic, and would probably not hinder anything that he felt would make a good story. Hopefully.

Without making a fuss about it, Jehan slipped out of his usual tunic and breeches, and put them onto the cloth blanket he had used for his bundle. Giraud needed a bit longer with his boots and tight trousers, but even though Jehan felt more than a little tempted, he managed not to stare.

When he was done, Giraud added his clothes to Jehan's pile and smiled at him a little awkwardly.

"Would you mind finding a place outside the clearing for all this?" Jehan asked while he packed their bundle back up. "I'll prepare everything here in the meantime."

Happy to have something to do, Giraud nodded and disappeared in the forest. He stepped cautiously on the unfamiliar terrain, and for a change, Jehan was happy he was used to not wearing shoes for most of the year. Still he ogled Giraud's backside for a little longer than appropriate.

Forcing himself to focus on the work ahead, he turned his attention back to the circle of equipment on the mossy ground. First things first, he decided, and took up a small pile of dry leaves and kindling he had brought together with the flint and firesteel.

Right in front of the little pond, he cleaned a small area until he was sufficiently certain he wouldn't start a forest fire, stacked up his kindling and started hitting up sparks. The first flames already flickered up when Giraud returned. Now, his antlers were faintly visible, showing up every now and then in the dancing light of the growing fire. He looked very much like a creature of legend, wild and civilised at the same time, and Jehan felt his breath go a little faster at the sight. If Giraud felt self-conscious about his lack of clothes, it didn't show, his eyes sparkling with excitement when he knelt down besides Jehan. There was so much confidence in his expression, confidence in Jehan's skill and willpower, that he almost believed it himself.

They exchanged a smile across the tiny fire, and when Jehan rose to pick up his next equipment, he didn't feel ungainly or lumbering under Giraud's gaze. They trusted each other unconditionally, he realised, and it gave him hope for tonight's ritual.

Jehan picked the bottle of wine from the ground. Its cork was secured by a few rows of twine, and he twisted it open on his way back to the fire. He took a first sip and grimaced when the taste seemed to numb his tongue, but he handed the bottle over to Giraud nonetheless.

"What's this?" he asked, drank, and coughed. "Good Lord."

"Wine." Jehan chuckled and took back the bottle. "Just wine. And wormwood root, and dried woodruff. Bits and bobs. The best I could do on such a short notice." A second sip, this time less startling, but still a little strong. He had just thrown together everything he had that would make both of them a little more receptive to magic, and a little less alien to the other world. He wasn't even entirely sure this stuff wouldn't kill them. It probably wouldn't. Hopefully.

He should be less enthusiastic with the herbs the next time. Good Lord. Was he really considering doing this more than once?

He took another sip, shuddered, and handed the bottle back. "Here. You don't need as much as I do, but still a little more."

Initially, he had planned on sharing the entire bottle between the two of them, hoping for the alcohol to encourage him. But in the light of things, they would have to do with just a few sips each.

Giraud grimaced and took another long sip. He shuddered violently as well, and wiped his mouth in disgust. But Jehan also noticed how his fae self grew more and more pronounced, his antlers looking rather substantial, now, the white blossoms in his hair clearly visible.

So at least he hadn't entirely misjudged the ingredients of his potion.

Quietly, he added some wood to the fire. He drank some more of his concoction when Giraud handed him back the bottle. By now, the taste wasn't even half bad, still bitter and astringent, but very aromatic. Interesting. Maybe worth another sip.

Jehan put down the bottle with a shaky smile. Maybe no more for him.

"Yeah. Well." All around him, he felt the forest whisper with anticipation, the trees around them looming high above them, tall and unconcerned. "So the wine is doing its job, at least for me. How do you feel?"

Giraud shrugged. "Quite normal, I guess. A bit tingling." In an unselfconscious gesture, he brushed a strand of hair off his shoulder, but then paused and cocked his head. He took his hair and looked at it with fascination. "Oh. That's new."

"You had hair before."

"Not this long, at least not in a way that I could actually touch." He reached back and his hand returned with a single white flower that he placed on the ground between them. "See what I mean?"

Jehan stared at the flower, not quite sure if it was real or if they were sharing an illusion. Seeing them in Giraud's hair was one thing, but apart from him like this, it seemed much more real. Whatever it was, his plan seemed to be working much better than he had expected. So far, at least. Time for the next step.

He gathered up the wolf pelts from the ground and gestured for Giraud to rise as well. He handed him one of the furs and slung the other one over his shoulders like a cape, with the poor beast's paws tied in front of his chest and the head dangling between his shoulders. He helped Giraud with tying his pelt and just like that found himself getting lost in his eyes. He had been admiring his strong arms and beautiful shoulders, there, just for a moment, and when he looked up, he found Giraud looking right into his eyes. His lips slightly parted, his nostrils moving ever so slightly with excitement – he was so beautiful Jehan thought his heart skipped a beat or two.

Giraud's smile widened after a while when he realised Jehan had lost track of time.

"Not now." Giraud admonished. "There'll be plenty of time for longing gazes once this night is over."

This time, it was Jehan who cast down his eyes, hiding a blush. But Giraud was right, of course. With a faint sigh that was barely more than a pronounced exhale, he separated from him and turned his attention back to the fire. The stuffed rabbit hide was lying there, as well as Giraud's knife, the drawings and a small wooden bowl.

There were probably chants for this kind of ritual. Or dances, things to shout at the moon and whisper to the trees. He knew nothing of those. But he knew that magic didn't come through specific words or deeds – only through intention, properly expressed. Yes, there was real danger in what he was attempting. But he was also tired of hiding, of running away. He would figure this out, and fight, if need be.

He picked up the knife.

"Give me your left hand," he said, and was a little surprised when Giraud obeyed without a heartbeat's hesitation. "This might hurt a little."

With a swift motion, Jehan pricked Giraud's thumb, just deep enough to draw blood and instantly did the same to his own.

"Where ever you go, you'll carry a bit of myself," he said and pressed his thumb onto Giraud's forehead, leaving a bloody print right between his eyes. "And I'll carry a bit of you."

Giraud nodded and returned the gesture, leaving a matching bloody smear on Jehan's forehead. It sent a tingle throughout his entire body, and it felt as if the entire forest drew a collective breath.

Yes. That kind of magic.

Next, Jehan picked up the three drawings and handed Giraud the one with the coat of arms of Castelfort.

"Your ancestors ruled Castelfort, while mine have served La Morangiasse." He left a drop of his blood on the coat of arms of his town and gestured to Giraud to do the same with his. "But there was a time when both of them were one." He held the slip of paper with the old shield of Beronsac between them, and they both placed another drop of their blood onto it. "We look for the beginning of this rift, so we might find a way to bridge it."

The forest around them had fallen dead silent, wide eyed with anticipation. He sensed his words reaching out, creating connections between the symbols they were holding and the places they stood for. Their blood bound those energies to their spirits, and hopefully, it would lead them to what they needed to find. He felt the connections tug at him with every breath he took, as if swimming with a net full of fish in his hands. This night would show if he was strong enough to bring them in.

He knelt down next to the fire, and Giraud did the same. There wasn't much left, but that was all he needed. Carefully, he took the drawing of La Morangiasse and lit its tip on fire. The heavy paper sizzled where he had soaked it with his blood, but it burned nonetheless. He took great caution to gather up the ashes in the small bowl he had brought, and did the same with the two remaining drawings. He mixed the ashes and rubbed then onto the rabbit's forehead, leaving a dark smudge in its pale, sand-coloured fur. The rest, he smudged onto his own eyelids and Giraud's.

"We look like savages," Giraud remarked, chuckling.

"We are, right now." Jehan took the stuffed rabbit hide and placed it between them. "If that rabbit moves, you follow him. Understood?"

Giraud looked at him, bewildered, but nodded.

"We must catch that rabbit. I do not know for sure what's going to happen, what shape this magic is going to take, so I cannot give any more advice. Whatever happens, just remember that we must catch the rabbit."

Again, Giraud nodded. His eyes returned to the dead creature between them and suddenly took on a feverish sheen, his entire body thrumming with energy barely held in check.

"Our blood binds us to the past, and much of our past is hidden." Jehan mumbled mostly to himself, focussing on the resonance he felt within the connections he had just woven. "But we are hungry for knowledge. Hungry like wolves in winter."

Giraud didn't look up, his eyes fixed to their prey, but he made the connection. 'Loup Garou', he mouthed almost soundlessly, full of wonder. Jehan wasn't trying to turn them into werewolves, tonight, but there was a good chance this ritual was at the root of the tale of the 'loup garou'. Like most stories, even that one had a grain of truth at its core.

"Focus on the rabbit," he said firmly, more to himself than Giraud, and took his hand. It was warm and strong and full of life, his heartbeat clear enough Jehan could feel it despite his own heart beating in his ears. "Hungry for the truth. Hungry to see what we need to know; hungry to learn."

With his free hand, he picked some moss off the ground and dropped it into the remaining embers of the fire, where it immediately started to smoulder. The smoke stung his eyes, and made breathing hard, but he didn't pause. With long, deliberate strokes, Jehan waved the smoke across the rabbit hide as if trying to shoo it away from them.

"Run, little rabbit, run," he whispered. "Run for your life. Run to where we need to be."

In his mind, Jehan felt the pull of magic growing stronger, casting a net out through all their ancestry, through the history of their towns, through ages and events long forgotten. And just like when fishing in murky waters, there was that one tiny movement when he realised something was tugging at his line.

"Did you see that?" Giraud's voice almost tilted with excitement. "It moved!"

"Run, little rabbit, run," Jehan repeated without looking, urgent, single-minded in his intention. This had to work. "Run!"

With an exited yelp, Giraud jumped to his feet. "Whoa, there, there it is! It's running away!"

Indeed, there was a pale shape at the far end of the clearing, a nervous little presence with flicking ears and a round white tail.

"Hunt it down," Jehan growled. "Don't let it get out of sight! Go!"

Giraud all but jumped in the direction of the rabbit, happy to be let loose, happy to finally have an outlet for all that energy inside of him. Of course, the rabbit instantly fled deeper into the forest, with Giraud directly behind in hot pursuit. Jehan followed the two of them, a little less excited, but just as eager.

The dark forest rushed past them, nothing but vague, blurry shapes of trees and shrubs and rocks. Dimly, Jehan realised they should watch out, lest they stumble and break anything on the uneven ground. But he didn't care, and neither did Giraud who dashed through the undergrowth just like a young wolf – lean and hungry, all focus and anticipation. The little rabbit dashed ahead, always merely a hand-width out of Giraud's reach, dodging and leaping, drawing them deeper into the forest. But even when it got out of sight, its scent remained clearly noticeable, the unusual mix of rosemary and lavender as clear as a line drawn in sand to both of them. Though admittedly, Jehan had it a lot easier – he merely followed that mixed scent of herbs and white flowers, and he smiled every time Giraud made another fruitless attempt at reaching that rabbit, lunging into the dark.

The chase went on, and soon enough, he stopped focussing on anything besides. There was the rabbit, there was Giraud, and nothing else mattered, really. They ran through the dark forest, uphill and downhill, and he didn't care. His paws found reliable hold wherever he stepped, and as long as he kept up, that was all that mattered. They ran through shallow water, splashing loudly, soaking the fur on his belly with cold, but he didn't have a mind to bother. Follow the rabbit, he told himself ceaselessly, don't you let it get away.

The water got deeper, and then shallow again, and the chase continued relentlessly. There was more forest, more rocks, sharp under his paws, uphill, downhill, uphill again. Lots of uphill. Rocks crunched left and right, Giraud's paws kicking up sand and dust in puffs that gleamed in the moonlight. A steep incline, a narrow path, the pale little rabbit running for its life. A hairpin turn, more shrubs, the bitter scent of butcher's broom, another rocky path. And the chase continued.

The rocky ground turned to gravel, and then to cobblestone, interrupted by shrubs and grass and then more cobblestone again. There was the scent of fire and horses, but Jehan didn't care. He had a rabbit to catch. Giraud was still a few steps ahead of him, right at the heels of that little beast, snarling and yapping. The ground changed one last time from cobblestone to wood and to large flagstones, and suddenly, the rabbit stopped running. It just stopped and sat down on its plumb little butt, looking over his shoulder right at Jehan. It's face was still smeared with ashes, but its eyes were wide and dark and full of something old and much larger than itself. And then it got buried under a pile of black fur when Giraud caught up with it, claws first, biting deep. He grabbed the poor thing with his mouth and shook it wildly, blood staining his teeth red.

With a sound very much like a soft sigh, the rabbit dissolved into nothing but moonlight.

Deeply confused, Giraud bit into the empty air two more times, but there just wasn't anything there. The rabbit was gone, the hunt was over. He looked at Jehan and gave him a questioning yelp.

But there was no easy answer. With a gentle nudge of his snout, Jehan motioned Giraud to step aside, where a crenellated fieldstone parapet framed the yard they were on. Their hunt had led them to something like a large terrace, a clear space covered with large slabs of yellow stone, with the massive walls of a castle rising in their back. Nothing of this seemed familiar. Many of the castle's windows were lit, with the scent of smoke hanging in the warm air, and they could hear the buzz of many people inside. At least, they were all alone out here.

The moon still hung above them, bright and full as it had been when they started their hunt, and it filled the empty yard with cool blue light.

Cautiously, Jehan looked around, trying to spot anything familiar. He was too short to look over the parapet, but he was tall enough that he could jump up and place his front paws into one of the crenellations. The view was disappointing, though. Just forested cliffs as far as he could see, with the familiar curve of the river far down to his right. If he looked closely, he could make out the lights of a town in the distance, but most of it was hidden by the curve of the cliff.

Again, Giraud gave a questioning yelp. Jehan hopped back down and gave him a shrug. Naturally, Giraud had to look for himself, jumped up into the crenellation, looked down, and hopped back with a disappointed snarl.

Jehan was just about to roll his eyes at him when a fluttering motion above caught his attention. He looked up, and for the first time really looked at the banners flying from the towers – all of them showed the white bridge of Beronsac on a field of green. Could it really be?

With his tail wildly wagging, he ran over to the other side of the terrace and jumped onto the parapet where it met the castle wall. And there it was, just as he had hoped: two cliffs further downriver and, on the other side, hunched on the clifftop like an armoured soldier on guard, there was the familiar outline of Castelfort.

This was the castle of Beronsac, long before it was conquered and fell to ruins. Truly a long, long time ago.

Jehan had no clue how and why the spirit hunt had led them here, but that question was pretty irrelevant. Full of wonder, he looked up the castle walls and found more and more flags flying the white bridge. They had to be at the back of the castle, looking out onto the rolling hills of Guyenne, with the bridge of Beronsac on the opposite side.

He gave a small yip to gain Giraud's attention and gestured him to come and look as well. The black wolf hesitated for a heartbeat, then scurried along the wall, his head and tail held low, until he was next to Jehan. It took him another few gestures to make him jump up the parapet to peer through another crenellation. But when he recognised the silhouette of Castelfort, he looked over to Jehan, wide-eyed and tongue lolling. It looked so weird and yet to very much like him that Jehan couldn't help but burst out in laughter. It came out more a rhythmic wheeze than anything, but Giraud got the drift.

He dropped off his vantage point and bit into Jehan's hind leg, and before long, they were rolling across the floor in a heap of black and brown fur, nipping and snarling and wheezing with laughter.

The sharp clack of a heavy lock being turned froze both of them mid-motion.

Instantly, they were hiding in the shadows where the parapet met the castle walls, huddling close together.

The lock was turned again, and the heavy, iron-bound door in the castle wall was opened from within. Armoured soldiers streamed out and took position along the parapet, each of them wearing chainmail under their green tabards, and bows and arrows on their backs.

Giraud shuffled nervously when one of them manned the wall mere steps away from them, but the soldier didn't seem to notice. Maybe they were invisible to them. Maybe they weren't even really here, just reliving this moment like a dream. Jehan didn't dwell too much on the thought. The details would just prove much too unsettling, and wouldn't serve any purpose. They were here, now, and they would learn as much as they could from the moment.

Voices rose inside the castle, a man and a woman, arguing loudly. Several of the soldiers turned their heads, visibly embarrassed.

Jehan dared to venture out of his dark corner, just to see what would happen. As expected, no one reacted to the large brown wolf peacefully sitting in their midst.

The argument grew louder.

"You knew this would happen," the woman shouted, firm and full of righteous anger. "You knew we would be outnumbered. And still you believe you can ignore what happens right in front of your own castle?"

The man's reply was too soft to make out, but by the growling tone of his voice, Jehan judged he wasn't having this argument for the first time.

"No so bad?!" The woman's voice, closer now.

The next few sentences were too soft again for Jehan to understand, and he inched closer towards the door. He was just about to peek into the castle when a tall, red-haired woman stepped out onto the terrace, all long limbs and long strides.

"Have you even seen the army that is camping at your gates?" she asked with a faint accent that Jehan couldn't place. "Have you looked?"

She wore a pale blue gown the colour of a robin's egg, narrow-waisted and with open sleeves so long their tips all but trailed on the ground. From the points of her shoes to the coronet among the red waves of her hair, every inch of her was slender and regal, and she bore herself with the natural command and grace of a ruling queen.

"Stop evading my questions." She threw up her hands in exasperation. "Come. Let me show you."

She gestured to someone still inside to follow and turned around towards the far end of the terrace. When he stepped out, Jehan wouldn't have needed Giraud's apprehensive snarl to recognise Prince Sylvain – he looked hardly any different. Yes, he wore heavy chainmail under a green tabard, now, with polished pauldrons on his shoulders and a sword at his side, but it was undeniably him. A little younger, perhaps, and with a little more of a spring to his step. But the arrogant cast to his chin and his calmly seething anger were exactly the same.

Oddly enough, Jehan didn't see anything of their fae trappings – no antlers growing out of Sylvain's forehead, no winter storm tugging at his hair. He tried not to dwell on it, either – he was grateful his sorcery had led them this far, and wouldn't start nagging for details.

"We have been over this many times, Givonne -"

"And you have never listened to what I said." They had reached the far end of the terrace, and she gestured out into the darkness. "Look. This is what I told you would happen."

Even from the distance, Jehan could hear Sylvain take in a sharp breath. If in surprise or in anger, he couldn't tell. But he couldn't see beyond the parapet from where he was standing. So he gathered what little courage he had, gestured to Giraud to follow him, and quietly slipped past the guards towards the noble couple. On his way, he noticed how the Lady Givonne was almost as tall as himself, at least half a head taller than her husband, and that her gold-wrought girdle held the sheath of a respectable-looking dagger. Definitely not a demure princess, waiting for her husband to take control of her life.

When they reached the two fae, both Jehan and Giraud jumped into the same crenellation, shuffling for space. But their scuffle died the instant they realised what they were looking at.

Beyond the fortifications, the rolling hills of the country stretched under a thick forest cover from here to the town of Sarlat half a day's ride up in the north. But the hills were not deserted, tonight. In a distance, campfires burned among the trees, hundreds of them, and the air over the hills was hazy with smoke. Dim noise carried across the land, the whinnies of horses and the clanging of metal on metal. There was an army camped outside Castle Beronsac, and even if there was only one man out there per campfire, the local forces had to be hopelessly outnumbered.

"You know I stand by my word," Sylvain pressed out between his teeth. "I will not surrender."

"And you know that this is utter folly," Givonne returned, just as tense. "Why do you insist on playing this charade to the bitter end? Have you forgotten that you are not really sworn to the Count of Beronsac?"

"These are my people. Those – " he pointed a chain-mail-gloved finger at the camping army. "Those are not."

"None of them are your people, Sylvain. They are all human. And you are throwing their lives away."

The prince drew in another sharp breath. "There are voices in court reminding everyone that those forces out there come from the same land as you do. And that your suggestion to surrender might be tainted by old loyalties."

Givonne's hand was up so quickly that Jehan almost missed the motion. She might have even managed to slap her husband across his face for the insult, but his arm was up just as quickly. He held her by the wrist, both staring at each other with barely contained fury. For a heartbeat, Jehan thought there was smoke rising from Givonne's hair, but that probably was just his imagination.

"How dare you!" she hissed. "You know my vows just as well as I do."

"Do I?" he asked, coldly. "All of them?"

Givonne gasped in affront. "Do you even understand how insulting your words are?" She shook her head as if wondering who she was looking at. The tension left her, and Sylvain let go of her wrist. "What has become of us, my love? What has changed?"

"We are getting to know each other," he grumbled in reply. Sylvain's eyes were fixed on the campfires in the forest below, but his thoughts seemed far away. "How can you be against me in such a matter? Why?"

"Because it is important." She sighed and rested a heavy hand against her husband's arm and her fingertips playfully flicked the rim of his pauldron. "When I met you, all those years ago, among the flowering orchids of this very hill, I knew you could have my heart, my soul, my everything – except my freedom. I married you under the one condition that I would never swear obedience to you, and you agreed. You shouldn't have said 'I do' if you had second thoughts."

"I never had."

"And now you do?"

Finally, he looked her in the eyes, very much like seeing a stranger for the first time. "I do not understand how you can even think of not standing by my side in this."

"And that lack of understanding makes me wonder who that man is that I have lain with all these years." Her voice turned brittle, like the first sharp spears of ice on a freezing lake. "What is human politics to you? Why do you care to whom these people swear allegiance? We were here long before there was a town of Beronsac, or Guyenne, or France, or England, for that matter, and we will be long after. Why fight their petty little wars, condemn the humans and our people to yet another struggle?"

"Because this is not just politics. This is about honour, about integrity. About faith in the continued history of our domain here. That there will be a next page in the story we have written here together."

"You are stuck in some silly human tale, Sylvain. Who cares about these rocks?" She gestured at the castle. "These trappings may be grand today, but give them a few years, and they return to dust like everything else. We remain. We, and the people under our care."

"You use them for your amusement, nothing else." Sylvain scoffed bitterly. "Can you name me one human who is not bound to you by a debt of one kind or another?"

Givonne tossed her head back, her expression very close to that of a snarling wolf. "As soon as you tell me the name of one human girl that you have neither slept with nor plan on doing so."

Icy silence spread between the two of them. With a slow, deliberate motion as if not to startle a wild beast, Givonne took her hand off her husband's arm and backed off.

"I will not see my towns condemned to a hundred years of fighting," she declared. "Whether you are by my side or not."

"There will be a hundred years of war whether we fight or not." He stretched his neck as if literally preparing to wade into battle. "But I will not allow foreigners to ruin what we have built here, and I will fight for what is mine." He paused, his breath heaving. "With or without you."

Another long moment passed in frigid silence, and Jehan and Giraud barely dared to breath.

Finally, Lady Givonne squared her shoulders. "So be it, then." She reached up to her hair, pulled out the fine silver coronet she had been wearing, and tossed it at Sylvain's feet. "There. Keep your trinkets."

She turned around on her heel and strode off the terrace and back into the castle, regal and cold and stunning. When she slammed the heavy door behind her, everyone on the terrace twitched.

Sylvain stared at the closed door, his face empty of every expression. Slowly, breath by breath, he seemed to age, the contours of his face growing sharper, his shoulders heavier, his expression darkening like an overcast sky at sunset. With visible effort, he forced himself to turn around and look past the parapet across the campfires that littered his forest. His jaws clenched, as did his fists.

"Man all the ramparts tonight!" he shouted all of a sudden. "Watch out for infiltrators, and make sure we are ready for battle come dawn!"

For the first time, the soldiers around the terrace reacted to anything that happened among them, nodding and mumbling their agreement.

"We are men of France! We will fight, and we will win! For France, for Guyenne, for victory!"

This time, his men answered with cheers and hoots, some of them yelling insults off the parapet down on the camping Englishmen. Of course they believed him.

"And if we do not win," Sylvain added wistfully, so softly only Jehan and Giraud could overhear, "then at least it will be over."

With a wave and a nod of his head, Prince Sylvain strode off and disappeared inside the castle as well, leaving his men and two stunned wolves behind.

Jehan cast a look over his shoulder and found his own feelings perfectly mirrored in Giraud's open-mouthed stare. What the hell had they just witnessed? And why had the spirit hunt led them here, to this very moment? Why didn't he see the solution they so desperately needed?

He jumped back up onto the parapet and stared through the crenellation. His head was swimming, the campfires little more than blurry spots in the night. Giraud had sat down on his behind next to him, scratching his face with his front paw as if he had something in his eyes. Why was everything so blurry, all of a sudden? And why were his feet so tired?

Quite inelegantly, he slipped out of his nook and back onto the flagstones of the terrace. The earth felt like gently rocking back and forth under his paws. Giraud blinked sluggishly, apparently feeling only slightly better. Everything was covered in cobwebs, they were even clinging to his thoughts, and his thoughts were all sticking together.

He decided to lie down and close his eyes, just for a moment.

Just a little while to clear his head.

Just a little moment...

Chapter Eleven - Preparing for Battle

It was cold. It was uncomfortable. Jehan tried his best to shift into a more comfortable position, but it only got worse. Like sleeping on a pile of beets, or a soggy forest floor. And the birds were making such a noise it was hardly bearable. Did he forget to close his windows?

A dim sense of alarm dragged Jehan's sluggish mind to consciousness.

That was indeed moss he was lying on. Soggy, springy moss, with leaves and twigs between. He shifted again, and realised that he was completely naked. What the hell...

He sat up and instantly regretted the decision. His head throbbed with pain and his vision remained blurry for an uncomfortably long time. Single beams of sunlight broke through the dense leaves overhead, like glowing spears of light, unforgivingly bright.

Bit by bit, his memories returned. He had been out here in the forest to find out more about the history between Prince Sylvain and Lady Givonne. He had drunk the herbed wine and whispered his wishes, wearing nothing but his wolfskin and hunted a pale rabbit that led them to where they needed to go. Giraud had been with him, laughing and running and panting like the happiest wolf there ever was.

Jehan looked around, but Giraud was nowhere to be seen. Good Lord, Giraud. He needed to find him.

With a deep groan, Jehan dragged himself to his feet. There were leaves sticking to his naked back, but at least he had mostly slept on top of his wolfpelt. He grimaced at the bitter taste in his mouth. That potion he had clobbered together had done its job, and hadn't killed him. A bitter aftertaste was a small price to pay. Less wormwood next time.

He slung the pelt over his shoulder and started walking. It took him a little while to get his bearings, but once he figured out where he was, it only took him a few moments to return to the small clearing and the pond where they had started their adventure last night. Their things littered the ground, but at least it didn't look as if there had been any wild animals rummaging through them. More like two drunk boys stumbling across the place and making a general mess of things.

Now where had Giraud stashed the proper clothes? He'd really like to get dressed...

He followed his memories and left the clearing towards the river. He didn't find their bundle of clothes, though, but a faint wheezing sound that was pleasantly familiar. Jehan turned further left into the forest and found Giraud curled up like a deer on a pile of dry leaves, using his wolf pelt as a makeshift blanket. Once again, the sight brought a smile to Jehan's face. How could a grown man be so adorable?

Trying not to startle him, Jehan knelt down next to Giraud and gently nudged his shoulder. "Hey handsome. Time to wake up."

Giraud blinked slowly, smiled and sat up. His dark curls were one huge cowlick, and there was a small snail sitting on his right cheekbone.

"Eugh," he mumbled, licking his teeth. "This is vile."

Jehan delicately picked the snail off his face. "It'll pass soon enough. But we need to leave, it's way past sunrise already."

Again, Giraud blinked, less sluggishly this time. "Shite."

He rose to his feet and swayed when his head protested pretty much the same way Jehan's had done earlier. Jehan was immediately at his side, steadying him. His body was warm under his hands, and Giraud leaned against him with unconditional trust.

"You alright?"

"Oh my." Giraud gave him a wobbly smile. "Hungover, nothing worse."

"Good. That will pass."

Giraud's left side was covered with brown leaves sticking to his skin, and Jehan seized the rare moment of him standing still to help pick them off.

He was just about to brush off his friend's lower back when Giraud insistently patted his shoulder.

"Jehan? Jehan, who is that?"

"Huh? What?" For a heartbeat, Jehan feared Giraud had taken more damage than a headache from last night's adventure. But then he followed his gesture and indeed found someone standing only a few trees away, watching them. A short, white figure in a flowing dress, Jehan first feared it was another White Lady. But the longer he looked, the more her dress seemed familiar to him.

"Grandmother?! Is that you?"

The apparition nodded, and only now Jehan realised that she was hiding her mouth behind her hands. She looked at him, clearly able to see, and the corners of her eyes crinkled with amusement.

"Are you laughing at us?"

The figure shook her head, but it was clear that she was about to keel over with laughter, even though Jehan couldn't hear a thing.

"It's really you..." Jehan mumbled and took a few hesitant steps in her direction. "But how can you – Why?"

She cocked her head, looking at him as if trying to tell him he was acting like an idiot once again. She really didn't need a voice to do that.

"Have you ... passed?"

She nodded hesitantly. Now that Jehan was closer to her, he could see that she looked a lot younger than he remembered. Her dress and bonnet were just the same as she had always worn, and there was a calm glow of contentment around her.

"You seem at peace," he stated. "Will you be alright?"

She shrugged and smiled. Apparently, she didn't feel too sure about her current state, but not in a bad way.

"We went on a spirit hunt, last night, can you imagine?" it suddenly burst out of Jehan. "Just like in the ancient stories. And it worked, we saw Prince Sylvain and the Lady Givonne, and we went all the way up to Castle Beronsac – " Her faint expression of disbelief made him hesitate. "We did, didn't we?" he asked Giraud over his shoulder.

Giraud nodded. His expression wasn't overly confident, but if he remembered being in Beronsac as well, it couldn't all have been a dream.

"See? We did it." He sighed, his shoulders dropping. "I know I should have understood this sooner. Learned more from you."

His grandmother nodded.

"But I get it now." Jehan nodded as vigorously as his aching head allowed. "I'll look after our family, and after our village. I promise."

Her mocking smile turned proud, and she folded her hands in a wordless prayer of gratitude to heaven. At least death didn't seem to have dulled her acerbic humour.

"Will I be seeing you again? Or is this a last farewell?" Iolande shrugged, adding half a nod. So she wasn't sure they were going to see each other again, but she expected it to happen eventually.

"Just take care of yourself, yes?" He took a few steps towards her and tried to hug her colourless shape, but she sifted through his arms like mist.

Again, she gave him that idiot glance.

"Sorry," Jehan replied sheepishly. "You know I had to try."

She nodded, mildly annoyed as one gets with an overeager child. But then she moved a little to the side so Giraud couldn't see her face. Her smile gained a decidedly naughty edge when she nodded in Giraud's direction and gestured Jehan that she definitely approved. She didn't use words, this time either, but the gesture she employed was rude enough to make him blush.

"Thanks, Grandma..." he mumbled.

With another happy smirk, she nodded her farewell and disappeared, the ghostly lines of her apparition dissolving like morning mist in the sun.

"That was admittedly unexpected," Giraud remarked while he walked up to stand beside Jehan and placed his hand on his shoulder. "I am sorry for your loss?"

"Thank you." He cast him a wry look. "It doesn't really feel like she is dead, and I mean, she obviously isn't as dead as other dead people."

"That kind of doesn't even make any sense at all." Giraud smirked. "Can we go fetch our clothes now? I'm starting to feel really exposed."

"Of course." Jehan nodded and gestured roughly in the direction Giraud must have stashed their bundle. "Do you remember where you put them?"

"Uh..." Giraud scratched his head, noticed his cowlick and made a half-hearted attempt to sort out his hair. "I am pretty sure I'll remember when I see the spot.

What about you pick up what's still lying around the clearing and I go and search for our clothes?"

"Sounds like a perfect idea to me."

But instead of leaving, Giraud smiled at him widely. "We really did it, didn't we?"

This time, it was Jehan who gave a half-convinced shrug. "I think yes. We were both in Castle Beronsac, weren't we?"

"Yep. Great war brewing, Prince Sylvain and the good Lady Givonne fighting... What a magical way to spend the night."

"If only I had the faintest idea why the spirits brought us there..."

"Oh, you'll figure it out, I am sure of that." Giraud walked past him, but not without smacking Jehan's backside as if he were a saucy tavern wench. "You're my hero."

Jehan was too flustered to reply anything witty. Instead, he remained standing at the spot, furiously trying to decide if he should feel angered or flattered or maybe even both at the same time. In the end, he decided that it was just too stupid standing around in the forest, naked and confused, and instead left for the clearing.

Gathering up their belongings wasn't much of a task, if for no other reason than there hadn't been much to begin with. The wooden bowl, the knife and the bottle of wine, the two pelts they had been wearing. The stuffed rabbit skin was nowhere to be found, and Jehan was half happy about it. Finding it lying here on the ground would have made the events of last night feel even more like a fevered dream.

Giraud returned with their clothes moments later and they got dressed in companionable silence. Only when they were already back on the way to Jehan's hut, it was Giraud who spoke up.

"So – I'll head back home, now, for work, yes? And you'll come talk to me once you know what we're going to do?"

Jehan mulled over his answer for a while before he replied. "I think I'll come to town with you. Now that Grandma has passed, I need to talk to my family and see if they need anything."

Giraud just gave him a noncommittal grunt.

"Also, I should come and see to your parents, you know? I can't lift the curse, but maybe I can do a little something that would make it less likely anything really bad happens to them. Maybe help your mother find something so her foot will heal better."

"You can do that?"

"Honestly? I don't know." Jehan shrugged with a smile. "But I didn't know I could turn both of us into wolves, either. And if I can help, I have to."

Giraud gave him a long glance, hard to read and somewhere between intrigue and admiration. "I knew it was a good idea to ask you for help."

"It was." Jehan nodded with conviction. "I still have no idea if my involvement will help anyone in the end. But I already learned a thing or two I otherwise wouldn't have. So yes, it was a good idea indeed. Thank you."

Giraud smiled warmly. "So you'll continue to keep an eye on things when my parents are safe again, aren't you?"

"If I am still around to do so, yes, absolutely."

"Well, if I am still around, then, I would very much like to help you. You will need someone to watch your back." His smile grew a little insecure. "I really like being around you, you know that, don't you?"

Jehan slowed his steps until they stood in the forest, facing each other. From Giraud's shy, hopeful expression, it was clear that he wasn't just talking about being friends. But he didn't seem to know what would be the alternative to that, and admittedly, Jehan wasn't sure either. But that wasn't important. Important was that tiny bit of hope in his heart, that little bit of a dream that Giraud had just given substance to.

"I would love that."

From afar, the wind carried the sound of church bells to them, and both looked up with the same, urgent expression. Without exchanging so much as a look, they postponed whatever it was they had just started, and hurried to reach Jehan's hut, to fetch Trajan and get back to La Morangiasse.

***

It seemed half the town was sitting underneath the chestnut tree in front of his family's house. Everyone had come to pay their respects, and the ones coming out of the house stayed for a little chat with the ones still waiting in line. It was an orderly, sober, but hospitable affair, and his grandmother would have been very pleased with it. Well, maybe she even was.

Ugs' daughters were milling among the guests, offering water and chestnut cookies to everyone. Little Luc was handing out *eau-de-vie* for the men, and quite a few of the women as well. Marianne was in charge of the outdoors happenings, while her parents were probably inside, busy accepting condolences.

When Marianne spotted him, her look mirrored that of her mother a few days ago.

"Mama knew we wouldn't have to send anyone for you," she said instead of a greeting, her expression a muted smile of relief and exhaustion. "She's inside." She looked at him suspiciously. "You look terrible. Didn't you sleep well either? There were wolves howling in the forest tonight, the kids were so frightened. Or is it because of Grandma? I am so sorry."

Had they been howling? Jehan had no recollection of it, but there probably hadn't been any other wolves on the prowl last night. He gave Marianne a vague nod and measured visitors waiting in line. It would take some time until he would be able to talk to Alienee, by the looks of it. But there was a handful of other people that he wanted to talk to, as well, so maybe he could just return later.

"Jehan, my boy," a slightly mumbled voice from the side pulled him out of his thoughts. *Père* Ancel, a little pale in his black frock, looking as if this was way too early in the day for him. So in essence, he looked like Jehan was feeling. "I am so sorry for your loss. But our beloved *Grand-mère Matrone* is in God's hands now, and we should rejoice for her soul."

Only in the very last moment, Jehan managed to swallow a flippant comment on the state of his grandmother's soul. "She was a pious woman, and dedicated her life to the service of this town. I am sure Heaven has welcomed her with open arms."

Père Ancel nodded and patted Jehan's shoulder. "We'll hold a beautiful service on Friday, in memory of her life. You will come, won't you?"

"Of course, Father." Jehan smiled at the rotund priest. "No less than she deserved."

Grandmother would have had a few choice words about *Père* Ancel and his ignorance of all things spiritual. But the Priest was a kind man and trying to do the best he could for La Morangiasse. As long as he got enough sleep and enough food, that was.

It seemed *Père* Ancel already considered their conversation over, and wandered off to someone else he thought he needed to talk to. Not without picking up a few more chestnut cookies on the way, of course.

On the few stairs that led up to their house, a mumbled conversation arose when guests leaving the house all but stumbled over those waiting on the stairs. It took them a while to sort out their paths, among muttered apologies and greetings, but eventually they found their way around to each other. It turned out the leaving party was *Capitaine* LaForge and his wife who had just paid their last respects.

Jehan gave them a passing nod, but the utterly distraught expression of LaForge's wife caught his attention. Yes, his grandmother had been well-liked all over town, but this was not a reaction he had expected. A nagging feeling that he couldn't place grabbed Jehan, and he followed them until they were a little out of the crowd.

"Captain!" he called out. "A word?"

LaForge turned around and his scowl changed to an expression of genuine care. "Jehan, I am so sorry for your loss. *Grand-mère Matrone* was part of the bedrock of this town."

"Thank you, captain. Would you mind a word or two? Alone?" He added a look at his wife, and even though LaForge's scowl returned, he nodded in agreement.

With a caring look, LaForge first ensured his wife would be alright without him for a moment before he followed Jehan a few steps along the road.

"What is it?"

"Maybe it's none of my business, captain, but I couldn't help but notice how distraught your wife looks today."

"She took the death of your grandmother very much to heart," LaForge replied without even trying to gloss over his utter lack of understanding.

"I ... I didn't grow up underneath my grandmother's kitchen table for nothing. Alienee for all her skill is maybe a bit brusque at time, and maybe not the best one to help a bruised heart."

LaForge's expression lit up with a grim smile in the corner of his eyes, clearly agreeing with Jehan's assessment, but he didn't say a word.

"Would you mind if I exchanged a few words with your wife, captain, alone?" Jehan continued. "I might be able to help."

It was hard to read LaForge's minimal expression, especially with his beard hiding most of his face. But after a moment's consideration, he nodded.

"Please, have words with her."

"Thank you, captain." Jehan gave him a deep nod of gratitude that might have been a bow before he walked back to his wife.

She looked at him with surprise and a little alarm, but remained standing where she was, her hands clutching an embroidered handkerchief.

"Good day, Madame," he offered in greeting, more formal than his usual self as they had never spoken before. "I am Jehan, the grandson of *Grand-mère Matrone*."

She nodded, still a little insecure. She definitely looked as if she wanted to be anywhere but here right now.

"I know you have regularly consulted with my grandmother, haven't you?" Jehan offered her his most disarming smile. "I also know that my grandmother offered services that went a little beyond the usual range of a midwife's. Services that Alienee doesn't see as her responsibility."

Her eyes were wide, dark orbs, and her voice wavered just a little when she replied.

"I have no idea what you are talking about."

"Of course you don't." Still, Jehan had the distinct feeling he was doing the right thing. "I just wanted to let you know that I will be picking up that part of my Grandmother's responsibilities. At least, to the extent I am able to."

This time, she blinked at him, slowly, cautiously hopeful.

"Your grandmother helped me greatly, and I don't know what to do without her." She hesitated, as if chewing on the words before she could speak them. "We should talk, then, I guess."

"What about you come down to the market next week, then?" Again, Jehan smiled at her, hoping to appear as non-threatening as a man could possibly appear. "We can talk about a few new recipes, then, and the herbs you'd need for them."

Her face lit up. "Herbs. Cooking herbs. Yes, I'd like to talk about those."

"Herbs are wonderful. For cooking. They have so many useful properties."

"Yes, they do, don't they?" She nodded, her mood rapidly brightening. "We will talk about those, on market day, at length."

"Madame LaForge," he replied with a polite nod of his head. "Looking forward to market day."

She returned his nod in like, and turned back towards her husband, who looked genuinely surprised at her visible relief. He looked back and forth between his wife and Jehan, then walked over to him.

"Whatever you said, it seems to have worked a small miracle. Thank you." He took Jehan's hand and shook it with gratitude, even placing a heavy hand on his shoulder. With a bittersweet expression, he added, "Do I even want to know what you talked about?"

Jehan gave him a conspiring smirk. "Cooking recipes." At LaForge's disbelieving look, he added, "No, I think we'll all be better off if you didn't know the details. Women things, you know?"

LaForge scrunched up his face, not happy, but not annoyed, either. "I trust your judgement, *Maître* Jehan."

"Thank you, captain," Jehan retorted with a smirk of his own. "I promise your trust is not misplaced."

The captain scoffed in amusement, tipped the brim of his hat and strode off to meet with his wife, who leaned her head against his shoulder in a gesture of exhaustion and relief. Jehan only hoped he would be able to help her. But then again, this wouldn't be the first time he had offered his help in matters far beyond his reach, would it?

He watched as they walked back to La Morangiasse. He knew he had to pick up some of grandmother's duties, but it was difficult to do so when he had never paid any particular attention to what those duties had exactly been. Maybe Madame LaForge was a good start. She was quiet, but well respected among the women in town. So if maybe he could help her with her 'woman problems', she would drop a word in the right ears here and there. And maybe that would bring those duties to him, hopefully.

A glance over his shoulder confirmed that there were still enough people waiting on the stairs of their house that there was little point in waiting. *Père* Ancel was still merrily milling among the crowd, dispensing kind words, and eating. He was gaining a little colour, by now, so all seemed well.

Jehan turned back onto the road and headed towards town. Maybe his grandmother had been the greatest repository of fairy tales in town, but there was at least one other person who knew a story or two. Maybe not stories in the traditional sense, but history. Standing in the same spot in the centre of the village for a century would do that to you.

He had a feeling Cassanoë was watching him the moment he turned from the road onto the market place. Did that dryad have nothing else to do?

"Cassanoë, are you there?" he asked in a whisper as soon as he had reached her oak. "Do you have time for a chat?"

A rustle in the leaves above answered him, but she didn't appear. Jehan glanced around – they were virtually alone on the square. There were a few people passing by on the road that followed the river, and a few others were walking up the road that led up onto the cliff and towards the smithy.

"Cassanoë?" he asked again. "Just a few moments."

The leaves remained silent, this time, but he spotted a handful of green curls around the massive trunk. Jehan peeked around the tree and found the dryad staring at him with a mix of caution and curiosity.

"What are you doing there?" he asked. "Since when don't you want to talk to me?"

She eyed him wordlessly, from a respectful distance.

"It's me, Jehan. We are friends."

"I know that." She pursed her lips. "But you have changed. A lot. But you humans usually don't change. You only grow old and die."

"Yes." The thought of his grandmother dimmed his smile for a heartbeat. "But sometimes, we do change. And I hope it is a change for the better."

"That is what I was trying to find out from a safe distance." Cassanoë sounded vaguely reproachful. "You have become a lot more dangerous over the last few days. I am not sure I like it."

"I have also become a lot better at protecting my friends," he offered. "I have a story to tell and I need someone to listen. Would you mind?"

Cassanoë was just about to reply when the door of the *Plume d'Or* opened and a large splash of dirty water and suds got hurled onto the square. It landed with a splat that resounded from all walls, the bone-dry stones soaking up the moisture with a soft crackling buzz. A tavern girl stood in the door, bucket in hand, and she smiled when she noticed Jehan standing next to the tree.

"Greetings, Jehan!" she chirped, only to look utterly crestfallen a heartbeat later. "Oh, I am so sorry about your grandmother."

"Thank you, Camille."

She smiled at him, a little sheepish, then offered, "Can I get you anything? You look like you could use a drink."

"No, please, nothing." He definitely had enough alcohol last night, and he still had that lingering bitter aftertaste from an overdose of wormwood clinging to the roof of his mouth. "I am good, thank you. I just was looking for a spot to be alone for a moment."

"Oh." Her eyes went wide with understanding. "And here I am, chatting and making pretty eyes at you like a silly tavern girl." She giggled and shrugged, smiled, then disappeared back into the darkness of the tavern. She left the door open, hopefully to air the place out, and not to have an eye on him. There were already enough people in town wondering about his odd behaviour.

He looked back at Cassanoë who still examined him with deep suspicion. She had completely ignored the tavern girl, secure in the knowledge she wouldn't be able to see her anyway.

"So your grandmother is dead?" She offered him the hint of a sympathetic smile. "I will remember her fondly. She was wise, for a human."

"She was, indeed." He let his shoulders drop, suddenly aware of the tension he had been building up. "I only wish I had understood that much earlier."

"There is no shame in being ignorant. Only in staying so."

Jehan nodded. There was a good reason he preferred talking to the oak on the market square to most other people. Cassanoë's unique point of view helped him sort his mind, and her natural patience made him feel a lot less silly.

"You said you had a story..." She pursed her dark green lips. "So what is it that you want in return?"

"Honestly? I don't know." He leaned his back against the trunk of her tree and slid down until he sat comfortably on the ground. "Me and Giraud, we walked in different skins last night."

She struggled visibly, but with a tiny, defeated sigh, her curiosity won out and she sat down next to him. "So that was you?"

"I guess? As far as I know there are no others nearby who could. Are there?"

"None that I know of, either."

245

"I am not sure how we did it, but we went back to when Beronsac was still standing," Jehan continued his explanations. "Sylvain was there, and Lady Givonne."

Cassanoë just looked at him, her eyes dark and cool and very unreadable.

"It was the night before the English attacked, I think. The hills were lit with their fires as far as we could see." Jehan craned his neck, hoping that would help him get rid of that sore feeling in his brain. "They were fighting like fishwives, the two of them."

"It must have been a sad day when their love broke apart."

"Yeah, I guess it must have been." He eyed Cassanoë carefully. "I understand that this night was important, how this is at the root of our problem. But I still cannot see how this is going to help us solve anything. Can you?"

She smiled enigmatically. "When you have the answer, but it doesn't fit your question, then maybe you are asking the wrong question."

"Really, more riddles?" Jehan scratched his head. "So you think I should ... what? I am sorry, I really am at a loss, here."

Cassanoë's smile grew warm. "Seems that in some ways, you haven't changed at all."

"Still a bumbling fool?"

She gave a non-committal sound, but by the sparkle in her eyes, it was a clear yes. "You went on a spirit hunt, didn't you?"

"Yes."

"And what did you ask the spirit for? What were your exact words?"

"I ... It wasn't so much words, I guess ... I just wanted to find out how to solve this entire mess, to make things right again."

She raised her elegant green eyebrows, clearly expecting some moment of enlightenment from him.

"And the spirit showed me that the entire mess comes from the two of them still being bitter about that night." Jehan nursed that thought in his aching head for a while. "It does make sense, in a way. Giraud, his parent's ... even the folks up in Castelfort and La Morangiasse constantly fighting in one way or another."

"And?"

"And... Are you saying that if they didn't hate each other any longer, all would be well?"

Cassanoë's expression lit up with a wide smile.

"But how? You can't make people fall in love, much less fae folk. And by God, I surely am not good enough a witch to enchant them."

Her smile disappeared as swiftly as it had come up. "My, but you are a dullard this morning, *Jehan Le Pêcheur*."

"My apologies, Lady of the Green House." He grinned at her sheepishly. "I am afraid I am still working off last night's potion, and I can barely think straight."

Her faintly annoyed expression remained unchanged, so he tried to sort his thoughts once again.

"To make things right, I need to make them love each other again. Or, at least not trying to hurt each other at every opportunity. So how do I mend bridges between two fae who hate each other with a passion..." He blinked, slowly. That last sentence felt like he had grabbed an eel by it's tail, slippery and trying to get away from him, but definitely within his grasp. Careful, now, don't let it slip... "Passion! They still have feelings for each other, or else they wouldn't be so ... passionate about it."

Cassanoë gave a deep sigh of relief. "Finally."

"So you mean I just have to – " His eyes went wide as his mind flooded with things he needed to prepare if he wanted to make this work. "Oh, Cassanoë, you are the best!"

He grabbed her face with both hand and placed a smacking kiss onto her cheek, which she reacted to with a hiss and a squirm very much like a cat, cuddled against her will.

But Jehan was already on his feet, his mind racing. He was two steps down the market place towards his family's home when he turned around on his heel and paced in the other direction, towards the end of town and the bridge of Beronsac. Finally, he threw his arms up in defeat and turned around again, this time heading uphill and towards the smithy, leaving Cassanoë behind, sitting at the base of her tree, still wiping her cheek but smiling widely.

Chapter Twelve - Midnight Orchids

"It's too late to change your mind, isn't it?" Giraud huffed with exertion from the long climb up the cliff, struggling with a steep incline a few meters behind. "I still think we shouldn't confront either of them, let alone both of them at once."

"You had no qualms confronting five brigands only a few days ago, and now you're afraid of two elderly fae?"

"Oh yes, I am afraid. I still remember vividly what happened the last time we stepped on the toes of one of them. And that was when we were surrounded by normal people."

Jehan acknowledged Giraud's concerns with a shrug. There was a distinct chance they might die tonight. Or get turned into frogs. Or worse. But then again, that wasn't much worse a risk than they had faced several other nights this week so far. And this time, there was hope he could end this, once and for all. And it was high time they finished this adventure. He really needed to get back to fishing and while Giraud's father didn't seem to mind his son spending some nights out, sowing his wild oats, he did mind when Giraud wasn't there to work in the morning.

If anything made him feel uncomfortable about what he had planned tonight, it was that he had roped others into helping them. But he had needed their help, and if it worked out, they would get out of this unscathed as well.

Jehan reached the edge of the cliff and scrambled onto the top. He stretched his back and tried to get his bearings – behind him, half hidden by another cliff, the lights of La Morangiasse blinked in the darkness. Straight ahead, tall walls rose in the darkness, roofless, cracked and toppled with age, but still tall enough to be visible from the valley down below – the ruins of Beronsac. Bats zipped and fluttered above the rocks, little black shapes barely distinguishable from the night sky.

"Oh this is uncanny." Giraud had reached the clifftop as well and looked around with a queasy look on his face. "The perspective is different, but I swear I remember how this looked when it was still standing."

Jehan nodded. "We need to find that terrace," he said with a glance to the moon, "there's not much time left."

"Alright." Giraud cracked his knuckles. "Just one last time – I think this is madness."

"Acknowledged." He shot him a smile. "So – any suggestions for an easy path?"

"Straight ahead, and then to the right. The main donjon and most outbuildings of the castle have collapsed, and I really have no desire to clamber across those piles. But the smaller building shouldn't make much of an obstacle."

"You lead the way, *Maître* Forgeron," Jehan decided with a tip to his imaginary hat.

They had left their hats down in the valley by the remnants of the road that had led up to Castle Beronsac in olden times. Overall, Jehan was proud of how they had both dressed appropriately for the occasion – sturdy clothes, with long trousers and little finery. He had even thought of wearing his sandals tonight, and already he was grateful for it. The road had been still intact in parts, but more often than not, it had collapsed and crumbled downhill, so they had been forced to cling to the cliffside like hungry goats. At least, these cliffs weren't as covered with butcher's broom as the last ones they had climbed together. Close to the top, they had abandoned the old road entirely and just sought out the easiest way upwards. Which, considering that it was well past nightfall, had been anything but easy.

But now they were here, and Jehan felt his heart in his throat, thumbing with excitement.

As requested, Giraud lit the small lantern he had wisely brought and led them through the sparse forest that grew here. There were several trees as tall and wide as anywhere else in the forest, but there were so many large stone blocks and paving slabs blocking the ground that it was relatively easy to get through. Compared to the messy tangle of plants around Raëlle's 'tower', this was a leisurely walk.

It was an eerie feeling, walking through the remains of a settlement like this. There had been people living here, working here, people just like him and Giraud. It felt more than a little bit like walking across a grave. But then again, that was why they had come. Too much was buried here, and not all of it was resting peacefully. This was a time to put old things behind, and maybe take that end as a new beginning.

"Careful, now," Giraud pointed out, shining his light ahead. "The old road ends here, we need to climb the last bit."

Up ahead of them, a dark slope rose into the night sky. Against the indigo backdrop, Jehan spotted the familiar outline of a crenellated wall. Giraud picked a path and they advanced up the incline, stepping across remnants of fieldstone walls, moss-covered roof tiles crunching under their feet, brittle with age. Jehan sensed the attention of the place turn in their direction. People rarely came here, and for good reasons. Enough blood had been spilled here that even after all this time, the place gave them goosebumps even if they were as mundane as a brick. Jehan had insisted they both wear sprigs of rosemary around their necks tonight, just in case there were any restless spirits lingering. They would have enough trouble dealing with the fae.

It turned out the incline was a lot steeper than they had expected, most of it still covered with tightly fitted stone blocks as tall as a man, and Giraud had to extinguish his lantern again and fasten it to his baldric so he could climb on with both hands. At least, a portion of the rampart had collapsed, and only the stones that littered the slope allowed them to climb up at all. They could already see the rim of the terrace through a breach in the wall when the ground became nothing but brittle gravel and dry sand, sliding under their feet. They were almost in grasping reach, but the last few meters seemed impossible to cover.

Giraud cursed silently and handed his satchel and baldric to Jehan.

"What are you -"

Jehan didn't manage to finish his question. Wordlessly, Giraud stepped back, took a run-up and jumped. With an inelegant grunt, he landed halfway over the edge of the terrace, a wave of sand drifting out from under the paving stone he lay upon. But it held fast, and Giraud managed to pull himself up.

He straightened himself and smoothed down his shirt, grimacing when he thought of the bruises he'd probably sport the other day.

"It's nice up here, don't you want to come, too?" he asked, his cocky grin so wide his teeth shone in the moonlight. "Toss me the bags."

Jehan did as he was told and hurled their stuff up at Giraud. He walked back a few steps as well, took a run-up himself and just as he felt his feet slipping and sliding away from under him, Giraud's strong hands grabbed his outstretched arm and pulled him up.

"Teamwork," he remarked, still grinning. " See, was a piece of cake, getting up here, wasn't it?"

Jehan didn't feel in the mood to share Giraud's enthusiasm, but there was no denying that they had made it, and in less time than he had feared, too. That left him a few precious moments to catch his breath and get a feel for the place.

The former castle was nothing but a dark pile of stones behind them, a few scraggly trees topping the shapeless mass. Only two of the main walls were still standing, at least partially so, their empty windows like eye sockets in the skull of an antediluvian beast.

The terrace itself was mostly like Jehan remembered from their spirit hunt. Only at the far end, where they had stood with the prince and his wife and watched the enemy fires burn in the night, the entire construction had collapsed and slid down into the forest. But there was no question that the place was still recognisable, and that was all that mattered to him. Maybe the decrepit and overgrown mood would even remind Sylvain and Givonne of how the place had looked before the castle had been built, of that time they had met right here on the meadows.

"Do you think you can lend me a hand?" Jehan smiled at Giraud winningly. "I need some time to focus, but I'd really like to do something to keep this place free of lingering ghosts, at least for tonight."

"I am all for not having any ghostly visitations, so if I can help, I gladly will." Giraud had walked over to the far side of the parapet to look across the valley towards Castelfort, but now he returned to Jehan's side. "What am I to do?"

"I have prepared these." Jehan dug into his satchel and produced a tightly bound bouquet of dry rosemary and lavender, wrapped in sage leaves. "Here. Light them on fire on one end, and blow out the flames again. It should glim and smoke nicely."

Giraud eyed the herbs suspiciously. "And then?"

"You walk around the terrace and make sure a bit of the smoke gets in every corner." Jehan had to smile at his doubtful expression. "The smoke of these herbs will appease spirits, and maybe even ease their passing. So while I doubt we'll change anything significant with what hasn't changed over the last few hundred years, at least for tonight it should ensure nothing from the realm of the dead will bother us. I hope."

"If you say so." Giraud knelt down and first lit his lantern again, then lit the herbs on the candle inside. "And now I just walk around in circles?"

"Along the border of the terrace, yes. If you have a few kind words to say to any ghosts listening, that might be a good thing, too."

"I think I'll just smoke them out, then," Giraud replied glumly, "I'd rather leave the incantations to you."

Jehan was about to reply that he had been talking about prayers, not incantations, and that it was simply a matter of intention and focus, but caught himself. Smoking out ghosts was still a lot better than not doing anything, so he was happy with whatever Giraud would do. Besides, he would do it with passion and focus, just as he did with everything else. Being half fae did have its advantages, sometimes.

"Just go ahead," he said. "But you might want to take off your necklace."

"Now you tell me?"

Giraud searched for a spot to put his smoking bundle of herbs. Not really willing to put it on the ground with all the dry leaves, he finally stuck it between his lips like a pipe and grinned at Jehan while he fumbled with the necklace.

Despite everything, his eyes sparkled with excitement, and Jehan's heart beat in his throat once again, though no longer from the exertion of the climb. Even the possibility of sharing a part of his life with this man made his heart skip a few beats with excitement. Each smile of him felt like an undeserved gift.

Giraud managed to untie his necklace and first tried to stuff the necklace into his own pocket, but then thought better of it and handed it to Jehan. Maybe he wasn't willing to say some prayers on the ramparts of a ruined castle, but obviously, he had given some thought to the matter, and clearly intended to enter tonight with nothing hampering his gifts. Staying away from cold iron was a smart choice.

Jehan watched as he left for the pile of rubble that had once been the castle, and started waving the smoking herbs around with enough enthusiasm that it looked almost as if he was trying to signal a ferryman. He did look good, doing so, Jehan admitted with a smile, before he returned his focus to the work ahead.

He took the large waterskin out of the bag he had brought and looked for the centre of what remained of the terrace. Cradling the waterskin in his lap, he sat down, cross-legged, and closed his eyes.

Breathe in, breathe out.

The tree tops of the forest around the terrace rustled softly in the night breeze, and the day's heat still radiated from the stones he was sitting on. An owl called in the forest below, the sound echoing across the hills. A whiff of burning herbs passed him by, followed by a gentle, persistent hint of white oleander. Jehan took another deep breath and let his concentration sink deeper into the ground below, past the flagstones and the sand. Before the castle had been built, this had been a meadow, a gentle slope surrounded by forest. And even though the forest had reclaimed most of this area these days, the ground still remembered. Jehan felt the roots of the trees reach down deeply, felt where the cracks in the paving allowed the rain to seep through and nurture the earth below. There was the network of roots that connected the occasional butcher's broom shrubs with each other, and the haze of mist-like threads that would turn into mushrooms come autumn.

But he wasn't looking for more oaks or grass, tonight. He was searching for plants a lot more delicate, a lot more sensitive and much less forgiving. Buried deep underground, dormant for centuries, he sensed an entire colony of seeds, tiny and long-forgotten, but not dead. Jehan took a long, long moment to familiarise himself with those seeds, until his mind could grasp them as easily as if he were reaching for them with his hands.

"*Ophrys, Ophrys*, can you hear me?" he whispered, calling out with his heart rather than his voice. "*Ophrys, Ophrys*, come on up!"

He opened the waterskin in his lap and allowed a trickle of its contents to spill before his feet, where it ran over the broken stones and disappeared between the cracks. He had brought water as a gift, water laced with earth from meadows where he knew the same flowers were growing in abundance, and a few drops of his blood. And together with the water, his powers reached down into the ground, finding each tiny, buried, sleeping seedling and tickling it awake. The sensation was so kind and playful Jehan broke into a wide smile. He could almost see the hard shells of the seeds crack open, the plants inside awakening like drowsy children.

"*Ophrys, Ophrys*, can you hear me?" he repeated, "*Ophrys, Ophrys*, time to wake up."

Slowly, without breaking his connection to the happenings underground, Jehan rose to his feet. His eyes half closed, he started walking around the spot where he had been sitting in ever widening circles, sprinkling more and more water all over the ground. The plants below craved the water, craved the fresh air, and he felt them being pulled upwards by the promise of nurture, pulled up by his will.

"Come on up, darlings, come to me," he whispered, smiling. "Come, there's plenty of water for you here."

From the corner of his eyes, Jehan noticed Giraud giving him that look again, half-impressed and half-doubtful at the same time. But Jehan just smiled wider, emboldened by Giraud's confidence in his powers. This was a vainglorious thing he was trying to do, taxing and straining his energy more than he had imagined – but it worked.

By the old gods, he felt it work!

Barely audible at first, but stronger and stronger, another sound joined the usual night time noises of the forest – a soft scraping, a rustling, like fresh leaves moving in the wind, or the sound of tall grass with a rabbit running through it. Giraud gave a startled curse when he noticed the movement all around him. Tiny shoots of green were breaking through every crack and cranny of the pavings, slender little plants as green as blades of grass in spring, everywhere. They twisted and turned and sprouted narrow leaves, going through the growth of an entire spring in just a few heartbeats.

Jehan felt sweat pearl down his forehead, his breath going in hard, focussed bursts. It felt like pushing them physically up himself, all at the same time, like carrying an overloaded backpack uphill. But he could still force them a little further, grow them a little taller, and each bit of progress gave him new strength to carry on.

The plants wanted to stop growing when they were barely longer than a forearm, but Jehan still pushed them on.

Gasping for air by now, it felt like swimming against a current, trying to fight against a force of nature, and really, that was what he was doing right now. It was late summer, not spring, but he didn't care. He needed this to work out, needed this to be as good as he could possibly manage.

The plants swelled with little buds along their stems, bulging within the span of a few heartbeats, and one by one, they began to bloom. Luscious petals unfolded, each blossom looking a little like a fat, happy bumble bee sitting on a three-petaled purple flower. Bee orchids, so common to this area, littering the terrace as if it were a meadow in spring.

With a final gasp, Jehan fell down onto his knees.

"Jehan!" Immediately, Giraud was at his side, steadying him. "Are you alright?"

Jehan felt as if he had swum the entire way upstream from his hut to La Morangiasse, his chest hurting and his heart hammering in his chest like a woodpecker, but what he saw was worth every bit of sweat and the shaking hands. Hundreds of orchids were scattered all across the terrace, all of then in full bloom, looking as full and lively as if this had been exactly what nature had intended.

"It worked," he gasped.

"Was there ever any doubt?" Giraud pulled him back to his feet. "I mean, I had no idea you could do this, but by God's wounds, this is impressive."

For a moment, they merely stood there, marvelling at this self-made miracle. Magic still hung in the air like the scent of a thunderstorm, but it didn't feel wrong. Yes, he had forced his will upon nature, but it was such a bold and beautiful thing that it seemed to warrant some magic of its own. It ebbed and flowed back and forth, like a lake disturbed by a stone thrown in, each wave a little smaller than the one before.

"I think this is the most beautiful thing I have ever seen," Giraud muttered softly. "Thank you."

"It rivals even the beauty standing right next to me," Jehan replied with a shaky smile. "And you are welcome."

It took Giraud a deliciously long moment to understand what Jehan was talking about, his expression changing from clueless to embarrassed to flattered and happy in a single instant. He was still holding Jehan around his shoulder, just to make sure he didn't stumble, and feeling him so close made Jehan wonder how he had managed to survive without another person in his life. A person to hold close, to share secrets with, to admire and mock and laugh together with. A person to love.

A warm wave of gratitude washed through Jehan, filling him with a joy he had rarely known in his life. Had he really found a kindred spirit in Giraud? Someone to walk through life by his side, whatever form that would take? In Giraud's eyes, large and impossibly green, he saw a reflection of his own happiness. With a tender gesture, Jehan took a strand of Giraud's hair that had escaped his short pony-tail and tugged it behind his ear, careful not to disturb any of the white flowers he could already guess in ghostly semblances.

"Thank you for being here with me," Jehan said, his voice still a little husky.

Giraud's smile widened another notch when he nodded calmly. "I was just about to say the same. I – I have never felt like this with anyone else before. It is as if you are making me whole, if that makes any sense to you."

Jehan's heart felt full to the point of bursting, but he had no way to express his feelings. He could think of a word for what they felt, but he feared naming it, worried it might dispel this particular magic if dragged out into the open. Instead, he put a finger underneath Giraud's chin and leaned down to –

An insistent rustle of a shrub nearby startled both of them out of it.

"What was that?!" Giraud whispered, alarmed, his hand on the handle of his hammer.

Jehan looked around, trying to figure out the source of the sound. A second rustle broke the relative silence of the night, and this time, Jehan could see where it had come from – a single shrub of butcher's broom, shaking vigorously as if tousled by an invisible hand.

"They're on their way," he said to Giraud and reluctantly untangled himself from his embrace. "They will be here any moment."

Not waiting for Giraud's reaction, he walked over to the shrub and gave him the last few sips from his waterskin. "Here, *Maître Fragon*, for you. Thank you for the warning."

The shrub rustled one more time, softly, and fell silent.

Giraud took an audible, deep breath.

"Couldn't they have waited for just a moment longer?"

Jehan gave him a smile and a shrug. "Alas, 'tis as it is. The nobles decide, and simple folks like us have to follow suit, willingly or not."

Giraud replied with a rude gesture and so much heartfelt emphasis that Jehan burst out laughing. It took him a while to calm down again, but once he did, he motioned Giraud to join him in the corner of the terrace where they had already hidden once before, centuries ago.

"With the shrubs and the few trees now growing here, this might be sufficient cover," he explained. "And I have prepared a little something so we won't be too obvious."

Giraud didn't look particularly convinced, but dutifully started moving their stuff into the corner. Jehan cast a last glance over the moonlit sea of flowers, trying to spot anything that could reveal their involvement with this. He didn't see anything.

With a huff, Giraud put down the last bits, sat down in the corner and blew out the candle in his lantern. With the moon still mostly full and hanging low over the horizon, enough light remained for Jehan to continue with his work. Quietly, he pulled out three small pouches from his satchel, and opened the first one.

With careful motions, he took out a pinch of its contents – finely ground cat's hair and owl feathers, both freely given – and began to lay out a circle with them around their little corner. He took care to make it as regular as he possibly could.

"Silence," he whispered once he had finished, sealing the little ward with his word as one would close a lock with a key.

Next, he took a handful of coarse iron filings from the second pouch, and placed them along a second circle around them, inside the first.

"Ignorance," he whispered.

Lastly, from the third pouch, he poured a thin line of white salt around them.

"Purity," he whispered, eliciting a stifled giggle from Giraud.

"What?" he asked under his breath, urgently gesturing him to stay calm, not to break the subtle spells he had set up. "What's so funny?"

"Purity, really?" He wriggled his eyebrows. "And besides – do you really think this is going to cloak us?"

"I can't make us invisible, if that's what you're asking." With a frown, Jehan looked at his triple ward. "This couldn't even keep a squirrel from noticing us. But that's not what it's supposed to do. We're up against fae, and as a very wise tree once said to me, they don't work like humans, at least not exactly so."

"So you think the intention of staying hidden will be enough?"

Again, Jehan shrugged. "They won't destroy our game unless it's part of their story, and right now, I tried to make this about them, not us, so – "

A heavy gust of wind rattled across the terrace, and both men immediately fell silent. The air suddenly carried an unexpected chill, a scent like the first warning of snow in autumn. Jehan felt the magic of the place ripple once again – this time, there was a big fish swimming right underneath the surface. The first of their guests had arrived, no doubt about that.

"Strange magic here, Sire," a voice from the far end of the terrace, the side of Castelfort, came through the night, coarse and thin, but filled with wonder, nonetheless. "Bumblebee flowers, so many..."

"I can see that." Another voice, clear and commanding. Even though they could barely make out anything, Jehan and Giraud instantly recognised Prince Sylvain. "What sorcery is this..."

Sylvain sounded more startled than angered, and they heard several pairs of of feet crunch on the dry ground as the newcomers wandered through the newly sprung meadow. Jehan felt how Giraud next to him tensed up and all but stopped breathing.

"Why would anyone..." they heard Sylvain voice his thoughts. "It's been centuries..."

He wore an embroidered overcoat again, tonight, and a slender épée at his side. No billowing cloak, though, but it was easy enough to imagine on him. With the air still crisp with magic, his sweeping antlers and ghostly armour were easily visible. He was trailed by two familiar shadows – one tall and lumpy looking, the other one short and weasely – and next to them, a much smaller figure walked.

Jehan and Giraud exchanged a hopeful look. So far, this was working as they had hoped.

"What do you know about this?!" Sylvain suddenly demanded, addressing his companion. "Who did this?"

"Sire, I don't know anything," the first voice said. "I'm just a lowly *lutin*, at your service, Sire."

Sylvain grunted something unintelligible, but apparently considered his question sufficiently answered. "Watch that little rat," he ordered his guards, "I need to find out if she is behind this."

"Yes, Sire," the tall guard replied, his voice rumbling like a pile of boulders rolling downhill.

A buzz of dragonfly wings was suddenly in the air, crossing the terrace from right to left, followed by another gust of wind – this one a little less forceful than the first one, but colder, and coming from the direction of La Morangiasse. As if suddenly revealed by a passing moonlight shadow, a slender woman stood close to the parapet, short steps away from them. But as Jehan had hoped, she ignored them completely as her eyes immediately locked on Sylvain.

"*You!*" She hurled the word through the night like a knife. "I knew there was something fishy about this, I should have known it was you."

"I bid you a good evening, Lady Givonne," Sylvain replied, a lot less hotheaded. "You look beautiful."

His friendly reaction took the wind out of her sails, and for a moment, she just looked at him, wordlessly. Lady Givonne wore the same colours she had when they had last seen her – robes the pale blue of a frozen lake, her skin as white as snow. But while her hair was still piled in luscious curls upon her head, there were noticeable streaks of grey among the fiery red.

"Did you do this?" she asked, doubtful. "You never had a hand for flowers..."

"I had no hand in this." Sylvain took a few steps in her direction, cautiously approaching her with the respect one had for an equally matched opponent. "Did you?"

"No."

They looked at each other, separated by just a few steps now.

Both Jehan and Giraud were holding their breaths, and it seemed Sylvain's guards had enough common sense to stay out of sight for the time being. Silently, they backed away from Sylvain, roughly in the direction where Jehan and Giraud were hiding. Between them walked the *lutin*, straight-backed and proud, with a single wild rose on the chest of his tunic like a medal of sorts.

Unlike all other fae on the terrace, though, the *lutin* looked across his shoulder, grinned and nodded at the two men hiding there, clearly ignoring Jehan's wards. Which made perfect sense to Jehan – after all, they were integral parts to his story.

"Captain," he whispered with an acknowledging nod towards the courageous *lutin*, tipping the rim of his imaginary hat. "Thank you."

"So if it's neither me nor you," Givonne said, "then who? This clearly is some ridiculous ploy."

"I don't find it so ridiculous," Sylvain replied, squaring his shoulders. "Is it truly impossible that we might find again what we found on this meadow, so many years ago?"

"We lost it, many years ago, in this very spot."

"What is lost can be found again."

"What is lost can just as well be dead forever."

Sylvain drew in a sharp breath. "Is that how you see it?"

She scoffed, the air suddenly brittle and humming with a sound like thin ice just before breaking underneath your feet. "Your decision has brought centuries of suffering over these lands. In a heart as cold as yours, I have to doubt love could have survived any length of time."

"Don't fool yourself into believing things would have been different if you'd had it your way," Sylvain retorted coldly. "If you hadn't split our forces, maybe we could have beaten them that day."

"Now who's fooling himself here?"

Another silence fell, cold and heavy. This absolutely wasn't how Jehan had hoped this conversation would play out. Yes, he had expected some bickering, maybe some insults, but not this ... bitterness. Next to him, Giraud was literally gnashing his teeth.

"I am not fooling myself, dearest." Sylvain's voice was heavy with defeat. "I am keenly aware how you betrayed me."

"Oh this is how you tell it these days?" Her voice resounded like large shoals of ice, grinding along each other. Around her feet, cold mist gathered on the stones, and the flowers around her wilted like salad caught in an early frost. "I only remember you abandoning me and my people to the enemy, leaving me all alone to negotiate a modicum of civility!"

"I would have fought beside you, if you had only been willing to fight!" Sylvain all but yelled these last words, and his hair moved with unseen storm.

"And I didn't want any part in that senseless slaughter. But that is what you men are all about, isn't it?!"

"Just like you women are all about backstabbing those who believe in you, right?!"

"Oh for heaven's sake!" Giraud jumped to his feet. "Just listen to the two of you!"

Every single face on the terrace turned to Giraud, everyone displaying various degrees of surprise and disbelief. Jehan just wished for a hole to disappear into, but Giraud didn't give a wet rat's ass about anyone's opinion right now.

"You style yourself as Lords and Ladies, and yet you bicker like toothless hags! Shame on you, both of you!" He walked up to them, his hands clenching with fury. "You play silly, inconsequential games, and all around you, people suffer. People who only have a few years to live, unlike you, people to whom every day is priceless. *How dare you?!*"

Both Sylvain and Givonne seemed utterly aghast, stunned out of words.

"You treat even me like a pawn in your games, and yet in my short life, I have done more for the people in the valley than either of you. And I haven't even tried!"

"How dare you talk to me like that?!" the Lady Givonne hissed, her voice humming like a furious swan's. "Do you still not know who I am? I should gut you like a fish, I should -"

"Oh, just cut it out." With grim determination, Giraud took the hammer out of his baldric and flipped it in his hand. "You want to gut me, yes? I'd like to see you try."

Immediately, Sylvain and his guards had their weapons out as well. The *lutin* captain did the only smart thing, gave a startled yelp and disappeared into the undergrowth.

"Everyone, hold your weapons!" Jehan rose from his crouch as well, his hands raised. "Everyone."

"You again!" Sylvain sounded surprised, and Jehan wondered for a heartbeat if he should feel relieved or insulted. "Did you do all this?"

"Yes, I did this," Jehan admitted and briskly crossed the distance between himself and Giraud. "Put that hammer down, Giraud."

"I am not going to stand by while these two pompous fobs continue ruining these lands."

"Yes." Jehan put a calming hand onto Giraud's shoulder. He shivered with rage as if it were a fever, but as much as Jehan felt with him, this wasn't the time. "Now put that hammer down."

Hesitantly, Giraud dropped his weapon back into his baldric.

"A wise choice, *Maître* Jehan," Sylvain commented, but immediately turned towards his guards. "Now grab him, you fools!"

Jehan hurled around and could only make out two dark shapes rushing forward towards them.

"*Stop!*" he yelled, and much to his own surprise, the two guards stopped dead in their tracks. Judging by the looks on their faces, they were just as surprised as Jehan. But there was no wasting a moment of luck, so he added in calm command, "Don't move."

A heartbeat passed in silence, and indeed, no one moved. Jehan realised how the entire place still reverberated with the power of his command, humming through the air and seeping down into the ground. A grim smile spread across his face.

"Now that we can talk uninterrupted," he continued, "I suggest we – "

"What have you done to my men?" Sylvain bellowed, his épée still raised. His fae cloak was almost as real as anything else around him, and his blade was encased in the ghostly image of a heavy-set, well-worn sword. "Release them, immediately!"

Jehan felt the order tug at the corners of his mind, but nothing stronger than that.

"No," he replied with a cold smile.

"What do you want of us, sorcerer?" Givonne hissed, still sounding more like an angry swan than a human being. Faint images of smoke were rising from her hair, and Jehan was almost sure he spotted glimpses of burning embers between her curls. "Your parlour tricks have no power over us, you know that, don't you?"

Again, he felt himself trying to believe her words, trying to convince himself he was powerless against creatures like them. But his heart wouldn't let him. If he gave up now, he'd abandon Giraud, abandon the duty he had sworn to take up. And for the moment, it was his own magic he felt hanging heavily in the night air, no one else's.

"I don't believe you," he replied calmly, smiling as her eyes widened in surprise and just a little bit of fear. "Giraud, would you hand me your knife, please?"

Again, Giraud looked half-worried, half impressed, but he handed him his old knife without hesitation. Jehan took the blade and cut himself across the palm of his left hand, deftly, grimacing at the pain. Blood pooled in the cup of his palm, black in the cold moonlight.

"That ground you are standing on," he said without taking his eyes off the blood in his palm, "that ground is soaked with my blood."

He allowed a few drops of his blood fall onto the ground and immediately felt his connection to the ground recharge.

"You are standing on ground that I have cleansed and watered and fed, you breathe the air that carries my magic." He gave them a grim smile. "This is my sanctuary."

"You are piling insult upon insult, child," Givonne snarled. "You will regret this moment for the rest of your – "

"Oh, just shut up!" he ordered.

She didn't say a word, though Jehan wasn't entirely sure if that was by his command or sheer manners.

"Maybe I am just a mortal, a creature of flesh and blood, but that doesn't mean I am entirely helpless." He sprinkled more of his blood onto the ground and dabbed some onto Giraud's forehead. "You will not change me unless I want to be changed. That's the rule, isn't it?"

Sylvain looked as if he was about to rip off Jehan's head by purely mundane means, but oddly enough, it was Givonne who nodded in acquiescence. She even looked vaguely respectful, didn't she?

"You're the grandson of *Grand-mère Matrone*, aren't you?" she asked.

"I am, Milady, and her successor," he replied with a polite bow of his head. "My name is Jehan, Lady Givonne."

She returned the nod, not as deeply, but still.

"Now." For lack of another option, Jehan dabbed the remaining blood in his palm across his own forehead, his chest and forearms, wearing it like an armour. "I called you here to talk to you, and I have used a ruse for that, yes. I will tell you why I called you here, but first, I need you to promise me something."

Both Sylvain and Givonne were listening intently, their fury and indignation all but swamped by their curiosity.

Jehan turned around and faced the dark ruins behind him. "*Lunette*? Captain? Will you please show yourself?"

For a heartbeat, nothing happened, but then the buzz of silver dragonfly wings filled the night air. A soft light appeared over Jehan's shoulder, and inside, he could make out the slender shape of the tiny *lunette* who had already helped him in Castelfort. She seemed more than just a little scared, but determined, judging by the way she had crossed her minute arms in front of her chest.

Next to Jehan's feet, some leaves rustled, and looking down, Jehan found the *lutin* captain of Raëlle's guard standing next to him with pretty much the same expression on his wide face.

"These two have helped me out of the kindness of their hearts, and I need your oath that they will not suffer for it." He gave them an expectant look. "There won't be any point in continuing this if you don't promise."

"You have my word," Givonne said, her voice finally sounding mostly human again. "They have my pardon for their role in this."

All eyes turned towards Sylvain. He had his chin out and his arms crossed in front of his chest, looking pretty much like a larger version of Lunette in his stubbornness. But the silent expectation of everyone on the terrace wore away his determination within heartbeats, and he nodded with a mumbled agreement.

"I need your word, Sire," Jehan insisted. "Do we have it?"

"Yes." He bared his teeth in the direction of Lunette and the captain with a silent snarl. "Those little buggers are pardoned."

"Thank you." Jehan let out a breath he hadn't realised he was holding and gestured for everyone to come closer. "I have called you here to talk to you about your marriage."

Sylvain took in another deep breath, clearly insulted, but Givonne just threw him a wry look.

"Dear, our marriage was a matter of public discourse even before we said the vows. Unruffle your feathers."

Sylvain frowned at her, but didn't comment on it either, so Jehan continued.

"You have been at each other's throats for long enough now. You are harming the lands, and our people. The people I have sworn to protect. So you will either bury the hatchet or, by the Old Gods, I will find a way to make you."

Silence fell between them, and Jehan heard the two guards in his back shuffle their feet awkwardly.

"It is not by my choice that we are separate," Sylvain finally said, soft and almost hesitantly.

"Neither by mine," Givonne replied, just as softly.

Jehan bit his tongue to keep himself from saying something rash, and hoped Giraud was doing the same. For a long moment, no one said a word, and Jehan took his time looking at the two fae closely. On first glance, Prince Sylvain looked just as he had the other day in Castelfort – strong, wilful, handsome. But now, Jehan could also see his fae self in clear detail, see his worn look and the deep frown that had burrowed sharp lines into his forehead. Lady Givonne also looked older than the last time he had seen her, centuries ago in this very spot. She was still a tall, willowy presence, her face long and noble, but she seemed weighed down by the years, tired and full of sorrow. It wasn't even that she looked old – she looked heartbroken.

"Give me your hands," Jehan ordered when an idea struck him.

Both fae hesitated.

"You are in my sanctuary, and I promise I will uphold the laws of hospitality," he reassured them. "I have sworn to protect and heal the people here, and are you not people? Now give me your hands."

Lady Givonne cocked her head, curious, and offered him her slender hand. Not willing to be outdone in courage by his wife, Sylvain followed her example immediately. As soon as he held their hands in his, Jehan felt the emotions running through them, much clearer than usual as his hands were still stained with his blood. A whole thunderstorm of hope and disappointment, of love and hatred and fear. Jehan groaned with the sheer volume of it, but suddenly there was a calming hand on his shoulder – Giraud, once again concerned about his wellbeing. His confidence helped him find his own facing the emotions of these two, and he gave Giraud a grateful smile and reassuring nod before he continued speaking.

"You have both been wounded, but you were both too proud to do what was necessary to allow a healing," he explained. "Prince Sylvain, why don't you offer your wife a long-due apology?"

"Never!" Sylvain jerked back, but Jehan didn't let go of his hand. "Why should I apologise? It was her who left in the middle of the – "

"Stop!" Jehan's simple command cut off Sylvain's torrent of words. "It doesn't matter. Do you hear me? It doesn't matter. That war lasted a hundred years, yes. But that was two-hundred years ago. We've had several other wars since then. It is over. It doesn't matter." Sylvain looked at him like a child, startled by a sudden thunderclap. "But you are still here, and so is your wife. And you swore an oath to her, to be at her side, for better and worse, in good days and bad days, didn't you?"

Hesitantly, Sylvain nodded, and Jehan felt the emotional turmoil inside of him recede to a single, deep sentiment of exhaustion and mild embarrassment.

"You swore that oath, and yet when she needed you most, you weren't at her side. Regardless of what she did or didn't do – I think you owe her an apology for that."

Sylvain looked at him, his green eyes large and full of wonder. Calmly, he took his hand out of Jehan's and bowed down to one knee in front of Lady Givonne.

"My Lady, I have failed my most sacred oath to you," he began, and his words brought a startled, half-choked sob from her lips. "Worse than that, I have failed to see my failure. I stand before you, humbled, and filled with only the hope that you will accept my sincerest apology."

He remained in his genuflection, waiting for her to reply. When that reply took longer than decent, Jehan asked: "Do you accept his apology, Milady?"

"I … " She looked at him from dark eyes, her emotions feeling like a roiling cloud of anguish to Jehan. "How can I forgive all the pain his arrogance caused?"

"It doesn't matter. Remember? That war is over. The people who got hurt are dead. Their children are dead, and so are their grandchildren and their children as well. It's been close to ten generations, now. It is over." He smiled at her. "You have grieved long enough. It is time to forgive."

She returned Jehan's smile, a little shaky, but hopeful, nonetheless.

"I accept your apology, husband. And I hope you will accept my apology, for I have sworn the same oath to you, and wasn't at your side when you needed me most."

Sylvain looked up in deep surprise, his eyes wide with hope. Cautiously, he rose to his feet, as if he barely dared to believe what was happening. "And I accept your apologies, wife, humbly and grateful."

Jehan sent a silent prayer of gratitude to whatever deity was willing to listen. This was more progress than he had ever hoped to achieve tonight. Now the healing could begin, and with a little bit of luck, Givonne would understand the error of her ways in time to free Giraud's parents from their curse.

"Will you join me in my castle," Prince Sylvain asked out of the blue, "one of these days?"

With Givonne's hand still resting in his, Jehan felt the new flare of anguish inside of her like a knife stabbing through his palm.

"No," she replied courtly, her eyes downcast. "No. I think I am happier these days on my own."

Sylvain flinched at her rejection, and Jehan could see how his eyes grew narrow.

"Well, seems I'll need to fetch myself someone else for company," he retaliated, his voice all but dripping with venom. "Your town has quite a few pretty ones, I remember. Younger ones."

She looked as if she was about to slap Sylvain, but even before Givonne could do anything, it was Giraud who shoved him aside.

"How dare you talk like this?! She is your wife, for God's sake!" He was bristling with righteous fury, his fists clenched at his side. "So you destroy people's lives just to hurt her? How is that going to help anyone? Does it make you feel better when you're so clearly being the villain in your own story? Are you happy with all the tears you have brought?"

"Giraud, please – " Jehan attempted to prevent a disaster. "We should – "

"Even that bastard has more honour than you, Sylvain." Lady Givonne cut him off to deliver right another blow to her husband. "He's defending his mother's honour and mine, where you did nothing but sully – "

"Oh, *you* keep quiet!" Giraud snapped around, pointing accusingly at her face. "You're about to kill my parents for no other reason than to hurt me, and to get rid of me. Don't talk to me about honour, you vengeful old – "

"*Silence!*" Jehan's command rolled over the terrace like thunder. "*Silence, everyone!*"

Everyone around him swallowed their words, and Jehan seized the moment of respite to rub his face in exasperation.

"Really, all three of you. Full of passion, lashing out at every opportunity just to make a point. Too proud, too headstrong." He looked at Sylvain first, then at Givonne. "I refuse to believe you two didn't love each other. It might have only been fairy tales, but I refuse to believe they weren't true. I refuse to believe yours wasn't the greatest love of its time. And I firmly believe true love never dies."

Givonne scoffed at him with a cold smile. "What do you know about 'true love', fisherman? Who are you to talk to me about love?"

Her blunt accusation left Jehan speechless. Indeed, what did he know about 'true love'? Was what he felt in his heart enough to make her see? But then he remembered how his heart had been about to burst when Giraud held him, only a short while ago in this very place. He glanced to his side and found Giraud biting his lip with a sparkle in his eyes, amused, indecent, breathtakingly handsome. It took Jehan a heartbeat or two to realise that he must have had exactly the same expression on his face right now. They clearly were of one mind about this, of one heart.

"For such a famous sorceress, you are pretty blind to the obvious," Jehan quipped to Givonne. "And about the subject of love – just watch" he said and placed a firm hand around Giraud's neck to pull him close and into a long, tender kiss.

At least that was the plan, but when his lips touched Giraud's, it went through both of them like lightning. With all the magic around, their kiss was like a spell of its own, and there was no doubt anymore that their love was true. Each breath, each heartbeat became one, as if their very souls were entwining, until the world dropped away around them. It was more than Jehan had ever hoped it could be. It was a promise of never being alone again.

After what felt like a small eternity and yet way too short, he let go of Giraud's neck, and Jehan straightened to look at the two fae watching them.

Prince Sylvain at least attempted to appear polite, and had his look cast down to the side, but it was obvious that he was in equal parts surprised and deeply moved.

Givonne, however, seemed stunned, staring at them as slack-jawed as a woman of her composure possibly could. Her cool eyes were wide with wonder, sparkling like dark stars. And the way she now took a deep, sensual breath with her lips slightly parted told Jehan that she definitely remembered.

Jehan pursed his lips, still tingling with the memory of that kiss, and smiled at her. "Love. It is the same whatever form it takes, isn't it? Between two men, or between two fae from different lands. It still is the strongest magic there is."

"I – I didn't..." she mumbled, her words trailing off. Her eyes sought out Sylvain, and memories seemed to flood her mind, memories of happier times, times when the touch of her husband made her swoon and forget the world around her. Wordlessly shaking her head, she reached out to Sylvain, her breath going deep and yearning. As soon as he made so much as a minute step into her direction, she grabbed his wrist and pulled him in, pulled him tightly into a scorching kiss that spoke of centuries spent in desperate longing. Like embers lighting up when the ashes are stirred, her hair glowed up with an inner fire, crackling and writhing and radiantly beautiful. In turn, lightning crackled around Sylvain. Much like Jehan and Giraud before, they lost themselves in their kiss, oblivious and uncaring of their audience, lost themselves in what they had denied each other for so long.

Giraud nodded to himself and wiped his hands as if he had just finished a particularly nasty piece of work. He turned to Jehan with the expression of a craftsman genuinely taking pride in his work.

"See? Told you it would work."

There was so much earnest conviction in his words that Jehan couldn't help but give a startled laugh. "I recall the events distinctively differently, *Maître* Forgeron," he said and pulled his lover into another close embrace. "But I won't complain as long as you kiss me again."

"Nothing I would rather do." This time, Giraud stood up on his toes to kiss him tenderly, with a grin so wide Jehan could feel it even with his eyes closed.

Somewhere in the distance, they could hear Lunette's muffled squee of delight.

Chapter Thirteen – Happily Ever After

The sun was setting over the far end of the valley, pouring golden highlights all over the river, and the air moved slow as honey. Swallows zipped across the water surface, hunting for mosquitoes that played there in dense clouds.

It was the end of another beautiful, warm summer day, and when Jehan looked up from mending the net on his knees, there was nothing that marred his view. Sitting on the bench in front of his hut, he enjoyed the last warm rays of sunlight after a long day of bringing out crayfish traps and catching trout. It had been a day filled with hard and honest work, and he wouldn't have wanted it any other way.

With a faint smile, he returned his attention back to his net, checking the next stitch in the row, and the next, and then the one after that. Quiet work, mindless work, good for his hands and his back and his soul. He closed his eyes while his hands continued working. Next stitch, check, move the net, next stitch.

From far inside the forest, quite a bit downriver, he heard a horse coming up the path to his hut at a reckless speed. And the sound made Jehan's heart beat faster with anticipation. Probably, the rider was not going much faster than a light canter, but the path hadn't been cleared for horseback riders in ages, and even a single low-hanging branch could be rather painful if it hit you smack in the face.

But of course, Giraud wouldn't care about that, would he?

It didn't take long for Giraud to arrive at the dyke, and Jehan heard him talk to Trajan in a low voice. He was calming him for the ascend onto the hill, so he would be able to stay on the chicken meadow.

Jehan decided that he had sufficiently repaired his net, rolled it up and stashed it with the others in the shed that leaned against his hut. He had done enough work for the day, and Giraud came with important news. Good news, hopefully.

Jehan found himself standing in front of his hut, his hands nervously searching for something to do, while he waited for Giraud to finally come into sight. He eventually did, first his hat with the green rooster feathers, then his smiling face and the rest of him and his horse that followed him peacefully uphill. So it was indeed good news he was bringing.

"God's blessing, Monsieur," Giraud offered as a greeting. "I come to deliver the new door hinges you ordered."

"I didn't order any door hinges."

"You sure?" Giraud pointed at the hut's door behind him. "That sure looks like it could use some better hinges. The door might even close properly, then."

"Who cares about that door?"

Laughing at Giraud's banter, he walked over and pulled him into a bearhug, just wrapping him in his arms and not quite intent on ever letting him go again. He felt warm and vibrantly alive, and even though he had washed after work, there were still streaks of dark soot down his neck.

His hair smelled of smoke, and faintly of white oleander. "Thank you for coming, my Blacksmith Prince."

Giraud gave him a startled chuckle at the expression, but didn't leave their embrace. "Of course. I said I'd come, and here I am." He leaned his head against Jehan's chest for a while, until Trajan got restless. "I think I should unsaddle him and tie him down, before he gets too bored and stroppy."

"Hm. No wonder you two get along so well."

Instead of a reply, Giraud stuck his tongue out at him. "My parents send their best regards, by the way. Mama is still utterly moved by the beautiful funeral, she said she can barely remember another ceremony where everyone was so touched."

They shared a silent smirk at the memory. Iolande's funeral had been beautiful, indeed, and tinged with a palpable sense of spirituality. Which, at least in parts, had been due to the fact that there had been a White Lady present, standing in a corner of their tiny church, deeply amused about all the pageantry. She simply hadn't been able to pass the opportunity to be a spectator at her own funeral. And even though his grandmother had mostly ignored her old family except for a nod to Jehan and Giraud, it had been good to see her around, to know that even though her mortal life was over, she still existed in some fashion. It had made the entire proceedings feel a little surreal, to say the least.

"And Mama says the salve you gave her for her feet worked like a charm," Giraud continued. "The pain is gone and her sores are finally healing."

Again, they shared a knowing smirk. Jehan had brought a simple chamomile concoction to the funeral so Giraud had something to give his ailing mother – hoping that indeed, the Lady Givonne would see her curse had been a misguided decision.

"So the curse is gone?" Jehan asked. "Did you talk to her?"

"Yep." Giraud's voice came across a little muffled as he was just taking the saddle off Trajan. He halted his rapport until he had stowed it properly and started wiping down Trajan with a handful of dry grass. "She agreed to meet me, despite everything, and she was ... I'm not sure, but I almost think she likes me now in some peculiar way. She didn't exactly apologise, but she assured me my parents would have nothing to fear from her any longer."

"But that is wonderful!" He walked over to Giraud and grabbed him by the shoulders. "How can you stay this calm? We did it!"

A big, naughty smile grew on Giraud's face. "Because maybe it's not the best news I am bringing?"

"No? Well, now you see me curious."

"There." Giraud pointed at one of his saddlebags. "Mama's given us some bits to add to dinner. Said you should at least eat well after losing your grandmother."

"That's the great news?" Jehan picked up the bag in mock disappointment. "Marette's food sure is nothing to frown about, but really, this is it?"

"No. This is me distracting you." Giraud wriggled his eyebrows at him and turned his attention back to his horse. "Now go, set the table, I'll be right with you."

For a heartbeat, Jehan was tempted to reply something brash, but in the end, he didn't bother. He had the entire evening to extract the news out of Giraud, and he had wanted to set the table anyway. So instead of a snarky remark, he waited for Giraud to pick something off the ground and patted his rear in just the same way one would show appreciation for a nice tavern wench. The glance he earned in return was surprised, furious, mortified and delighted all at the same time, so Jehan counted that as sufficient payback.

He left Giraud and his horse to their business and instead added the contents of the saddlebag to their table. Two dried boar sausages, two bottles of wine, half a loaf of bread, a tiny jar of mustard, some pickled gherkins and an entire rabbit paté. Together with the fish and cheese and plate of over-ripe figs that Jehan had already put out, that was a veritable feast.

Calmly, he watched the sun set over the river, and uncorked the first bottle of wine with only half his mind present. They had done it. Not only had they meddled with powers far above their own, but had also come out living, happy, and with Giraud's parents safe from future harassment. At least, as safe as one could be.

He poured himself a cup of wine and silently toasted the setting sun. Work never ended, but today's work was definitely done. And he was more than willing to enjoy his little rewards.

As if on cue, Giraud appeared at his side, smiling. He flung his hat onto a peg in the hut's wall, hitting it perfectly without even looking. "Can I get a cup as well?"

"Of course." Jehan poured him some wine, toasting once they both had a drink. "To jobs well done."

"To jobs well done, and to adventures." Giraud returned with a widening grin. He took a long sip before he drew a deep, relaxed breath, and nodded. "But really, this has been almost entirely your doing. I wouldn't know how to thank you properly. Or at least, that is what I thought it would be like."

"And now you do?" Jehan couldn't help himself, but a soft note of apprehension crept in his voice. Giraud's growing smile only confirmed his suspicions.

"I think I have a little something." He opened the second saddlebag he had brought over and dug out a small velvet purse. "Because, you know, I talked to my father, today, as well."

"Which one? The one you call father, or the one you call 'that wanton cockscomb'?"

"Uh – the latter." Now, Giraud's grin gained a decidedly guilty edge. "But, he was civil, and so was I. He thanked me for what we did for him and Givonne, and wanted me to express his gratitude to you."

"That admittedly sounds a lot more civil than our last meeting."

"It does, doesn't it?" Giraud took a deep breath as if bracing himself for something. "So, when he asked if there was a favour he could do us, at first I wasn't sure what to say."

"Do I have a reason to feel as apprehensive as I suddenly do?"

"I have no idea." Trying to feign innocence didn't suit Giraud well, and he knew it, so he didn't try for very long. "Anyway, he still feels well amused by our kiss that night, and even though he has some reservations when it comes to you, he genuinely thinks we should … well, enjoy each other's company for as long as it lasts. And so, he gave us these." Giraud upended the purse into his palm, two simple silver rings tumbling out. Seeing Jehan's apprehensive look growing even more pronounced, Giraud laughed out loud. "Oh, I am not going to propose to you, don't worry. I am of half a mind, but I do not make promises I can't keep."

"How gallant of you."

"Just can't help myself." Giraud took one of the rings and handed it to Jehan. There was a pleasant weight to it, and also the unmistakeable tingle of strong magic.

"He gave you enchanted rings?" Jehan asked, not sure what to make of this gift. He frowned in concentration, trying to make sense of the intricate spell he felt woven into the metal. "What is this – is it a spell of misunderstanding? What?"

"Of course that's what you'd call it." Giraud chuckled with delight as he put the remaining ring onto the third finger of his left hand and gestured Jehan to do the same. "I think one could call it a spell of misunderstanding, alright. But it's going to be useful to us, you know?" He stepped up right to Jehan and gingerly took him by the collar of his tunic. "Because, every time I do this – ", he pulled Jehan down and placed a light kiss onto his lips, "every time anyone see us doing this, they will misunderstand. Because, you know, we're such good friends, and there is nothing untoward in our behaviour."

Now that really sounded like a present worthy of a fairy prince.

"So you say, each time I do something like this – " Jehan laced his fingers into Giraud's dark curls and turned his head up to face him, "or something like this," he kissed him in return, a littler longer and more intense than before, "each time everyone seeing us will just be happy seeing two men be such good friends?"

Giraud looked up at him, his lips flushed and half-parted, his voice husky. "Yes..."

"Even ... if I'd do this?" Emboldened by by the way Giraud remained in his close embrace, Jehan started unlacing the other man's shirt, slowly and meticulously, savouring each motion.

"They'd probably think that you're just helping me."

That indeed sounded very much like a spell Sylvain would have a particular joy in concocting.

Unwilling to stop with what he had just started, Jehan let his hands wander down Giraud's chest, feeling him warm and firm through the thin fabric of his shirt. Giraud seemed to soak up the caress like a cat would bask in sunlight, and he twitched with nervous energy.

"Even if I did something like this?"

"I think so, yes."

Jehan sneaked his hand around Giraud's waist and drew him close, their bodies now fully leaning against each other, separated by nothing but a whisper of cloth.

"Also this?"

"I – I am not sure."

For several heartbeats, they just remained standing as they were, their eyes locked, breathing, feeling each other. They leaned into one another and kissed, their hands exploring each other's body with unfamiliar delight. Dinner on the wonky table nearby could clearly wait.

"Do you want me to stop?" Jehan asked, softly, almost whispering.

Giraud's reply came just as softly, but no less firm. "No. Please, no."

Wordlessly, Jehan took his lover by the hand and pulled him up the few steps and into his home. Tonight, he wouldn't care about the people of La Morangiasse, or the other denizens of the domain. Tonight, it would just be the two of them, and the love they had for each other.

And maybe, with a little bit of luck, this would only be the first of many more such nights to come.

~ And they lived happily ever after. ~

We hope you enjoyed this story.
Learn more about our books here:
www.brackhaus.com

'Loving Djinni' is a charming, screwball-y paranormal m/m romance about ancient magic meeting modern men, and how true love still is the strongest magic of them all.

Left to die in a sealed tomb, David, an educated and good-natured New York arts dealer and part-time forger, stumbles over an old oil lamp. But instead of producing a little light for David's last hours, it conjures forth a veritable djinni.

An ancient, tempting, puckish djinni, who in David's company prefers to show himself as an irresistibly handsome, fit and barely legal teenager. Quite literally an incarnation of trouble waiting to happen.

So what's a modern man to do with his three wishes, when he can wish for anything except the one thing the truly desires - to mend his broken heart?

'Loving Djinni' is a 2016 Rainbow Book Award Winner for Best Romantic Comedy (Gay).

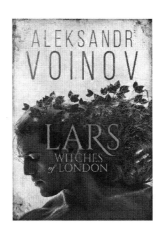

Some problems you can't solve with magick—and some you can.

After a homophobic pagan group rejected him, Lars Kendall is a solitary heathen on the Northern Path, loyal to the gods of the Norse pantheon. But being on his own sucks. So when he finally meets a mixed group of other queer witches and magick-users, it's like finding family. If family involved exploring past lives and casting spells.

Rhys Turner quit a stressful job in the City after his high-strung boyfriend of six years walked out. He sold the expensive flat in central London and bought a run-down house out in the suburbs. Never mind that it needs walls knocked down, its garden landscaped, and what the hell is up with that carpet?

With his health failing, Rhys is desperate for a clean slate and a new start. He isn't ready to fall in love with anybody, least of all the hunky builder who looks like he's stepped out of a TV show about Vikings—tattoos, long hair, and all. But as strong and loyal as Lars is, he also has a very soft heart, which might be the hardest thing for Rhys to resist.

Made in the USA
Columbia, SC
05 June 2017